Fo

or Worse

ALSO IN THE WEDDING BELLES SERIES
BY LAUREN LAYNE

To Have and to Hold
From This Day Forward

Lauren Layne

For Better or Worse

POCKET BOOKS

New York   London   Toronto   Sydney   New Delhi

Pocket Books
An Imprint of Simon & Schuster, Inc.
1230 Avenue of the Americas
New York, NY 10020

First Pocket Books paperback edition September 2016

POCKET and colophon are registered trademarks of Simon & Schuster, Inc.

For information about special discounts for bulk purchases, please contact Simon & Schuster Special Sales at 1-866-506-1949 or business@simonandschuster.com.

The Simon & Schuster Speakers Bureau can bring authors to your live event. For more information or to book an event, contact the Simon & Schuster Speakers Bureau at 1-866-248-3049 or visit our website at www.simonspeakers.com.

Interior design by Devan Norman

Manufactured in the United States of America

10 9 8 7 6 5 4 3 2 1

ISBN 978-1-5011-3515-6
ISBN 978-1-5011-3516-3 (ebook)

*For everyone whose life has been
touched by cancer in some way.
I long for a world in which everyone beats it.
Until then, be brave and stick together.*

Chapter One

FOR AS LONG AS Heather Fowler could remember, living in Manhattan had been The Dream.

The one she talked about as a precocious eight-year-old when her mom's best friend, turned chatty by one too many glasses of the Franzia she chugged like water, asked her what she wanted to be when she grew up.

At eight, Heather hadn't been exactly sure about the *what* in her future. But she absolutely knew the where.

New York City.

Manhattan, specifically.

The obsession had started with *Friends* reruns, and had only grown as she'd moved on to her mother's *Sex and the City* DVD collection, which she'd watched covertly while her mother had worked double shifts at the diner.

People in New York were vibrant, sparkling. They were *doing* something. Important things. Fun things.

She wanted to be one of them.

By the time Heather was in high school, The Dream was still going strong.

While the overachievers had dreams of going to Mars, and the smaller-thinking ones had aspirations of getting to the mall, for Heather it had always and *only* been NYC.

Her mother had never pretended to understand Heather's dream. Joan Fowler had lived her entire life in Merryville, Michigan, with only two addresses: her lower-middle-class parents' split-level and the trailer she'd rented when her parents had kicked her out, four months pregnant.

And while Heather had wanted something more for her mother—something more for *herself*—than hand-me-down clothes and a two-bedroom trailer that smelled constantly like peroxide (courtesy of her mother's hairdressing side job), Joan had always seemed content.

But to Heather's mother's credit, Joan had never been anything less than encouraging.

If you want New York, you do New York. Simple as that.

And so Heather had.

Though it hadn't been simple. There had been detours. College at Michigan State. A tiny apartment in Brooklyn Heights with four roommates that, while *technically* located in New York City, wasn't quite the urbane sophistication she'd pictured.

But Heather's resolve had never wavered. In one of her college internships, a mentor had told Heather to dress for the job she wanted, not the one she had.

Heather did that, but she'd also broadened the idiom: *Live the life you want, not the one you have.*

In this case, that meant saving up enough to cover rent that was more expensive than she could comfortably afford. *Yet.* More than she could afford *yet.* Because Heather was close to a promotion from assistant wedding planner to actual wedding planner. She could feel it.

The apartment was going to help her get there.

An apartment in zip code 10128, just east of Central Park.

She'd done it. She'd achieved The Dream, or at least part of it.

And it was . . .

Terrible.

It was two a.m., and she wasn't even close to anything resembling slumber. Heather's eyes snapped open after yet another failed sleep attempt. Her nostrils flared in an unsuccessful bid for patience before she turned and banged her palm against the wall over her Ikea headboard.

She'd purposely left the walls of her bedroom white because she'd read it was soothing. The curtains were also white, as were the area rug at the foot of the bed, the flowers on her table, and the lamp shades.

White is soothing, white is soothing, white is soothing . . .

She waited. And waited. There was a pause, and Heather held her breath.

Then: *Bum ba-dum bum bum bum . . .*

White wasn't soothing enough for this shit.

Heather fought the urge to scream. Was the music actually getting *louder*? Was that even possible?

Apparently. Because whoever lived on the other side of her bedroom wall either couldn't hear her banging or straight-up didn't care.

Heather closed her eyes and tried to tell herself that it was peaceful. Tried to pretend that the mediocre pounding of the drums and the squeal of some sort of guitar was a lullaby.

Her eyes snapped open again. Nope.

Heather threw back the covers—a fancy new white duvet for her fancy new place—and shoved her feet into her slippers as she pulled a hair band off the nightstand and dragged her messy dark blond curls into a knot on top of her head. She slid on her glasses, threw on a gray hoodie that she didn't bother to zip, opened the front door of her apartment, and made the short journey to the door of 4A.

The building was old, hence the thin walls, but it was also recently renovated, hence the modern-style doorbell, which Heather pressed firmly with one manicured finger.

And again, when there was no answer.

And again and again and again.

She pressed it until her finger started to cramp, and until—

Whoa.

The door jerked open, and Heather was suddenly face-to-face with a male chest. A *shirtless* male chest, replete with rippling abs and pectoral muscles that she'd seen the likes of only in magazine ads or on billboards. An upper body so spectacularly shaped that it was downright tacky.

Yes, tacky was definitely what it was.

Not hot. Not hot at all.

Heather ordered her gaze upward and found it meeting the greenish-blue eyes of a dude who looked *highly* amused for someone who'd nearly had his doorbell torn off.

The guy leaned one forearm—every bit as tackily muscular as the chest—against the doorjamb as the other scratched idly at his six-pack.

"Hi there," he said, giving her a crooked smile. It was a good smile. It was a good voice, too, but Heather was *soooooo* not in the mood to be charmed.

"Let me guess," she said, gifting him with a wide fake smile. "You're in the midst of a quarter-life crisis, maybe it's taking a little longer to get the corner office than you hoped, and you decided to scratch the itch by, wait for it . . . starting a band."

He was seemingly oblivious to her sleep-deprived bitchiness, as his smile only grew wider. "You're the new neighbor."

She pointed at her front door just a few feet away. "4C."

"Nice," he said appreciatively.

For a second she could have sworn his eyes drifted down toward her chest, but when she narrowed her eyes back up at him, he was all innocent smiles.

"So that's a yes on the new band, then?"

Instead of answering her question, he extended his hand. "Josh Tanner."

"Pretty manners for someone with no neighborly consideration," she muttered as she reluctantly put her hand in his. "Heather Fowler."

"Heather Fowler," he repeated slowly, as though trying to decide whether or not her name fit and coming up undecided.

Before she could respond, he reached out, his thumb and forefinger tugging at a curl that had come loose from her messy bun. "Pretty."

"Okay, enough," she snapped. "Are you going to stop with the music or not?"

"Well now, that's hard to say." He crossed his arms over his impressive chest. "I'm very volatile, what with the . . . what was it? Quarter-life crisis?"

"Just keep it down," she said wearily, rubbing at her forehead.

"Mrs. Calvin never used to mind," he said.

"Who the hell is Mrs. Calvin?"

"Lady who lived in 4C before you. She used to bake banana bread every Wednesday and make me a loaf. I don't suppose you bake?"

"Was Mrs. Calvin deaf?" Heather asked, ignoring the baking question. She *did* like to bake, but not for this guy, no matter how great the upper body.

"Definitely," Josh confirmed. "Turned her hearing aid off every night at eight p.m., which is when my band and I started practice."

"Aha!" she said, pointing a finger in his face. "You are in a band."

"Of course."

"Well, I need you guys to knock it off."

"Oh, they're not here tonight," he said simply.

"That was just me practicing along with one of our recordings. Can't get the intro quite right."

"Can you get it right some other time?"

"It's Friday night, babe. You need to loosen up. Want to come in for a beer?"

"No," she said, sounding out the word slowly with what she thought was admirable patience. "What I want is for you to stop the hideous music so that when my alarm goes off in four hours, I won't have to stop by here and kill you before I go to work."

"Work? On a Saturday? Dare I hope this means you're a professional baker and like to get in early to make delicious sweet buns?"

"Do I look like the type that makes delicious sweet buns?"

"You look like the type that *has* delicious sweet buns."

Heather made a face. "You're a pig."

"I'm lashing out," he said with a grin. "My ego's stinging from the fact that you didn't show any appreciation for how hard I work on all of this."

He spread his arms to the side and glanced down at his body.

Heather rolled her eyes. Great body or not, this guy was disgusting. "What *normally* happens when a woman bangs on your door at two in the morning?" she asked irritably.

He wiggled his eyebrows.

"Never mind," she muttered, embarrassed at having set herself up. "Can you please, *please* just shut up until after I leave at seven tomorrow?"

"To go . . . to the bakery?" he asked hopefully.

Yep. It was official. The new neighbor had to die.

Heather let out an audibly annoyed sigh. "To Park Avenue United Methodist Church to ensure the florist is there with the pew bows and to set up the guest book table, and to the bride room to make sure it doesn't still smell like onions. And then to the Bleecker Hotel to make sure the gift table's under way, that the florist is on time, that the caterers will be able to get into the kitchen, that they set up the good dance floor, not the crappy one that splits right down the middle, because if they do, so help me God—"

"And this is why modern men avoid the altar," Josh interrupted. "You're one scary-ass bride, 4C."

"I'm not the bride," she grumbled, rubbing her increasingly tired eyes. "I'm the assistant wedding planner."

"*Assistant* wedding planner. What does that mean?"

It means I need to get some freaking sleep so I can become the real deal.

"I see," Josh said, even though she hadn't said anything. He leaned toward her. "You want to come in and talk about it?"

"Better idea. How about you go to bed like any normal person over the age of twenty-two," she snapped.

"I thought you'd never ask," he said, stepping aside and sweeping an arm inward as though to usher her inside.

Heather put a hand over her heart and made a

dramatic gasping sound. "You mean . . . you mean a big handsome hunk like you would actually bed little old me?"

"Like I said, gotta verify that the sweet buns are, in fact, sweet," he said, flashing her another one of those easy grins.

Heather's fake smile dropped, and she stepped forward, getting in his face and ignoring—mostly—the heat radiating off him. "I'm going back into my apartment, and I'm going to sleep, and if I hear one more peep from your side of the wall, I'm going to get my hands on a loaf of Mrs. Calvin's glorious banana bread and shove it up your—"

Josh's head dropped to hers, and he stamped a kiss on her mouth. Hard.

Heather lifted her hands to shove him back, and they made it as far as his shoulders before she registered that it was a good kiss. A really good kiss. His mouth was warm and firm, and he tasted a bit like chocolate and a *really* good time.

For a second, Heather was tempted. It had been a while since she'd done something fun, just for her. Something that didn't have to do with the Wedding Belles, or moving to Manhattan, or making sure her mom remembered to pay her bills, or . . .

Reality crept back in just as her new neighbor's skilled lips nudged hers open.

She pulled back before he could deepen the kiss and make things *really* interesting. "What the hell was that?" she spat at him, wiping her mouth with the back of her hand.

Josh's shoulders lifted. "The quickest way to shut

you up, apparently. Should have tried it five minutes ago before you started rambling about bows and pews."

"Fine," she said through gritted teeth. "Let's make a deal. I'll shut up about bows if you stop the music. Deal?"

"You need to lighten up, Assistant Wedding Planner."

"Yeah, we're not calling me that," she said, already turning toward her apartment.

"Hey, 4C," he called, just as she was about to step back into her place.

In spite of her better judgment, Heather glanced over. "What?"

He winked. "See you around."

His door shut with a firm click, leaving Heather staring like an idiot with her mouth gaping open. She clenched her fists, walked back into her new apartment, locked the door, and got back into bed. But while it was finally quiet, her mind was racing a million miles a minute.

What. In the fresh hell. Was *that*?

Chapter Two

"HONEY, IS THAT YOUR third cup of coffee?" Brooke Baldwin asked. Heather's friend and colleague gave her a curious look.

Heather let out a snort. "Try fifth," she said sourly, topping off her cup from the elegant silver carafe the Wedding Belles always put out for the various vendors on wedding days. Caffeine didn't necessarily make the never-ending chaos of a Saturday wedding easy, but it certainly helped.

"Okay, well at least eat something to soak up all the caffeine," her friend said, plucking a muffin out of the pastry basket and handing it and a napkin to Heather.

"I'm not hungry," Heather said, lifting her coffee cup to her lips and turning to watch with a critical eye as some of the florist's assistants scattered the gold glittery fall leaves on the table with less care than Heather would have liked.

The muffin reappeared in front of Heather's face. "Come on. It's delicious. Banana walnut."

"Ugh, then I *definitely* don't want it," Heather said, the mention of banana reminding her of the reason she was on her fifth cup of coffee. The adolescent-brained nutcase in 4A.

"What do you have against bananas?" Brooke asked, taking a huge bite of the rejected muffin.

Heather liked that about Brooke—the way she ate whatever she wanted to eat, no apologies. Chocolate, cupcakes, banana muffins . . . all fair game. Sometimes Heather wondered if it was all the sweetness going into Brooke's body that resulted in the constant *output* of sweetness. She doubted it though. Heather was no stranger to chocolate herself, and she had a serious weakness for ice cream, but there was no sweet goodness flowing through her veins.

Brooke Baldwin though—she was good people. Brooke was the newest member of the Belles. She'd moved from California to New York this past January to escape a doozy of an ex-fiancé, and Alexis, the owner of the Belles, had snapped her up to join the team.

If Heather was *all*-the-way honest with herself, and she usually was, she'd been a tiny bit resentful when her boss told her that they were hiring a new wedding planner rather than promoting one they already had. *cough, Heather, cough.*

Brooke had come on board simply as wedding planner. Not *assistant* wedding planner, as Heather had. It had stung, a tad, knowing that Heather had put in two years of her life with the Belles and had been outranked by a newcomer.

But after about five seconds of looking at Brooke's

portfolio, she knew that the woman had deserved absolutely every bit of the full title. Not only had she started her own company in Los Angeles, but Brooke was good. *Really* good.

It helped that Heather and Brooke had hit it off almost immediately, and it was hard to hate someone as nice and decent as Brooke. Case in point, Brooke had managed to land the hottest, richest bachelor in the city within just a few months of arriving. Seth Tyler had hired the Belles to plan his sister's wedding, and Brooke had been given the plum job as her first assignment. Only, *that* wedding didn't happen once it turned out the sister's fiancé wasn't quite who she thought he was. It hadn't mattered. By then, the billionaire hotel god had fallen hard and fast for Brooke's sunny California girl charm.

They now lived downtown in a gorgeously renovated old building, complete with a built-in bar, a hot tub big enough to fit a family of four, and no wannabe musician neighbor.

Heather would be seriously hating Brooke right about now if the gorgeous blonde wasn't such a good friend.

"How about I go buy you a breakfast sandwich with some protein?" Brooke said around another bite of muffin. "You're looking hangry."

Damn. She *was* kind of hangry.

"Nah, I'll go get it," Heather said distractedly as she noted that some of the gold chair bows looked a little crooked and reached out to fix one.

"No way," Brooke said, washing down her muffin

with a sip from her bottle of water. "This is your gig. I'll get the dang sandwich."

Heather glanced at her in surprise. "This is your and Alexis's gig, too. We agreed all three of us would tag team this one, since it was last-minute and you were overbooked."

Brooke shrugged. "Sure, but you've done the most work out of the three of us. It's your vision, babe, and it's a good one."

"It *is* a good one," said a third voice from behind them.

Heather turned around to see the founding member of the Belles trio standing behind them, elegant arms crossed, nodding approvingly as she surveyed the surroundings.

Heather rolled her eyes at her friend and boss. "Seriously? How the heck are you pulling off that dress right now?"

Alexis was wearing a sleeveless sweater dress in a shade that could only be described as *nude*. But whereas the formfitting beige sheath would have looked hideous on Heather—and just about any other woman she knew—Alexis looked effortlessly chic.

But then, when was Alexis not effortlessly chic? The Belles' founder was one of those women who managed to channel old-school glamour right alongside modern-woman girl power. She was pretty, yes, but it was more that she was so damn *together*. Her dark brown hair was in a slick chignon more often than not, her makeup always natural and polished, her posture straight out of an etiquette manual.

Alexis glanced down at her dress. "Is it no good? I bought it online, but the model had considerably bigger boobs than me, and I'm a little worried it makes me look like a stuffed condom."

Brooke choked on her water. "*So* not what I thought you were going to say."

Heather let out a laugh. That was the other thing she loved about Alexis—the woman had the look of a 1920s film starlet and the mouth of a trucker when it suited her. It had taken Heather a while to figure that out. When Heather had all but thrown herself across the stone steps of the Belles' headquarters after seeing a write-up of Alexis Morgan's hot new wedding planning venture in *The Knot*, Heather had at first been intimidated as all heck by the other woman's chilly sophistication—though not quite enough not to practically beg that Alexis hire her on as an apprentice.

But little by little, Alexis had loosened up, revealing a woman who was kind, generous, and a little bit badass. Heather wasn't sure at what point they'd crossed from boss and employee to friends, but the two of them got each other, in an opposites attract kind of way. Heather was a little bit noisy, a touch crass when her trailer-park slipped in; Alexis, former country-club darling, was the opposite.

Stuffed condom comments not withstanding.

As though reading Heather's thoughts, Alexis pursed her lips. "I think my lack of recent sexual exposure is starting to manifest."

"Hear, hear," Heather said, raising a hand before fixing yet another bow. "I can't remember the last time I've *seen* a stuffed condom."

"Okay, is nobody else thinking that's a gross visual?" Brooke said. "It makes me think of sausage."

"Ooh, speaking of sausage . . ." Heather's head snapped up.

"On it," Brooke said, finishing off her water bottle. "Alexis, want anything from Starbucks? I need to feed Heather before she kills someone."

"Ooh, get me a coffee, too," Heather said. "A big one."

"Only if it's decaf," Brooke replied, holding up Heather's fifth cup of coffee, which was nearly empty, and looking at her pointedly.

"Decaf coffee is like an *un*stuffed condom," Heather argued. "Completely useless to me."

"I give up," Brooke said, throwing her hands in the air. "If you start levitating later, it's on you."

Alexis gave Heather a concerned glance. "You didn't sleep? I can recommend a nice tea."

"Is it a nice tea that will turn my noisy musician neighbor into a nice, quiet accountant?"

"Oh, but musicians are kind of hot," Brooke said interestedly.

Alexis gave a nod. "They are, rather."

Heather narrowed her eyes at both of them. "First of all, they're only hot when they're not next door. Second of all, I didn't peg either of you as the musician type."

"I think every woman is the musician type. At least a little," Brooke argued.

"Nope." Heather shook her head. "Your type," she said, pointing at Brooke, "is tall, dark, and grumpy. And yours," she said, pointing at Alexis, "is . . ."

Alexis's eyebrows lifted. "Yes? Believe me, I'm dying to know."

Heather exchanged a quick look with Brooke. "Um, I was going to say wickedly brilliant, a little bit serious, and gloriously British?"

Brooke nodded in enthusiastic agreement as Alexis groaned. "Not this again."

Heather shrugged. "Hey, you asked. And I don't know why you're complaining. I *just* got done saying how nice a quiet accountant neighbor would be."

Heather had just described Logan Harris, the Belles' longtime accountant and Alexis's friend-but-supposedly-never-lover. The man was *ridiculously* sexy, especially with his English accent. Objectively speaking, of course. Heather had never been truly interested, because despite her boss's constant denials, Logan had always seemed to belong to Alexis somehow.

It's like they *went* together, only neither had realized it yet.

But Alexis was getting that stubborn look that she always wore whenever they brought up Logan in a romantic light.

Brooke changed the subject, probably sensing Alexis's impending shift in mood. "Are you seriously telling us that you don't *kind of* get the appeal of a hot musician?" she asked.

Heather pursed her lips, a picture of Josh's chiseled abs and very nice biceps coming to mind.

"Aha," Brooke crowed. "Busted."

"Okay, he's good-looking," Heather allowed. "But in that too-many-martinis-fling kind of way, not like a throw-your-heart-at-him kind of way."

"Flings have their place."

"They do," Heather said slowly. "But I'm not going to have one with the guy whose mailbox is next to mine. Plus, I'm sort of . . ."

"Tired of flings?" Alexis finished for her.

Heather shrugged. "I don't know. It all just seems like a waste of time, you know? This fruitless wait for The One, who's statistically likely to break your heart. I'm not saying it'll *never* happen for me, I'm just not . . . holding my breath, you know?"

And that, right there, was the heart of the matter. Heather had never been in love. Not even close. Lust, yes. Affection, sure. But she'd never experienced that head-over-heels, lose-your-heart-to-him *love*.

And at twenty-seven, she was *way* past due, and yet she was also all too aware of how disastrous it could be to fall too hard and fast for the wrong type of guy. She'd seen it time and time again with her mom. Not that her mom had dated jerks—well, okay, a couple had been rotten—but Joan Fowler had always moved fast. Every guy she'd brought home was "The One," every guy who'd lasted a week, her soul mate.

Heather's mom was a smart woman. Scrappy, feisty, and street-smart. Except when it came to men. But while Joan Fowler *still* hadn't learned from her romantic mistakes, Heather had. Sometime around the age of fourteen, Heather had learned to stop hoping for happily ever after. For her mother or for herself.

Still, it didn't stop her from fantasizing. Sometimes,

in moments of weakness, she wanted. She wanted the white knight, the white horse, the whole gig.

But even in the *weakest* of moments, Heather knew that too-good-looking musicians were not the guys that smart girls fell for.

"Much as I wish I had the love of your life in my back pocket, the best I can offer up is breakfast meat," Brooke said sympathetically.

"I'll take it," Heather said, shoving aside her pity party for a better time. "Bacon, egg, and gouda? And don't forget the coffee."

"Got it," Brooke said. "Alexis?"

"No, I'm good, thanks. And before you go . . ."

Heather and Brooke both looked at their boss expectantly. Alexis's smile was slow and victorious. "We got the Robinson wedding."

There was a moment of stunned silence, followed by a whole lot of squealing, most of it coming from Heather's own mouth.

"Seriously?" Heather said, wrapping her arms around her boss's shoulders and squeezing happily while unabashedly jumping up and down.

Danica Robinson was the biggest thing in socialite culture since the Kardashians broke onto the scene. The daughter of Hollywood's biggest director and an international supermodel, Danica had the stunning looks and unlimited income that made for legendary weddings.

The types of weddings that were featured not just in all of the biggest bridal magazines, but on E! and in *Us Weekly* and *People* and *Vogue* and . . .

"And she wants you."

It took Heather a full thirty seconds to register that Alexis was talking to her.

"Wait, what?" Heather asked incredulously.

Alexis's eyes were twinkling in happiness, and Brooke was grinning at her, too.

"What do you mean, she wants *me*?" Heather asked, not daring to hope.

It's not that Heather thought she lacked the skills. She *knew* she was good. She knew that Alexis knew she was good. But she was woefully short on experience.

Alexis had been giving her more and more responsibility in the last few months, but Heather didn't have a mile-long resume of famous clients like Brooke and Alexis did. She'd assisted with a bunch of weddings, definitely, but she'd never had one to claim as hers, *all* hers.

But if she was understanding Alexis correctly . . .

Heather's heart began to pound in excitement.

"She saw the pictures from the Monteith wedding in August on our website" Alexis was explaining, referring to the swanky but small black-tie wedding that Heather had put together for a middle-aged congressman and his second wife. "Danica said it was exactly the kind of class she was looking for. *Insisted* that whoever did that wedding do hers."

"The Monteith wedding was yours," Heather said hesitantly, even though she didn't exactly want to remind her boss whose name had been attached to the project.

Alexis shook her head. "You know as well as I do that the cold turned laryngitis rendered me mostly useless. You stepped in and killed it. You know it, I know it, and now Danica Robinson knows it."

Holy crap.

Never one to play it cool, Heather squealed again, doing a little happy dance before spreading her arms wide. "Seriously? *Seriously!* Group hug, everyone. Group hug up in here."

"I'm so happy for you," Brooke said as she stepped into Heather's waiting embrace. "This is it. Your big break!"

"Brooke's right," Alexis said, half stepping into the circle and giving Heather something that resembled a pat on the shoulder. Alexis wasn't one to show her affection physically. "I know you can do this, Heather. Let's see how you do running the thing all by yourself, and then I think it'll be time to talk about a change in your title, don't you?"

Heather resisted the urge to give a little fist pump of victory. This was it. This was *it*. The chance to be the real deal.

"Does Jessie know?" Heather asked, referring to the Belles' longtime receptionist, who was back at the office, manning the ever-ringing telephone.

"Yup. And she's already ensured your favorite champagne is chilled and ordered Shorty's for later." It was a Belles' tradition for every time they nabbed an especially significant client, and the wedding planner of choice always got to select the celebratory food and beverage.

"Shorty's," Heather said dreamily. "And she knows I like Whiz, right? Extra?"

Alexis rolled her eyes. "Yes, I think by now she

knows your penchant for sprayable cheese on your Philly steak sandwiches."

"You're just mad because they don't have a triple-cream brie option," Heather said, giving Alexis a smacking kiss on the cheek. "And you better not have ordered a salad again."

Instead of answering, Alexis held up a warning finger. "There is one teeny, *tiny* detail I should mention about the Robinson wedding."

"Bring it," Heather said.

At this point, nothing could bring her down. Not turkey bacon instead of the real thing, or a droopy chair bow, or even a noisy neighbor.

"Are you familiar with Heidi Rivera?"

"Sure. She's Danica Robinson's frenemy, currently trending toward the enemy side." Heather made it her business to keep up with all the latest celebrity goings-on.

"Exactly. Heidi's getting married at the Plaza in February."

"So?"

"Soo . . . Danica also wants to get married at the Plaza. Before Heidi does."

"Before?" Heather asked. "It's October. How can she possibly think we're going to pull a Plaza wedding together in less than four months?"

"She doesn't," Alexis said in a wary voice. "She wants it in three."

Chapter Three

❧

THINGS THAT COULD ANNOY a grown man:

His mother stopping by at seven a.m.

Things that could *kill* a grown man:

His mother stopping by at seven a.m. before he'd figured out how to gently get rid of last night's female companion.

Josh Tanner was still in bed, mentally running through his list of fail-proof methods for getting a woman out of his apartment in the kindest way possible, when he heard his front door open and close.

His eyes closed and he groaned audibly. There was only one person in his life who had a key to his apartment, and Sue Tanner had yet to fully absorb what Josh meant by *for emergencies only*.

The cute brunette came out of the bathroom, where she'd been borrowing Josh's toothbrush without asking, and gave him a puzzled look. "Is someone here?"

As if on cue, there was a cheerful knock on his bedroom door. "Joshy? Are you decent?"

Josh sighed as he swung his legs over the side of the bed and walked unabashedly naked, and decidedly *not* decent, to the dresser.

"April, honey," he said to the woman as he pulled out T-shirts and sweatpants for them both, "prepare yourself to meet my mother."

"Your mother?" she squeaked in a high voice that sounded remarkably similar to the sound she'd made when she'd—

"I'm sorry," he said, meaning it. For her sake and his own.

"Joshy?"

Good Lord.

"Mom. A minute?" he called.

April hurriedly took the clothes he handed her. They'd be huge on her tiny frame, but they didn't have time for her to wiggle back into her skintight dress.

He pulled a plain white tee over his head, tugged on the blue sweats, and after a glance to make sure that all of April's crucial bits were covered, opened the door.

"Oh hi, honey," his mom said, all smiles. "I thought you might still be asleep."

"Sure you did," he said, automatically sidestepping to block his mom's attempt to peek into his bedroom.

Just because he'd learned to endure Sue Tanner's meddling didn't mean poor April had to.

But just as he was about to suggest his mother come back a bit later, he caught a waft of vanilla perfume as April crowded around him, already reaching for his mother's hand.

"Mrs. Tanner. It's so nice to meet you."

Oh boy.

The only thing worse than a woman who didn't want to meet his mother was one who did.

He needed to get rid of both. Pronto.

But first . . . caffeine.

He bent to peck his chatty mother's cheek before moving into the kitchen to get some much-needed coffee.

"Well aren't you lovely, dear," Sue was cooing to April. "You have just the prettiest eyes. I bet my son noticed those right off."

Josh held back a snort of laughter as he reached for the canister where he kept his expensive Italian-roast coffee beans. Yeah. That had been it. Her *eyes*.

April had a fantastic body and a great smile. She'd found him after his band's set last night at the Irish pub around the corner, and after the requisite five-minute conversation to make sure she didn't set off any of his *crazy* warning bells, he'd brought her back to his place.

Truthfully, she wasn't the best lay he'd ever had. But that didn't mean she deserved an interrogation from his mother.

"Leave her alone, Mom," he called.

His mother ignored him as she led a beaming April into the kitchen. "I'm so sorry to intrude on your morning like this!" his mother exclaimed.

Now Josh *did* let out a snort.

"Oh gosh, no problem at all," April gushed. "I'm just disappointed you got here before I could make us all some breakfast."

His mug clattered to the counter. *What now?*

"Oh, aren't you sweet as sugar. Now you just let me take care of that. I'm here to make pancakes! Josh loves when I make pancakes."

"You know what else I love?" he muttered loudly over the whir of his coffee grinder. "When you call first."

"So you *don't* want my pancakes?" his mom said, finally shifting her attention away from April.

Josh considered as he turned to face the women and crossed his arms over his chest, leaning against the counter.

On one hand, he had two women eager to cook breakfast for him.

On the other hand . . . *he had two women eager to cook breakfast for him.*

But what the hell was he *supposed* to do? It was hard enough figuring out how to convince one woman that leaving was her own idea. No way could he handle two at the same time.

Josh sighed. "Pancakes would be great, Mom. Perfect fuel for that conversation we're about to have about boundaries."

But neither woman was paying attention to him anymore.

"So what do you do, April?" Sue asked, going to Josh's tiny pantry and pulling out the container of flour she'd stocked for him, again without his asking.

"I'm a marketing analyst," April bubbled. Josh rubbed his temples. Good God, had her voice been that chirpy and annoying last night? "Technically, I'm based here, but I travel a lot."

Sue made a *tsk*ing noise as she pushed Josh out of the way so she could place all of her dry ingredients on his counter. "Traveling's no good. Must be hard to maintain relationships."

Josh turned around so April wouldn't see his grimace. "Coffee, ladies?" he asked.

"Always," his mother said. "Your father insists on buying that cheap stuff whenever he does the shopping."

"Is that why you're here unannounced?" Josh asked. "Because my coffee's better?"

"That, and I want a pancake. If I make them at home, your father will eat them, and if he eats them, he'll put syrup on them, and the diet I've put him on will be for nothing."

"The diet you were doing . . . together?"

"You hold your tongue, son," she said with a little wink.

His parents had both put on a bit of weight after turning sixty. Something Josh's dad had accepted just fine, but his mom was always on a "lose a dress size" mission.

At least until she got a pancake craving.

"Oh darn" came a quiet mutter from Josh's kitchen table.

Josh's one-night stand turned breakfast companion looked up from her cell phone with an apologetic look on her face.

"I'm so sorry, but I have to get going," April said. "One of my coworkers has a stomach bug and needs me to cover a conference call for her."

"No problem," Josh said, just as his mother exclaimed, "Oh no!"

"Rain check?" April said, standing and coming over to touch his mom's arm.

Absolutely not.

He liked April. She was a nice woman. Cute. Smart. Likable.

But he'd made it perfectly clear last night that he was only looking for *last night. Only* last night.

His mother's unexpected appearance had bought her a reprieve for this morning, but no way was he looking to turn this into a thing. That wasn't his style—at least not anymore.

Josh was already braced to counteract whatever invitation to dinner his mother had at the ready, but to his surprise, Sue Tanner gave April a noncommittal pat on the back of the hand.

"It was just lovely meeting you, dear. Good luck with your meeting."

"Thanks," April said, gracious enough not to press any further. She turned toward Josh and opened her mouth to say something. Then, seemingly seeing there was nothing to say, simply glanced down at the oversized clothing he'd shoved at her. Probably debating leaving wearing something three times too big versus putting on last night's dress, which if he remembered correctly was flesh-toned, skintight, and probably not what she'd hoped to meet a guy's mother in.

"They're yours if you want them," Josh said, jerking his chin at the clothes.

Her head snapped up. "Really?"

Josh smiled. "Really. Keep them."

The light in her eyes dimmed just a little bit as

she put the pieces together that *keep them* had a very different meaning from *you can give them back later*.

There would be no later.

Not for April.

Not for any of the women that came by.

Five minutes later, April was teetering across his living room in her high heels and last night's dress, apparently deciding that a going-out dress at seven in the morning was a better option than wearing a one-night stand's T-shirt back home.

"It was really nice meeting you," April said, giving Josh's mom a little wave.

"And you, honey," his mom said with a wave, helping herself to the rest of Josh's French press.

And because he wasn't a complete ass, Josh walked April to the door, even though there wasn't much to be said at this point.

Even still, she hesitated briefly, giving him a chance to ask for her number.

He did not.

"See you around," April said, giving him the same awkward wave she'd given his mother.

"Absolutely," he said, bending to kiss her cheek.

He wouldn't be seeing her around, and they both knew it. Or if he did see her around, there wouldn't be a repeat of last night. They both knew that, too.

Josh let out a little sigh of relief as the door shut behind her. Bachelor status firmly in place, exactly as he wanted it. *Needed* it. Life was too short—way too short to sleep with only one person.

Did that make him an ass? Maybe. Did he care? Not particularly.

"Well. She seemed nice," Sue said, holding her mug in both hands and taking a sip as she watched him over the rising steam.

"Thanks for not asking her to Christmas dinner," he said, heading back into the kitchen to make another pot of coffee, since his mother was drinking faster than him.

"I wouldn't have done that," she said, sounding scandalized.

"No? Just ask her to breakfast?"

"You don't feed them after you're done with them?"

"Mom." He winced.

"Am I wrong?" she said. "This is the third one in as many months I've seen that's left just like that. Nothing but a good-bye."

"Well, perhaps if you called once in a while, I could spare you that," he said pointedly.

Sue sighed. "I know. I'm sorry. I just . . . sometimes I need to see you. You know?"

Josh's chest constricted, understanding immediately what his mother was saying as well as what she wasn't saying, and grateful for it.

He didn't need reminders about those days. Didn't need a reminder of just how fiercely he'd needed her and his father.

And yet he knew that he wasn't the only one with scars. Just like he was trying to put those days behind him, Sue Tanner was trying desperately to make sure they never came back.

And if that meant her stopping by, looking him over, all but checking his temperature . . . he could deal.

Josh glanced over, held his mother's blue-green gaze, her eyes the same color as his own. "Mom. I do know. I understand, and I don't mind. It's why you have the key to my apartment. Just . . . some warning next time, okay?"

Her eyes crinkled as she smiled at him. "But if I call first, you might tell me not to come."

"I'll just tell you to come over later. You know. *After*."

"After you're done wham-bam-thank-you-ma'am-ing, you mean."

"*Jesus*. Mom. Did you spike your coffee?"

His mother had never been the frail and dainty type, but she wasn't quite normally so bald in talking about his . . . *relationships*.

"I'm sorry if I'm embarrassing you, dear. Just once I'd like to come over here and see a girl that you actually *look* at."

"What?" he grunted, scooping beans into his grinder.

Sue gestured with her mug in the direction of the front door. "That girl right there was beautiful and sweet, and I'm not even sure you noticed."

"I noticed."

Last night.

He'd noticed this morning, too, he just . . .

Didn't care.

His mom was shaking her head as she went to the fridge. "One day you're going to find a girl that you can't look away from and I hope I'm there to relish every minute."

"Oh, I'm sure you will be," he muttered.

"Josh Tanner, you're out of milk!"

"Yeah, well, I eat cereal most days," he said, mentally adding milk to his grocery list. "It happens."

"Well, I can't make pancakes without it. What about buttermilk?"

"Of course I keep buttermilk on hand. What thirty-three-year-old bachelor doesn't?"

His mom shut the fridge door. "Sarcasm's not going to get you pancakes."

Josh sighed. "I'll run to the bodega."

"Nonsense. Just ask Mrs. Calvin for some. That's what neighbors are for."

"Moved out," Josh said, drinking the last swallow of his coffee. "Wanted to be closer to her family."

"Well, that's too bad. She was a nice lady. And deaf, which meant she didn't have to suffer through the late-night band practice."

"You too, huh?" he asked, heading toward the bedroom for shoes.

"Me too what?"

"The new girl in 4C's all in a tizzy because of my music."

It had been a week since she'd banged on his door, and he'd played his music just a little too loud nearly every night since then in hopes she'd come over for a repeat of that kiss. For a short, shut-her-up kind of kiss, it had been surprisingly hot. He wouldn't mind a repeat, followed by something a little more naked than kissing.

"A band member's hardly the ideal neighbor, dear," his mother said.

"Yeah, she let me know that in no uncertain

terms," he muttered, flashing back to the way the curly-haired firecracker all but ripped him a new one. Hideous, uptight creature.

Hot though. Definitely hot.

Inspiration struck, and Josh halted on his way to the bedroom, instead turning left toward the front door.

"Where are you going?" Sue asked.

"I think you're right, Mom. Borrowing milk is *exactly* what neighbors are for."

Chapter Four

JOSH TANNER'S HANDS WERE all over her, and oh *God* they were good hands. Brooke and Alexis had been onto something with the hot musician thing, because he played her every bit as well as he played the guitar.

His palms skimmed up her sides, his fingers dragging over her rib cage teasingly before gliding over her breasts, circling her nipples teasingly while he sucked at a deliciously sensitive part of her neck. Heather shifted beneath him, spreading her thighs and moaning in need when he settled between them, rubbing his erection where she was wet and throbbing.

Her hands found his ass, grabbing greedily as she tilted up to him, suddenly aware that they had on too many clothes, aware of—

A rude knocking on her door.

Heather's eyes snapped open, unsure which was more horrifying. The fact that someone was knocking on her door at seven thirty on a Sunday or the fact that she'd been having a dirty dream about her annoying neighbor.

It was a definite toss-up, but when she rolled out of bed, shuffled grumpily to the front door, and looked out the peephole, it was decided for her:

The neighbor was the more annoying part.

"Are you kidding me with this?" she muttered, resting her forehead against the door.

"Heather, *darling*, it's me. 4A."

As if she could forget the abs. And the face. And the voice. And the hands. The really *skilled* hands.

Although the abs were covered up today with a T-shirt, she noticed with just the slightest pang of disappointment. A tight, nicely fitting T-shirt, but still. She'd barely gotten over the six-pack hangover from the last time she'd seen her horrible neighbor shirtless.

"What. Do. You. Want." She didn't lift her head, much less open the door.

"Are you wearing those cute little pajamas again?" he asked.

"Tell me that's not why you came over to wake me up."

"Oh, were you asleep?"

His voice was all innocence, and Heather narrowed her eyes in suspicion, raising her face to the peephole once more, only to squeak in surprise when she saw his eye right there staring back at her.

"Damn it," she said, jerking the door open so suddenly he nearly fell inside. "Who does that above the age of seven?"

He looked her up and down before a slow grin slid over his face. "Nice."

Heather couldn't help taking a quick glance down to affirm no strap had accidentally fallen. Nope. Technically she was covered, but she liked to sleep with her windows open to keep her bedroom cool, which meant she had a little headlight situation happening.

"Can I borrow some milk?" he asked.

She looked back at him. "Milk."

"Yeah. You know, white, creamy, delicious, comes from teats . . ."

His gaze dropped to her chest again, and Heather cursed, reaching for the gray zippered hoodie on the hook by the door and pulling it around her.

"I don't know if I have any milk," she said.

But he was already moving past her, entering her apartment uninvited. "Cute," he said, glancing around.

Heather didn't bother to say thank you. She already knew it was cute. Had deliberately made it so, with endless hours searching Pinterest for inspiration followed by *more* endless hours searching every vintage furniture shop in the city. She'd wanted a combination of minimalist and Bohemian chic, and she'd nailed it, if she did say so herself.

The walls were painted a dark teal, with plenty of original and slightly beat-up-looking canvas prints adding contrast. The area rugs were bright and slightly tattered, and intentionally so. The white couch was kept from looking stark by a handful of bold throw pillows, and a bunch of stubby pillar candles in varying heights covered her coffee table, end tables, and the windowsill.

But the real crown of the room was her window

seat. An actual window seat with a view of Central Park.

Hell. Yes.

"Mrs. Calvin used to love sitting here," he said, running a finger over the purple cushion. "Although she had an ugly yellow pad."

"Insisted on taking it with her," Heather said dryly.

"I'm sure you were *crushed*. You have no idea how many times I watched her drop a glob of cottage cheese onto the cushion before the Chihuahua gobbled it up."

Heather refused to engage or be charmed. "I don't think I have any milk."

"Now, now, neighbor," he said, turning to face her. "You didn't even look."

"Fine. If it'll get you to leave . . ."

She stomped into the kitchen to look for milk.

"The other night when you were so cranky, I thought for sure you must be a morning person." He followed her into the kitchen and leaned his forearms on her counter as she jerked open the fridge door. "I see now that that this irritable thing you have going on is more of a twenty-four/seven thing."

"Since you remember last weekend so well, I don't suppose you also remember that I mentioned that I'm a wedding planner, with Saturdays being my biggest days?"

"Today's Sunday."

"I know it's Sunday," she said, yanking out a carton of milk and slamming the door shut as she turned to face him. "I know it's Sunday because I spent all of yesterday on my feet, trying to pry champagne out of drunken teenagers' hands before they could get into a car, and then got felt up by the bride's drunken uncle."

He studied her for several moments, his eyes searching her face, before he rapped his palm lightly on the counter and stood up. "You know what you need, 4C?"

"Yes. Sleep."

"Pancakes," he countered.

"Pancakes?"

"Exactly." He came toward her and plucked the milk from her hand, glancing down at it. "Nonfat. Not my usual jam, but I think Mom can make this work."

"Mom?"

Before Heather could register what was happening, Josh had placed a big warm hand on the small of her back and was ushering her toward the front door of her own apartment.

"I don't want pancakes," she said through gritted teeth as she tried to push herself backward against his hand, to no avail. Jesus, those muscles didn't lie—the guy was strong as an ox.

"Everybody wants pancakes, 4C."

And apparently, just as stubborn.

"Heather. My name is Heather."

"That's way too pretty a name for someone as snippy as you."

"I'm not snippy, I'm *tired*," she said, meaning it. She knew she was sort of a bitch around this guy, and she wasn't loving herself right now, but he really did have the worst timing.

Heather just wanted one good night's sleep before she faced him again, and then maybe she could find her smile, find something nice to say, maybe even flirt.

But because she was exhausted, neither her brain nor her legs were working as well as usual, and before she knew it, she'd let herself be ushered toward 4A.

Josh shoved the door open and nudged her inside. "Mom, I brought you something sour," he called out.

"The milk was no good?" came a female voice from the other room.

"The milk was fine," Josh told the older lady who entered the living room. "It's 4C here who's a bit curdled."

"I'm not curdled," Heather muttered.

She wanted nothing more than to run for the door, but then the other woman was coming toward her with a wide smile. "You must be the nice girl that moved into Mrs. Calvin's place! Oh my, aren't you pretty."

Heather did find a smile for that, because, well, who wouldn't?

"Don't get excited," Josh said in a loud whisper as he headed toward his kitchen. "She says that to all the girls."

"I do," Josh's mom said with a wide smile. "But I don't always mean it. Today I do."

"Oh, well, thank you," Heather said, lifting a self-conscious hand to her hair and trying to wrap it into a loose bun at the nape of her neck. She liked her curls most of the time. Early morning before they'd seen shampoo or hair product was not one of those times.

"I'm Sue Tanner," the other woman said, extending a hand.

"Heather Fowler."

The other woman looked exactly as a mom who made pancakes was supposed to look. Short, a little bit plump, her hair short and curly and graying. She was well dressed but not Manhattan trendy. The smile, though, was the best part. Wide and friendly and genuine.

"So, you're sure your last name isn't Heather Foul?" Josh asked, glancing up from where he was reheating an electric kettle.

She would have given him the finger if not for the presence of his sweet mother.

"I should go," Heather said, ignoring Josh altogether and pasting on a smile for Sue. "You're welcome to the milk."

Sue frowned. "You don't like pancakes?"

"I—"

"Don't fight it, 4C," Josh said. "Coffee?"

He poured the water into a French press, the smell of dark roasty beans hitting her nostrils within seconds, and . . . damn. Heather was a sucker for a good cup of coffee, and somehow she *knew* this was going to be a good cup of coffee.

Josh caught her eye and winked. "Gotcha."

"Shut up," she muttered, earning a delighted laugh from Josh's mom, who led her to the kitchen table.

"Sit," Sue said. "You sit right there, and I'm going to make you the most delicious pancakes you've ever had while you tell me all about yourself."

"She's a wedding planner who's not a night

person, and apparently not a morning person, either," Josh said. "She also hates music."

"I don't hate music, I hate *you*," Heather said.

She glanced at Josh's mom in apology for hating her son—but really, she did sort of hate him—and saw Sue giving Josh a curious look.

Josh noticed, too. "Mom. What."

"You know what Heather does for a living," Sue said, her eyes sparkling as she assembled a whole slew of ingredients on the counter.

"Because she told me."

"You didn't know what April did for a living."

"Who's April?" Heather asked, mostly because she sensed Josh was almost squirming, and it was lovely to turn the tables a bit.

"Josh's overnight guest," Sue said.

Heather glanced around. "I thought it smelled like bachelor pad in here."

And it really was the quintessential man-space. From the dark leather couch and the TV the size of Montana right down to the guitar in the corner.

The guitar made her remember their first meeting, and she looked around curiously. "Where are the rest of your noisemakers?"

"Second bedroom," Sue answered, apparently understanding Heather's meaning perfectly. "Drums, more guitars, the whole deal."

"I can't believe the landlord lets you do that," Heather said.

Josh shrugged. "The unit below me is the community space. As long as nobody has the room reserved for something, nobody's there to hear us make noise or care. The staircase is on the other side, and on the other side is . . ."

"Me."

"Yup." He plunged the coffeepot. "And I just want you to know, I'd be happy to take any requests for your favorite songs. A nice lullaby to get you to sleep, perhaps?"

"You are not playing that"—she pointed at the guitar—"while I go to sleep," she said.

"Well now, how's that going to work, 4C? Because best I can tell, you're always just off to bed or just out of bed."

"I've seen you exactly twice. At two a.m. on a Saturday and seven a.m. on a Sunday, and I'm—"

"A wedding planner?"

"I was going to say a light sleeper," she said through gritted teeth.

"Huh. Your hair seems to take the whole bed thing pretty seriously. Cream and sugar?"

Heather ignored the slight on her hair. "Black, please."

He lifted his eyebrows and walked toward her with two steaming cups in hand. Heather tried to find a way to accept the plain white mug without touching his hand, but he'd seemed to arrange his fingers to make that impossible. Deliberate, probably.

"Thank you," she muttered, ignoring the little fissure of awareness she felt at his closeness.

"Heather, honey, do you like music?" Sue asked, glancing up from where she was alternating between watching Heather and Josh and scooping flour into a mixing bowl.

"Um, sure?"

"Liar," Josh said, dropping into the chair beside her.

He smelled a bit like soap and coffee, and Heather tried really hard to remember that he'd just had a woman in his apartment last night. That there'd probably been a constant stream of women in this apartment, and that she didn't want to be one of them.

"I do like music," she replied.

"Just not my music?"

"Not your music at two a.m.," she clarified, lifting her mug and pointing it at him.

Then she took a sip and moaned in pleasure. "Oh my God, what is this?"

"Italian roast from that little place around the corner." His voice was a little bit husky, and she wasn't entirely sure if it was because he shared her pleasure in the coffee or because he was appreciating her pleasure, and right now she didn't care.

"It's incredible," she said reverently, glancing down at the coffee with what could have only been described as love before looking back at him with something decidedly less so but also with a bit less animosity than before. Any man who appreciated coffee like this couldn't be all bad.

Their eyes locked, and for a moment, Heather lost her breath. He was just so darn good-looking, with his sleepy sexy eyes and his casual charm, and his really yummy Italian roast coffee. And then there was the matter of that dream . . .

"What about hedge fund managers?" Sue asked, slowly whisking some of Heather's milk into the bowl.

Heather was still looking at Josh when his mother asked the random question, and she was surprised to see something that looked like pain cross his face, followed by a complete shutdown.

It was as though the guy she'd been talking to vanished and was replaced by someone a hell of a lot more broody.

"Um, what?" Heather asked, forcing her attention back to Josh's mother and trying to figure out if she'd blacked out and missed some sort of transition. Why were they talking about hedge fund managers?

"Josh used to be one of those," Sue said as she placed a skillet on the stove and dropped a blob of butter onto it.

"Mom."

Josh's voice was sharp, and Sue glanced at him in confusion. "Am I not allowed to say that? It's not something to be ashamed of, honey."

He lifted a thumb to his face, pressing his thumbnail along the crease between his eyebrows just briefly as he closed his eyes. "I'm not ashamed. I'm just not that person anymore."

"I didn't say you were," Sue said in a happy voice. Too happy. As though she knew full well that she was pushing her son's buttons but was determined to feign ignorance. "I said you *used* to be a hedge fund manager."

"Which was relevant to the conversation how?" he snapped.

"Well, we were talking about careers, and I know you're taking a break from Wall Street for a little while, but *eventually* . . ."

"Mom, enough."

Heather took another sip of coffee as she debated the most subtle way to take her leave and let them settle what was obviously a personal, family matter.

Josh apparently read her thoughts, because he reached out a hand to stop her. Not touching her, but there was no question that he wanted her to stay.

She shouldn't, and yet . . .

Heather glanced at his profile, taking in the sudden tension and the rawness that had replaced his easy cockiness. And though she didn't know him, she *ached* for him.

And she wasn't completely immune to the pain on Sue Tanner's face, either, as she pressed her lips together and focused on ladling scoops of pancake batter into the now sizzling skillet.

"I just want you to be happy," his mom said quietly.

Josh exhaled a tiny sigh that only Heather could hear before he stood and walked over to his mother, wrapping his arms around her in a hug that tugged at Heather's heart.

Sue reached up a hand and patted her son's cheek in reassurance that they were okay, and when Josh stepped away, Heather's heart twisted even further when she saw his mother swipe a tear from her cheek.

What the heck had she stumbled into?

"Don't do it, 4C."

Heather glanced at Josh as he came and sat back in the chair next to hers, reaching for his coffee.

"Don't do what?"

"Don't go all soft on me now and let me think you're nice. I won't be able to handle it."

"I am nice," she insisted. "Super nice."

"Excellent," he said, back to his easy charm and wide smile. "So would now be a good time to tell you that my band's coming over to practice tonight?"

Heather shoved her empty coffee mug his way. "Let's just say that you making me more of that heavenly coffee is your best chance of me not strangling you with a guitar string."

He scooped up her mug and stood with a wink. "Damned if I don't like you a little bit, 4C, especially when you're all pissy and shit."

Heather ignored this, pointedly looking out the window as she waited for him to return with more of the insanely good coffee.

But damned if she didn't like him a little bit, too.

Chapter Five

WHEN JOSH HAD QUIT his old life cold turkey, he'd figured that the best part of "new Josh" would be the lack of rigid routine. No more five a.m. wake-up calls after a two a.m. nights. No more seven thirty meetings followed by coffee obligations and lunch obligations and happy hour obligations and dinner obligations.

Hell, no obligations of any kind. No commitments. No routine. He'd be able to do whatever he wanted, whenever he wanted. To live each day free and clear of yesterday, and more importantly, to live each day free and clear of *tomorrow*, because if he'd learned anything, it was that *tomorrow* was far from a guarantee.

Which was why it was so annoying to realize that despite his very deliberate intentions to embrace the carefree musician lifestyle, complete with its odd hours, one-night stands, and don't-give-a-fuck mentality, he was still very much a creature of habit.

Grocery runs on Sunday nights. Wake up at six

without an alarm, regardless of how late he'd gone to
bed the night before. Breakfast of smoothie and veg-
etable omelet to offset his penchant for pizza. Out the
door by eight to get to the gym, followed by a stop
for an extra large cup of coffee, followed by shower,
followed by a lunch of protein shake and salad . . .

Fuck he was tired of himself.

Which was why, as Josh let himself out of his
apartment at 7:55, the way he did every morning,
he felt a slow smile creep over his face as Heather
stepped into the hallway and pulled her door shut at
the exact same time.

Sure, he could have done without her wince and
sigh of dismay as she spotted him, but then again,
maybe that was part of the appeal. Josh was desperate for a change—desperate for a challenge—and the
neighbor in 4C with her determination not to like
him was exactly what the doctor ordered.

"Morning, 4C," he said with an easy smile, giving
her a slow once-over as they locked their respective
doors.

She looked . . . hot. White blouse tucked into a
gray pencil skirt with sky-high blue stilettos. Nice if
you liked the polished-career-woman look, and he
normally did. And yet . . . Josh's eyes narrowed a little
because it didn't seem quite like *her*. She pulled it off
nicely, but he'd seen the inside of her apartment; he
knew that she liked just a little bit of funk, and nothing about her clothing choices represented the quirky
personality that he was pretty sure lurked beneath the
surface. Still, he supposed he knew as well as anybody
that sometimes you had to dress the part.

"Leaving the house before noon," Heather said, dropping her keys into her purse and turning to face him. "I'm shocked. Where's your redheaded friend?"

"Ginger?" he asked as they headed toward the stairs. Technically, their building had an elevator, but it was slow as molasses and not much good for anything other than furniture delivery.

Heather halted at the top of the stairs. "Tell me you did not just call your red-haired one-night stand *Ginger*."

"That was her name."

"A ginger named Ginger?" Heather asked skeptically.

"Don't know if it was her real name," Josh said with a shrug. "Didn't ask."

"You're a pig," she muttered.

"Hurtful, 4C. Very hurtful."

"Yeah, you seem like a real softie underneath all those muscles," she muttered.

Josh moved quickly, descending onto the first step while she was still at the top of the stairs, minimizing the height difference between them and leaving them almost at eye level.

He leaned in slightly and lifted his eyebrows. "Noticed those, did you?"

Heather raked her gaze over him. "Hard not to, what with the too-small shirts and all. Do you shop in the children's section?"

Josh gave her the slow, lopsided smile that had coaxed more than one girl into his bed, but Heather Fowler was no adoring groupie and merely narrowed her eyes.

This time when he smiled it was a quick and genuine grin. Yup, definitely a challenge. Just what he needed.

"You'd better watch yourself, 4C. I'm going to figure out what softens you up. Other than pancakes."

"Don't sound so smug," she retorted. "Yesterday's pancakes were all your mother's doing."

"Ah," he said, holding up a finger. "But the *coffee* was all me."

Heather's eyes narrowed further. "Are you seriously trying to seduce me with coffee right now?"

His eyebrows lifted. "Is it working?"

"No. I made my *own* coffee this morning."

Josh's grin grew. "Dear God, please tell me that's a sexy euphemism for . . ."

He trailed off, and Heather frowned as she followed his train of thought, then her mouth dropped open when she put the pieces together.

"Did you just ask me if I masturbated this morning?" she hissed.

"No, I begged you to *tell* me that you masturbated. Willing it to be true is not the same as asking a woman if she did. That would be rude."

"You're unbelievable," she said, stepping to the right and trying to move around him.

He sidestepped, blocking her departure. "Okay, but did you?"

"I'm not answering that!"

Josh sighed and shook his head. "No wonder you're all keyed up. You could use a little . . . you know."

"Not all of us run on orgasms," she snapped.

"Maybe if you did, you wouldn't be so riled up all the time."

"I'm not riled up *all* the time. Just when work's crazy."

"Best I can tell, your work's always crazy," he countered.

"Because I like it that way."

"Bullshit," he shot back. "Nobody likes it that way."

"A little PTSD from your hedge fund days?" she asked.

This time it was Josh's turn to narrow his eyes. "Don't go there, 4C."

"No problem, 4A," she said sweetly. "You stay out of my business, I stay out of yours, and maybe, just maybe, we can refrain from killing each other."

"If anything kills you, it's going to be a heart attack. You're a workaholic, sweetheart," he said, falling into step beside her as they walked down together.

"Just because I'm not sleeping with a different woman every night and strumming my guitar into the wee hours doesn't mean I don't enjoy my life."

"I don't sleep with a different woman every night," he countered as they stepped onto the scuffed marble floor of the lobby.

"Oh, so there are repeats?"

"God, no," Josh said. "I meant that I take some nights off."

"Gotta give the little guy a chance to recover?" Heather asked with a pointed look at his crotch.

"More like the other nights are devoted to band practice. The guys don't like it when I'm distracted by girls, the girls don't like when I'm distracted by the band."

Heather put a hand over her chest. "You poor thing. And you've lived this long?"

Barely. He'd *barely* lived this long.

Josh frowned as the dark thought overtook him. He didn't let his mind go that direction these days. Figured that his storm cloud of a neighbor would rub off on him.

Time for a subject change. "Where you from, 4C?"

"None of your business."

"Would you quit being prickly for two minutes?" he asked, exasperated. "I'm just making friendly conversation."

"You are not, you're trying to get in my pants."

"Honey, if I wanted to be in your pants, I'd be there already," he said, even though he wasn't at all sure it was true. She seemed *very* determined to dislike him.

"Go away," she muttered as they stepped out onto the sidewalk.

"Tell me where you're from, and I'll leave you alone."

For now.

She rolled her eyes. "Midwest."

"Where in the Midwest?"

"What do you want, like, a map?"

Josh's head fell backward as he stared at the sky. "How about a state, 4C. Jesus. Why of all the women did you put this one next door to me?"

"It's not like I'm begging you to talk to me," she grumbled. "I'm just trying to go about my business."

Josh let out a little laugh. "Fine. You win. I'll leave you to take over the world of weddings."

He lifted his own hand for a cab. One stopped immediately, and she huffed in annoyance. "Of course."

Josh opened the car door and gestured for her to get in.

"No, go ahead," she said grumpily.

"I don't need a cab."

"Oh," she said, frowning, as though trying to figure out how to spin his gentlemanly gesture into something else. "Where are you going?"

He shook his head. "Too late for small talk, 4C. This chatty thing has to go both ways or not at all."

"Not at all sounds *great*," she said enthusiastically, stepping down from the curb to get into the cab.

Then, at the last minute, she looked up and caught his eye. "Hey. 4A."

"Yeah."

"I'm from Michigan. Specifically, Merryville, a little town you've never heard of and likely never will again."

He studied her for a moment. "That wasn't so hard, was it?"

She didn't answer, starting to drop into the taxi when his fingers brushed hers where they rested on the top of the cab door.

"Hey, wait, you didn't answer my most interesting question of the day," he asked.

"What?" she asked warily.

He tried again with the slow, sexy smile. "Did you touch yourself this morning? And, important follow-up question, did you think of me?"

"Oh, for the love of— Good-bye, Josh," Heather

said, pulling her hand free and dropping into the cab and slamming the door shut.

He watched the cab pull away, feeling a stab of victory when she turned to look at him over her shoulder. Her head whipped back around the second their eyes made contact, and he barked out a short laugh.

Yup, Heather Fowler of 4C was going to be a challenge, all right.

Chapter Six

THE WEDDING BELLES KEPT two kinds of champagne on hand in the main office.

Good and *really* good.

Alexis had even taken a trip to the Champagne region of France in the company's early days to be able to speak knowledgeably about the topic of all things bubbly. And she'd paid for all the members of the team, including Jessie the receptionist, to attend champagne-tasting class so they were able to identify both the diamonds in the rough and the overhyped brands whose tastes didn't live up to their price tags.

In other words, the Belles only served the good stuff.

But apparently, none was good enough for Danica Robinson.

After expressing snobby disbelief that they didn't have any Dom chilled, the celebrity reluctantly agreed to give the Krug Brut Rosé a try. It was a bubbly, layered concoction that Heather knew to be perfectly delicious, even to the most discerning of champagne palates, but Danica had merely wrinkled her perfectly shaped nose and pushed it away as if it had personally offended her.

It had been like that since the second the bride walked in the door. She didn't like the lighting, the music was a touch too loud, and she didn't appreciate being kept waiting on her busy schedule, when Heather had entered the room literally less than sixty seconds after Danica's arrival.

Danica's mother wasn't much better. Although still an attractive woman, Mariah Robinson hadn't exactly embraced the concept of aging with grace. While Heather was all for covering one's grays and stocking up on antiaging serums, Mariah had taken it to a whole other level. Her duck lips, Botoxed forehead, and too-tight clothes were the sad cliché of a woman who thought being attractive only came in one form.

On the plus side, Mama Robinson didn't seem to have a problem with the champagne. She was on her second glass.

"So *you're* the one who put together the Monteith wedding," Danica said, giving Heather a slow once-over that made her doubt her entire outfit and *definitely* doubt her decision to let her hair do its naturally curly thing rather than straighten it, as had been her original plan.

Heather was quite sure that Danica had never had a messy hair day in her entire life. Heck, the woman probably hadn't had so much as a single flyaway hair.

Danica's hair was long and sleek, falling in a

chestnut waterfall down to the middle of her back with just the slightest amount of curl at the end to give it a sort of "I woke up like this" look.

She was wearing a flawless navy-blue silk jumpsuit that at once made Heather feel uncomfortably corporate by comparison.

Truth be told, she'd been uncomfortable the second she'd stepped into the Alexis-esque pencil skirt this morning. She'd expected that dressing like her boss would make her feel accomplished and confident, but mostly she felt like an imposter.

Even more annoying, she had the strangest sense that her annoying neighbor had known it. When he'd given her his usual manwhore up-and-down, she'd seen something akin to pity on his face.

Imagine.

Josh Tanner pitying *her*. A struggling musician feeling sorry for a successful wedding planner.

No, not a wedding planner. Not yet.

First she needed to nail this meeting.

Heather took a deep breath and gave a confident smile, hoping to reset the tone of the meeting.

Danica didn't smile back, but somehow the slightly haughty expression made her even more striking. The woman—or whatever team made her look this way each morning—also had her makeup routine *down*. Heather had been around for enough bridal makeup sessions to know a master when she saw one, and Danica's eye makeup was definitely the work of a master. She'd done some smoky, smudgy thing that drew attention to her round blue eyes without making it look like she had loaded up on the eyeliner.

The woman was gorgeous, from her shiny brown hair to her Jimmy Choo–clad feet.

The jury was still out, however, on what was on the inside.

"I was happy with the way the Monteith wedding turned out," Heather said in a smooth, no-big-deal voice she'd heard Alexis use.

"Huh," Danica said, taking a sip of the champagne she didn't like.

"I'd love if you could tell me a little bit about what you liked about it," Heather said, opening up her notebook.

They were in the Belles' consultation room, a bright, airy conference room complete with a built-in champagne bar, all-white furniture, and gorgeous prints of some of the Belles' biggest weddings over the years.

It was Heather's secret wish that one of her weddings would end up among the oversized canvas prints one day.

Maybe *this* wedding.

"I liked that it was different, but not different for different's sake," Danica said, sitting forward in her chair and fixing Heather with an intense stare.

"Was that the one with all the green?" Mrs. Robinson (bet that made for some fun jokes) asked. "I didn't like the green."

"No, that was the Swafton wedding," Danica said with a dismissive wave. "That wasn't you, was it?"

"No, the Belles didn't work that wedding," Heather replied.

"Good. The green totally didn't work. It made Hannah look sallow."

"Not something you'll ever have to worry about, dear," Danica's mother said, patting her daughter's hand.

Danica lifted her slim shoulders in a little shrug. "I look good in most all colors," she explained to Heather in a matter-of-fact tone.

"That's great!" Heather said with false brightness. "It'll make finding the right dress color easier."

Danica gave her a snotty sneer. "I'm going with white. I should think that'd be obvious."

Heather couldn't help the little surge of smugness she felt at knowing something this snobby woman didn't. "Actually, the nuances of the wedding white are a good deal more complicated than most people realize. There's white versus ivory, yes, but then there are also multiple shades on that scale. Plus, when you start to play with textures, lace versus silk, et cetera, it can be important to know what works best with your complexion."

"Oh." Danica blinked. "Well, I think it'll all work well with my complexion. And my figure, too. I may not even need alterations."

Her mother nodded in agreement.

Seriously? Were these women for real?

"Actually, speaking of alterations, there's something I wanted to discuss with you ladies," Heather said as she stood and picked up the champagne bottle to refill each of their glasses. She noticed Danica didn't protest despite her disdain for the fact that it wasn't Dom Pérignon.

"Are you absolutely positive about this three-month timeline?" Heather asked once she'd sat back down.

"Why, can you not do it?" Mrs. Robinson pounced.

Easy there, tiger.

"Of course I can do it," Heather said smoothly. "We're absolutely committed to making our clients' dream weddings come true within any timeline. But the Monteith wedding you mentioned was a fourteen-month timeline. To get that level of customization, it's going to take—"

"Money isn't an issue," Danica interrupted.

Heather nodded in acknowledgment before continuing. "It's going to be rushed. I won't lie to you. There will be something wedding related to handle every day of the week. You may not be able to get your dream designer to put something together on that timeline, that sort of thing."

Danica snorted. "I don't think there's a designer alive who wouldn't drop everything to have me wear their dress. I have fifty million Instagram followers."

"That may very well be the case," Heather said in what she hoped was a measured tone that belied her increasing dislike for this person. "But that doesn't change the fact that the wedding-planning process will be more enjoyable for you if you're not making big decisions in haste."

The stubborn expression on both women's faces told Heather she was wasting her breath. Clearly beating Heidi Rivera to the altar was more important than their sanity.

Or Heather's.

"Okay, then," she said. "Three months it is. As I said, I'm confident we can get your dream wedding in that time, but one hurdle even your Instagram followers might have no sway over is the Plaza. Are you open to a non-weekend wedding, or—"

"No. It has to be on a Saturday," Danica said, already shaking her head.

Of course it does.

"I've already called," Heather said quietly. "They don't have any Saturdays available until April."

"April?" Mariah Robinson screeched. "That's way later than we wanted."

"Which is why I'm bringing it up," Heather said calmly. "There are plenty of venues in the city that are every bit as beautiful and classic, and we're sure to find an open date at one of them—"

"No. The Plaza," Danica said as though she were a five-year-old talking to the mall Santa Claus and had zero doubt that he was the real deal and could deliver on her wish for a pink pony.

"Ms. Robinson—"

"Call me Danica," she said, her tone indicating that this was a great privilege.

"Danica," Heather said, her smile growing more and more strained by the minute. "I've of course put us on their waiting list, and they'll let us know if there's a cancellation, but we really need to have an alternate in place."

Danica pulled her champagne glass toward her and downed half of it in one long sip. Somehow she made the gesture look classy and elegant. Heather suspected it was the hair. Women with shiny, straight hair could get away with just about anything.

Danica and her mother stood in unison, despite

the fact that there'd been no words exchanged or even eye contact.

Annnd, the weirdness continues.

"I'm confident you'll take care of it," Danica said with a bright smile. "Unless you think maybe one of the other planners might be better suited for the job?"

Heather stood, her heart skipping a beat at the thought of handing this wedding off to Alexis or Brooke. They'd never take her seriously enough to promote her to full-fledged planner if her biggest client to date fired her on the first day. "No, of course not," she said smoothly. "I'll absolutely take care of it."

You idiot. How will you "take care of" securing a Saturday reservation at the freaking Plaza in three months?

Heather ignored the voice of reason in her head. She'd deal with her later. If this were Alexis's wedding, she'd make it work.

"I do have a few more questions about what you're looking for," Heather said, trying not to panic as Danica started looking around for her coat.

And by a few questions, Heather meant *all* of them. She hadn't even started the questionnaire that the Belles opened each of their consultation with.

Mariah gave a derisive laugh. "Um, Helen, was it? Isn't it *your* job to come up with the ideas?"

"It's Heather," Heather said through gritted teeth. "And yes, it is. But I want to make sure this wedding is your vision. Not my own."

"You'll handle it," Danica said, moving toward the main reception area in her impossibly high-heeled suede Jimmy Choo boots. "I'll be in touch for questions. Text is best, but call as needed for emergencies."

Heather's mouth dropped open. "You don't want to be more . . . involved?"

"What for?" Danica said as she pulled on her white coat and tugged her long hair out of the collar.

"Well, for the dress, for starters."

"Oh. Yes, of course, I'll be involved for that. Set up some dates for next week and text me where to be. I'll fit it in."

Oh, could you fit it in? I'd be ever *so grateful.*

"All right," Heather said slowly. "And as for the flowers, the colors, the cake, food, music, seating, ceremony, tuxes, bridesmaid dresses, honeymoon transportation—"

"All you," Danica said sweetly. "I'll want final approval, of course, but quite frankly I really don't have time to be assessing the merits of different kinds of cake, you know? I'm more of a show up and have it be fabulous kind of girl."

"Then fabulous is what you'll get," Heather said, trying to ignore the way her hands had turned completely clammy at the thought of putting together the biggest wedding of her career *without the bride.*

And based on what she'd seen so far, if the Robinsons weren't happy with her choices, they'd have absolutely no problem tearing Heather's career to shreds.

Publicly.

To all fifty freaking million Instagram followers.

Somehow Heather managed to keep her smile in place until the two women left, choosing to ignore the loudly uttered *I can't believe they didn't have Dom* as she closed the door behind them.

Heather turned slowly on her heel, her eyes searching and immediately finding Jessie's. The adorable Belles receptionist looked torn between laughter and horror, and she wasn't alone.

Alexis and Brooke stood nearby as well. Brooke had her hand over her mouth, and even the implacable Alexis looked a little wide-eyed.

"Sooooo," Heather said slowly. "Did I hear that wrong, or are they thinking that I'm going to do this whole thing? Alone. And that I'm just to *text* her for her approval?"

Brooke's hand slowly dropped from her mouth. "Look on the bright side. At least she won't be a bridezilla?"

Heather gave her a look.

"Okay, she won't be a *hands-on* bridezilla. The ones that try to control every little detail are *way* worse."

"Are they?" Heather muttered as she rubbed her temples.

"Absolutely," Alexis said. "This will work out. How often do we wedding planners get carte blanche to do whatever we want?"

"*Never*, and for good reason," Heather muttered. "Everyone knows that an uninvolved bride is the kiss of death. What if I pick chocolate cake, and the groom's allergic to chocolate? What if I pick a DJ when they wanted a live band? What if—"

"What if we open up a bottle of champagne, toss in some orange juice to make it before-noon appropriate, and have a brainstorming session over mimosas?"

"No, no," Heather said quickly. "You guys all have your own work to do, and I can handle this. Really."

"We want to help," Brooke said quietly.

"I need to do this myself," Heather said, just a little bit sharply.

She gave Brooke a pleading look to soften the rebuke. *Please. I need to prove myself.*

Brooke's eyes narrowed slightly as she studied Heather, but eventually she gave a small nod. "Okay. But if you need anything . . ."

"I'll ask," Heather reassured her friend, even though she knew she wouldn't be asking for anything. She would nail this wedding, all on her own.

She had to. She was so close to achieving her dreams. She had the apartment, the wardrobe, and in three short months, she'd have the job.

And if there was a tiny nagging part in the back of Heather's mind wondering if she was missing something crucial, Heather ignored it.

Chapter Seven

❧

O KAY, GUYS, THAT WAS good," Josh said, pulling his guitar strap over his head and setting the guitar aside after the final chord he'd played to end the band's latest song had faded away. "Really good."

"Wait. We're done?" Felix Mendoza asked from behind the drum set, an incredulous look on his face. "It's only been, what, an hour?"

"Two," Josh replied, looking at his watch.

"Boss has a date," the lead singer said, making a lewd hand gesture. Of course, Trevor Cain could get away with just about any gesture and still have any woman he wanted. Such was the perk of being a kick-ass vocalist with one of those low, gravelly rock voices the women lost their panties over.

"I wish it was a date," Josh said. "More like a curfew."

"News flash, dude. You're in your own home. Can't have a curfew."

"Yes, thank you for that bit of wisdom, Donny." Josh clamped a hand on the shoulder of his high-more-often-than-not bassist as he headed toward the kitchen.

"Seriously though, what gives?" Trevor asked, following Josh into the kitchen.

Josh held up a beer in offering, and Trevor nodded. He was about to shout to the other guys, but Felix and Donny had already started in again on the music, working their way through the trickier part of the chorus.

He opened his mouth to tell them to knock it off, but he figured they probably had another ten minutes before 4C came over and busted their balls.

Today was Friday, which meant tomorrow was Saturday, and as she'd reminded him at least a dozen times, Saturdays were her big show days.

Excuse him, *wedding* days.

Although as uptight as she got about her job, they sure as hell seemed more like performances than ceremonies.

"Not feeling it tonight?" Trevor asked, taking a sip of the beer.

"Nah, it's this new neighbor. Not one of our biggest fans."

"Shit. That sucks. But we knew it was a risk when Mrs. Calvin moved out. Man, I miss that banana bread."

"Trust me, no banana bread coming from the new resident. I doubt she bakes, and if she did, it'd probably be, like, sour apple cyanide cake or something," Josh said, leaning against the counter and rubbing at the back of his neck.

"Bitchy neighbor sure got under your skin," Trevor said, already opening the fridge for another beer.

Josh didn't have the heart to tell Trevor that it wasn't Heather who was getting him down. Yeah, his hot neighbor was sort of a pain in the ass, and he'd sell a little piece of his soul to be the one she came to when she finally decided to get rid of all that wound-up energy, but . . . she wasn't what was bugging him.

Instead it was a tiny, annoying nagging sense that he didn't mind that they had to wrap up their practice early. Even worse: that Josh might be just a little bit relieved.

Which didn't make sense. Josh loved music. Loved listening to it, writing it, playing it. He knew that without vanity or conceit, he was the center. Most of the band's songs were *his* songs; the band was together because *he'd* brought them together.

Josh was the heart of the Weathered Gentlemen.

But lately, he hadn't been feeling the whole band thing.

He'd been feeling the *music*, yeah. At the risk of sounding like a douche, even to himself, Josh had *always* felt the music. He was the kid that had happily squeezed choir in alongside baseball practice all the way through high school.

And though his baseball prowess had maxed out in high school, his voice was good enough to get him into an a cappella group in college, where he'd continued to write songs at night to give himself a break from finance homework and economics papers.

And that was the tricky part. Josh had been every bit as good with numbers as he was with music.

Only, it wasn't just a matter of having two separate skills; it was as though they'd been intertwined. Music had been the counterpoint to the numbers, and vice versa.

Hence the problem. Josh still had the music, and was damn glad of it.

But he didn't have the numbers.

Not since he'd quit the firm. First because he'd had to, and then because when it had been time to go back, he'd realized he hadn't wanted to.

Hadn't wanted to go back to the suits and the power lunches and the power drinks followed by power dinners, and then . . . repeat. Days had blended into nights, weekdays blended into weekends, and though objectively he'd known that it wasn't his long hours that had caused his entire life to fall apart, it certainly hadn't helped matters any.

Maybe if he hadn't been so damn tired all the time, stressed to the max, living on frozen dinners and cocktails, he might have caught the signs a little earlier. Could have saved himself and his family a whole lot of fear.

And so he'd politely turned down his boss's offer of having his old job back, and had become, well . . . whatever he was now.

He'd founded the band from a mix of old acquaintances and friends of friends a year ago. The Weathered Gentlemen were good, but they weren't *great*. There was plenty of talent, good enough looks to get them into small weeknight gigs if one of the guys knew a guy. But with three out of the four holding down full-time jobs and four out of the four committed to an active social life, they weren't going anywhere in a hurry. And Josh had been okay with that. He had more than enough money in the bank from his old job to sustain his new appreciation for the simple life.

For the other guys, he always figured this was more of a hobby. The kind of thing where they'd gladly be along for the ride if the band hit the big time, but music wasn't their whole life.

And Josh was realizing slowly that it wasn't his, either.

He needed music in his life, definitely. It just wasn't *enough*. As if it wasn't bad enough that his routine was boring the shit out of him lately, now even the band—the one thing he'd thought he wanted—wasn't doing it for him.

Which begged the question: What was he missing?

A loud, repeated banging at his front door scattered his thoughts.

Heather.

Just like that, Josh felt his bad mood lift in spite of himself as he pushed away from the counter and went to open the door.

"That the neighbor?" Trevor called.

"Probably."

"Then what's the lady-killer smile for?" Trevor's asked. "I thought you said she was a bitch."

For once in Trevor's charmed life, his timing sucked, the last part of his statement coming just as Josh had opened the front door and at the exact moment Donny and Felix stopped playing.

The word *bitch* hovered in the awkward silence.

Josh braced for Heather to tear him a new one. He deserved it. He hadn't called her a bitch explicitly, but he hadn't exactly said anything nice, either.

The woman was annoying, yes, but she was also . . . interesting.

And despite all those badass walls she tried to put up, he'd bet his guitar that there was a sweetheart hiding beneath all the curls and sass.

Maybe.

One could always hope, at least.

To his surprise, she didn't mention the bitch comment at all. Knowing her, she was probably saving it for another time, planning to let it marinate good and long in her woman vault of Things You Did That One Time and haul it out and make him pay later.

Instead she merely lifted her eyebrows. "Do I need to do the whole 'do you know what time it is' routine, or is it pretty clear why I'm here?"

"Ahhh—"

For a moment Josh's brain turned off, because the way her purple tank top hugged her firm, round, slightly perfect breasts made him wish she were here for an entirely different reason.

"Well, hello there. You must be 4C," Trevor said, coming to the door and giving Josh a reprieve.

Heather shook Trevor's hand. "My reputation precedes me, I see."

Josh's eyes narrowed. Was that *flirting* he heard in Heather's voice? He didn't think the ballbuster was capable of it, but . . .

Yup, that was definitely an eyelash flutter he just saw.

"Can I get you a beer?" Trevor asked.

"Don't bother," Josh said. "She's here to kill all joy in the world."

"Not all joy, Josh. Just yours," Heather said, still smiling prettily at Trevor. "*And* I would also like a beer."

Josh's mouth dropped open as Heather came inside.

"Do you want to borrow a sweatshirt?" he asked her gruffly, surprised at himself even as the question came out unbidden.

Finally she looked at him, those wide eyes narrowing. "Why would I want to borrow a sweatshirt?"

"Just thought you might be cold," he muttered, shutting the door.

"Hey, who's this?" Felix asked, coming out of the practice room with Donny.

"This is 4C," Trevor said before Josh could respond.

"Heather," his neighbor corrected sweetly, going to shake Felix's hand as well as Donny's.

"So, you guys must be the band keeping me awake," she said good-naturedly, as though she didn't secretly want them all to die a painful death for stealing her precious sleep time. Josh felt like he'd just stepped into the twilight zone. Who was this smiling, friendly creature? Why was she not waving her hand around all crazy-like, forcing him to kiss her to shut her up?

And from the speculating look on Trevor's face, he wasn't the only one who noticed that Heather Fowler in her skimpy little tank top and flowing pajama pants looked ridiculously kissable.

"What kind of beer?" Josh asked Heather.

"I've got it," Trevor said, appearing at Heather's side and pressing a bottle into her hand as she stuck her head into the practice room.

"So this is where the noise happens, huh?" she asked.

Josh's eyes narrowed as his friend's hand touched Heather's back briefly. "Absolutely," Trevor said. "We're sorry it keeps you up though."

"Oh, it's okay," she said, waving her hand. "I mean . . . it's not. But tonight I couldn't sleep anyway, so you get a free pass. What do you all play?"

"Donny's bass, Felix is on drums. Josh is lead guitar, and I, as the most important member, have the pipes."

"Oh! I thought Josh was the singer," Heather said with a quick glance over her shoulder at him.

Their eyes locked, and Josh felt a flicker of . . . something.

"Ah, is that what he's telling the women these days?" Trevor joked.

"No, I just . . . I hear him, singing sometimes," Heather muttered.

"Our boy can carry a tune well enough, but wait until you hear *me*, love," Trevor said.

Josh turned away in mild disgust, pulling a beer out of the fridge as Trevor and the other guys coaxed Heather into the practice room, thrilled to have any sort of audience, even a reluctant one.

"Yo, Tanner," Felix called.

"What?" he called, popping the lid off the bottle and tilting the beer to his lips as he tried to shake off whatever was bringing down his mood tonight.

"Let's show Heather here that we're more than a bit of noise coming through her bedroom wall."

Josh turned around to see Donny dragging one of his kitchen chairs across the room, disappearing into the practice room.

"All right, love, you just sit down and get comfortable," Trevor said. "Tanner! Come on, man."

Josh heard the low strum of Donny's bass guitar, heard Felix do a little warm-up rhythm, and knew there was no way of getting out of it. If he refused to play a song now, he'd look like an ass.

Still, his feet didn't move, and he took another sip of beer.

Feeling eyes on him, he glanced up to see Heather in the doorway, leaning one shoulder against the doorjamb as she studied him.

"Okay, 4A?" she asked.

Her tone was lighthearted, almost slightly reluctant, as though she didn't want to care about why he was out here alone, feeling oddly itchy with his life.

He appreciated it. He'd spent enough time in the past few years dealing with people who walked on eggshells around him, cooing sweetness. Some of it genuine, some of it not so much.

Heather's no-nonsense question was refreshing—and exactly what he needed.

He was happy and healthy and living the dream, damn it.

Even if he was no longer sure it was *his* dream.

"You going soft on me?" he asked, taking one last sip of his beer before setting it aside and strolling toward her.

Heather's eyes narrowed. "Hardly. I just wanted you to get your shit together so I can see your cute lead singer work his magic."

He deliberately stepped into the doorway so she couldn't move in either direction without brushing against him, grinning at her discomfort.

"You're in a better mood tonight," he said, his eyes skimming over her crazy curls and relaxed expression. "Why?"

"Believe it or not, I'm not a shrew."

"Huh."

Heather shoved his shoulder with a little scowl. "I'm not!"

"Does that mean you're going to start making banana bread like Mrs. Calvin?"

"Yes, definitely. And coffee cake and sugar cookies and whatever other goodies you might like. All while wearing a frilly, feminine apron."

"Dare I hope there's nothing under the apron?" he asked, leaning in slightly.

"Right again!" she said, in mock delight. "I just love to bake naked."

Josh's pulse leapt, but Trevor interrupted before the sudden X-rated picture in his mind could turn into a full-fledged fantasy.

"Dude, we doing this or what?"

Josh looked at Heather.

"One song," she said, holding up a finger. "I may

as well hear what the music sounds like on this side of the wall."

She slipped back into the practice room, sitting in the stuffed armchair in the corner. Josh followed her in, reaching for his guitar and slipping the strap over his head before catching her eye and giving her a wink.

Heather rolled her eyes, and Josh couldn't hide the grin as he ripped his first chord.

Once again, it was this snotty, mouthy woman who'd managed to shake him out of his funk.

It was becoming increasingly clear that his intriguing new neighbor might be *exactly* what he needed to make him feel alive.

Chapter Eight

I T HAD BEEN A long time since Heather had let her-self enjoy a weekend night.

Hell, it had been *years* since she'd stayed up too late, had one too many drinks, which, considering she was only twenty-seven, was a little sad. But that was the nature of the wedding business. Her slowest days were Mondays and Tuesdays, when the rest of her social group was recovering from their weekend festivities, and her busiest workdays were on weekends, when everyone else was cutting loose.

Most of the time she didn't mind, even if the lack of overlap with other people's schedules left her feeling a little lonely. She wanted to be a wedding planner more than anything, and if that meant a limited social life, so be it.

But that didn't take away the joy she felt at sitting curled up on a cute guy's couch, with another cute guy's arm slung casually around her shoulder. And if she was maybe a tiny bit disappointed that the arm around her didn't belong to Josh, then she blamed it on her third—fourth?—beer.

"So, 4C, you never told us why you're living on the edge on a Friday night," Josh said, tilting his beer toward his lips as he studied her. His gaze flicked just briefly to where Trevor's hand had come to rest on her shoulder, but he looked away almost as quickly.

Trevor glanced at his watch. "Living on the edge? It's not even midnight."

"Way past the wedding planner's bedtime," Josh explained.

"Not tonight it's not," Heather said, scooching down on the couch and resting her bare feet on Josh's coffee table. When had she ditched her shoes? And why was she so dang comfortable here?

Josh's eyes narrowed. "Thought Saturdays were your big days."

"Usually they are. But I have tomorrow off."

Off.

It was a strange concept, not having to work tomorrow. But her work on the Robinson wedding meant that she didn't have as much time to help out with Alexis's and Brooke's weddings, which meant she was off the hook for tomorrow. She'd offered to help, but they'd both refused. And normally she'd have insisted, wanting to make herself as indispensable as possible, but the truth was, Heather had wanted the day off.

She needed a day to think, although about what she wasn't entirely sure. And maybe that was the whole point of taking a day off. To think about what you needed to think about.

Oh boy.

Heather glanced down at her half-drunk beer and set it on the table. Probably had had enough of those.

"What's it like being a wedding planner?" Trevor asked, his hand shifting slightly as he toyed with a piece of her hair. This time, Heather was positive Josh's eyes tracked the motion, although his expression betrayed nothing. Certainly not jealousy.

"Assistant wedding planner," she corrected, out of habit. "For now."

Her eyes locked with Josh's even as she sat hip-to-hip with Trevor. "What do you mean, for now?" Josh asked.

"I'm up for a promotion," she said, leaning forward and reaching for her beer again, although more to have something to do with her hands than because she wanted to drink it.

"Hey, that's great!" Trevor said, tugging at a curl again.

Again, Josh's eyes tracked the motion. Narrowing this time, before they came back to hers.

"How do you feel about that?" Josh asked.

She let out a surprised laugh. "How do I feel about a promotion? How do most people feel about a promotion?"

"I didn't ask about most people," Josh said, taking a sip of beer. "I asked about you."

She narrowed her eyes. "You're being weird tonight. What's up?"

"Yeah," Trevor echoed. "You are being a little weird, man."

"All I'm saying is that there's more to life than work," he muttered.

"Right, like this," Heather said, gesturing around his apartment in irritation to where the three of them sat like bumps on a log with too much beer, and while his other two bandmates had been glued to a shoot-'em-up video game for the past hour. "This is a *much* better use of one's life."

"Hey, at least we're not pissed off and cranky all the time," he shot back.

"If I'm pissed off and cranky, it's because I have a man-child living next door to me, whose life consists of pumping iron, screwing random girls, and having his mom make him pancakes," she snapped, pushing off the couch and stomping toward the kitchen to dump the rest of her beer and be on her way.

"No way, sweetheart, you don't get to back-pedal," Josh said, following her into the kitchen. "You knocked on *my* door, remember? I'd already told the band we needed to keep it down; you're the one who proudly waved around your day off like it's some sort of national holiday."

"Hey, take it easy, guys," Trevor said, following them into the kitchen and moving between them.

She ignored Trevor, hurling her beer bottle into the recycling bin, even though she really wanted to throw it at Josh's head. "Well, excuse *me* if we all can't have every day be an endless string of working out and fucking."

"Maybe if *you* did a little fucking, you wouldn't be so bitchy all the time," Josh said, his face tight and angry.

Heather's mouth dropped open in outrage, but she closed it as she realized there was far better retaliation than a saucy comeback.

"You know what, 4A? I think you're exactly right." She gave him a slow, sultry smile, saw his expression flicker in confusion as she stepped toward him.

Only she course-corrected at the last minute, moving toward Trevor instead, her hand hooking behind the lead singer's head and tugging his face down to hers for a thorough kiss.

A kiss that was—fine.

She tried to lose herself in it, she really did. Trevor was sexy and fun, and hadn't been the least bit shy in his flirting all night. But as he recovered from his surprise and wound an arm around her waist, deepening the kiss, Heather realized she felt little more than an awareness that it had been way too long since she'd been thoroughly kissed, and that this wasn't the right guy to break her streak with.

Still she made it look good for Josh's sake, arching her body into Trevor's, making a hungry little moan in the back of her throat before slowly stepping away.

She kept her eyes locked on Trevor's mouth as though it was the yummiest thing on the planet, even as all of her being was vitally aware of Josh Tanner and the barely contained anger coming off him in waves.

A trickle of guilt snuck in as she realized she was using Trevor, but his quick, friendly wink told her he didn't mind in the slightest. And the amused tilt of his mouth said he knew exactly what she was up to, even if Josh didn't.

"We should do that again sometime," he said in a low, bedroom voice.

Josh made a growling noise as Heather smiled at Trevor. "I'd like that."

She slowly took a step backward, shifting her attention to Josh as though just now remembering that he was there. "See you around, 4A."

He didn't respond, just glared, first at her, then at Trevor.

It was her victory, and they both knew it.

But as she went back to her apartment alone, and with the taste of the wrong guy on her lips, it didn't feel like a win so much as the start of a very dangerous game.

Chapter Nine

❦

ONE THING HEATHER HAD learned pretty quickly since moving to Manhattan was that Sundays in New York City meant one thing:

Brunch.

And while Heather was certainly no stranger to mimosas and fluffy omelets, today she was kicking it up a notch.

Today she was *hosting* brunch.

Saturdays were the Belles' bread and butter, but Sundays were increasingly popular for wedding-related events, so it was rare that all three of them plus Jessie had a free Sunday. Heather had decided to make the most of it by inviting them all over for a housewarming brunch at her place.

She'd even included Logan Harris in the invitation, the Belles' quietly dead-sexy accountant, as well as Brooke's new boyfriend, Seth. She'd invited Jessie's guy as well, but he was out of town.

It had seemed like a good idea at the time. Heather had pictured a perfectly set table, orange juice in a crystal pitcher alongside champagne nestled in the polka-dot ice bucket she'd gotten on clearance at Kate Spade, a freshly baked quiche, and a mint and vanilla fruit salad, all of which would be ready to go in time for Heather to wash and dry her hair and put on that green dress that she'd like to think made her eyes all kinds of sparkly and bright.

And then . . .

She'd slept through her alarm.

Make that alarms. All three of them.

She was an utter and absolute hot mess.

Yesterday had been crazy, running all over the city to check out alternates to the Plaza for the Robinson wedding, and by the time she'd dragged her weary body home at nine o'clock last night without a single viable option, the last thing she'd wanted to do was head to the store or set the table.

Instead she'd put together her shopping list last night, and then set her alarm for five. And then five fifteen. And five thirty, just to be safe, so she could be out the door by six to pick up the stuff for the quiche and the fresh bread and the fruit, plus everything she'd need for a new coffee cake recipe she'd found on Pinterest.

Her brain had the whole thing planned down to the minute.

Her body, however, had other ideas.

Namely, *sleep*.

One too many sleep-deprived nights had decided now would be a good time to catch up with her, and a groggy Heather had managed to turn off all three alarms.

So instead of getting out the door at six, it was nine, and she was unshowered, didn't have a single ingredient, hadn't set the table, and everyone would be here at eleven.

Two hours to do . . . everything.

Heather hurriedly pulled on her boots and debated texting everyone to beg for another hour, but that was so *not* the impression she was going for. She wanted the other Belles to see that this was the official start of the new Heather: savvy, sophisticated, and totally capable of being promoted to full-on planner. Moving into this apartment had been step one, but actually having people over to said apartment, complete with a very chic meal of food and beverage, was the next—and essential—step two. And Heather was not going to screw it up.

Heather was locking up when Josh's door opened, and his annoying now-familiar face appeared, along with . . . holy hell, a lot of skin.

It had been a little over a week since their semifight and her kiss with Trevor, and though she'd seen him plenty of times, none of their interactions had been anything resembling civil. There were still plenty of the quips and banter that had been a hallmark of their relationship since the beginning, but gone was the easy teasing, and in its place, an odd tension that had her feeling regretful, although she wasn't at all sure why.

She lifted a hand to shield her eyes from the expanse of taut, muscled flesh on display. "Can you please put that away?"

"Put what away? The crucials are covered."

"Barely," she muttered, trying to rid her brain of the image of Josh Tanner wearing nothing but black boxers. "Seriously, Josh. You can't just go opening the door naked."

"Noted," he said, bending down to pick up his newspaper.

"And that's another thing," she said, still shielding her eyes. "A real newspaper? Really? You've heard of the Internet, right?"

"I'm an old soul, 4C. Nothing like a little newsprint on the fingers while sipping that first cup of coffee."

His mention of coffee reminded her that she hadn't had any yet, and she withheld a whimper. Barely.

"I'm walking away now," she grumbled, too tired and stressed to engage.

"Hey, wait," he said, his voice sharpening slightly as he came into the hallway and blocked her path. "Something's wrong."

Yesterday, she would have either ignored him or lied, but since she was about thirty seconds away from a breakdown, she found herself babbling out the whole mess: the craziness that was yesterday's running around, last night's exhaustion, this morning's alarm mishap, as well as a frantic accounting of everything that needed to happen within the next two hours.

"And it's all your fault," she finished, pointing a finger at him.

He grinned, looking a little like the old Josh. "Of *course* it is."

"You and your band have been practicing way more this week, at all hours."

"What's wrong? Pissed that Trevor didn't come stick his tongue in your mouth and feel you up?" he said sarcastically, crossing his arms over his naked chest and clearly still not caring that he was close to nude in the hallway.

No, I'm pissed that you didn't feel me up.

"Whatever," she muttered, starting to push past him. "I'm wasting time."

Josh's arm shot out, his hand resting low on her hip and stopping her from walking by. "Hold up."

His fingers lingered just for a second, and she sucked in a little breath, not realizing how much she missed being touched until her brain registered how good he felt. And smelled. And . . .

"You're not naked because there's a woman in there, are you?" she blurted out.

His eyebrows lifted. "Jealous?"

"Disgusted," she shot back.

"Well then, you're in luck, because I'm going through a bit of a dry spell lately."

"Lately, meaning . . . a week?"

"Yeah, well, some of us don't think it's reasonable to go an entire year without sex, 4C."

"It hasn't been an entire year," she muttered.

Close though. Very close.

Heather stepped back from his closeness, only not fast enough, because his hand reached out and pulled her phone out of her purse.

"What are you doing?" She tried to snatch it back, and he lifted it higher.

"Well, considering your outrage at my newspaper, I assumed—correctly so, I might add—that you keep everything on your phone. Including your shopping list."

"So? What are you doing? What are you typing?"

"My phone number," he said.

"I don't want your phone number. If I need to yell at you, I'll come next door."

"There," he said, ignoring her comment and handing her phone back.

"There what?" she asked. "Did you just sign me up for some sex site?"

"A sex site? You mean porn, 4C? And how exactly do you think that works?"

"Well, what did you do?"

"I forwarded your grocery list."

"To whom?"

"To me," he said, heading back into his apartment and leaving the door open.

"Creepy, even for you," she called after him.

Josh sighed and turned around, walking back toward her until they were toe-to-toe and she had to tilt her head back to look at him.

"You are so dense, 4C."

She frowned.

"I'm going to the store for you," he said.

Her mouth dropped open, and he put his hand over it before she could respond. "Don't say no. I'm a nice guy. Let me prove it. Please."

He slowly lowered his hand, and Heather swallowed. "I never said you weren't a nice guy."

He grinned. "Sure you did. Multiple times."

"I can't let you go to the store for me," she said firmly.

Josh put both hands on her shoulders and pivoted her around so that she was facing her own door, and then marched her toward it.

"Here's the plan. You get your cute butt in there, take a shower, make yourself pretty, and then go about fussing around your table with your pink place mats or whatever."

Her head whipped around. "How did you know I have pink place mats?"

He merely smiled. "I'll go the store. Get all of your crap. Then you'll cook. No quiche though. You're doing scrambled eggs, maybe an omelet."

Her eyes narrowed. "You know that I have pink place mats and that I was going to be making quiche?"

"Women love quiche," he said. "I've never understood that."

"Well, I'm a woman, and most of the people coming over are women, so . . ."

"Most?"

"Three girls and two guys."

He studied her. "Guys? Huh."

It was on the tip of her tongue to explain who Logan and Seth were—but for some reason, she kept it to herself. Maybe she wanted to let him wonder. Just a little.

"You don't have to go to the store for me," she said. "Truly."

"I know," he said, moving to his own door. "But you're going to take me up on it."

"I am?" she asked, even though she was pretty sure he was right. Hell, she was already digging her keys back out of her purse.

"You are."

"What do you get out of this?" she asked suspiciously as he was about to close the door.

His head poked back out and he lifted his eyebrows meaningfully.

"No," she said, pointing her keys at him. "I am not sleeping with you in gratitude for going to buy eggs."

His grin only grew wider. "I'll be back in thirty. Feel free to still be in a towel when I knock on the door."

"Never gonna happen!" she called.

But then she was grinning, too, because she and Josh were *back*.

Chapter Ten

"EXACTLY HOW MANY BANANAS did I put on my shopping list?" Heather asked as she pulled out a second bunch from the grocery bag. "I only need a couple for the fruit salad."

"Sure, but you're going to need a lot for the banana bread," Josh said, moving some things around in her fridge to make room for the multiple cartons of eggs he'd picked up.

She turned and stared at his back. "I'm not making banana bread."

"Well, not today you're not," he said. "They have to get all ripe and brown first."

"Sorry, I'll clarify. I'm not making banana bread ever."

"Sure you are," he said, pulling a bundle of Italian parsley from the bag. "As a thank-you."

"Okay, I'll admit that I owe you a thank-you," she said slowly. "But I don't know how to make banana bread."

"Don't worry." He winked. "I do."

Heather rolled her eyes, even as she felt an odd little stab of happiness at the thought that they'd be making banana bread together in the near future. She didn't actually like banana bread, but she was pretty sure she was starting to like her neighbor. A lot.

Not in the romantic sense. She wasn't quite crazy enough to get involved with a man who had *heart-breaker* scrawled across his six-pack. But she couldn't deny that the guy was growing on her. Big-time. Nor could she deny that she was attracted. Big-time.

They unpacked the groceries, and Heather pulled up the coffee cake recipe on her iPad. Wow. *Wow.* Had it always been this complicated? So many ingredients. So many steps.

So little time.

Josh shoved his hands in his pockets, wandering around her apartment. "Table looks nice."

The table did look nice, thanks to him giving her time to fuss with it. Heather had taken a speed shower, leaving her hair to air-dry as she'd carefully arranged the freshly cut flowers she'd picked up on her way home yesterday and made homemade napkin rings of sorts out of gorgeous silver ribbon left over from one of her summer weddings.

She didn't have fancy china, but her plain white plates contrasted nicely with the pink place mats, and she'd completed the look with silver glittery candles that were maybe just a touch fancy for a daytime brunch but gave her otherwise pedestrian apartment a flare of formal.

"Yeah, well, that's the easy part," Heather said as she dashed around the kitchen, gathering the necessary supplies. The metal bowl balanced on top of a million other things crashed to the ground, followed by the bag of flour, the wooden spatula, and a box of salt, which thankfully wasn't open and thus didn't spill everywhere.

Heather set the stuff aside, bending down to clean up at the same moment Josh did.

They both reached for the bowl, and she glanced up when he didn't let go when she tugged. He was searching her face. "4C, exactly how bad are you in the kitchen?"

She bit her lip. "Um, I make a mean chocolate chip cookie?"

He gave a little sigh as he stood, extending a hand down to her. "Somehow I knew you were going to say something like that. All right, 4C, let's do this."

She frowned. "Do what?"

Josh pulled out two cutting boards and placed one in front of her. "You're on fruit salad."

"Not a manly enough dish for you to concern yourself with?" she asked.

"Absolutely not. I don't suppose you're planning on serving steak? Just a big, juicy hunk of beef?"

"Big, huh? Compensating for something, Tanner?"

"Sorry, if you wanted to see the goods, you should have done so earlier this morning *before* I put my pants on."

Heather rolled her eyes. "I'm confident it won't be the last time you prance around in your boxers. And no steak. But seriously, you don't have to help me."

"Shut up, 4C. You've pissed me off enough in the past week. Okay, let's talk egg prep. You skilled enough to do omelets, or you want me to just prep it all so that you can put it into one big scramble when they get here?"

"Scramble, I guess," she said, unable to keep the glum out of her voice. "Not as fancy as I was hoping, but I've never made an omelet before, and I'm not sure cooking for five guests is the time to start."

"Tell me about these people you're so determined to impress," he said, cracking an egg into a mixing bowl with surprising aptitude for a man who had his mother make him pancakes.

"The women are my colleagues," Heather said, flipping open the carton of strawberries and beginning to wash and slice them. "The rest of the Belles and our receptionist."

"The Belles?"

"The Wedding Belles," she explained. "That's the name of our wedding-planning company."

"And these belles," he said as he dug around in her drawer for a whisk. "They're the fussy quiche types?"

"For the record, quiche is delicious," Heather said, pointing her knife at him. "And no, they're not fussy. Not really. Brooke is sort of bubbly and sweet, Jessie's a little firecracker and probably the most outgoing person you'll ever meet. And Alexis is . . ."

Heather broke off. How did one explain Alexis Morgan?

"Complicated," she said.

"Is that your girl way of saying you don't like her?"

"No, I love her!" Heather said, scooping up a handful of the sliced berries and dropping them into the bowl. "I mean, yeah, she's my boss, but she's become a friend, too. When I say she's complicated, I just mean more . . . I sometimes think that I don't know her. I'm not sure that anybody does."

"A mystery woman," Josh said as he began slicing mushrooms. "That's hot."

"Says the man whose bedmates are all giggles and lip gloss."

"You bashing your fellow kind, 4C?" he asked.

"Absolutely not, 4A. I've been known to giggle and rock the lip gloss myself. To be clear, I was bashing *you*."

He nodded. "Sure, sure. Gotta keep up your walls, I get it."

"Oh, I'm not the one with walls," she said confidently as she opened the container of blueberries and went to the sink to rinse them.

To Heather's surprise, Josh came back with neither a defensive remark nor a quip. Instead he kept his focus on his mushrooms, almost as though relying on the fungi to provide a buffer from whatever dark thoughts had caused a little line to form between his eyebrows. Heather bit her lip as she studied his profile, torn between the urge to dig a little and the desire to respect his privacy.

She'd hardly spilled her guts to him; it's not as though she could fairly expect him to do the same. And yet, the more she got to know him, the more she wanted to really *know* him.

Because she suspected Josh was just as much as a mystery as Alexis. He just was a hell of a lot better at hiding it than Heather's reticent boss.

They fell into companionable silence as she finished up the fruit salad, and he set out the rest of the ingredients for the eggs. It wouldn't be quiche, but as far as scrambled eggs went, they'd be the high-class variety. Mixed mushrooms, scallions, and some grated Swiss cheese.

"Yes or no on the bacon?" Heather asked, holding up the package as she glanced nervously at the clock. There were only twenty minutes left.

"Seriously?" he asked, plucking the package from her hand. "The answer is always yes to bacon. Do you have a cookie sheet?"

Heather blinked. "For what?"

"The bacon."

"You don't cook bacon on a cookie sheet."

"Maybe *you* don't," Josh said, shoving at her hip as he correctly guessed which cupboard she kept the cookie sheets in.

Heather watched skeptically as he placed foil on the cookie sheet, then placed a cooling rack on top of that before laying out the bacon in neat strips.

"You forgot to preheat it," she said as he opened her oven door and slid the sheet in.

"It goes into a cold oven. Set it for four hundred degrees. Check on it in twelve to fifteen minutes."

"Are you trying to sabotage my brunch?" Heather asked. Her mother had never cooked bacon—or much of anything—but when Heather's grandmother had been alive, she'd always done it in a cast-iron skillet on the stove.

"Guess you'll have to trust me," he said, fishing

a grape out of her fruit salad, popping it into his mouth, and giving her a maddeningly smug grin.

"Yeah, because that's what smart women in New York City do. Trust strange men who prefer to walk around naked and bed a new woman every other night."

Josh hoisted himself onto her counter. "Strange? Really? You've seen me in my underwear, you've listened to my band practice, I just went grocery shopping for you, *and* you've met my mother. I'd say we're well beyond being strangers, 4C."

"True," Heather said as she arranged the ingredients for her coffee cake. It wouldn't be done by the time they got here, but she could pop it into the oven after the bacon came out. "You know, now that I think about it, I don't think a boyfriend has ever done my grocery shopping. And I've certainly never met a guy's mother."

"Really?" he asked.

She glanced at him as she measured out sugar. "You seem surprised."

"I am. Beneath all the girl-power energy, you've got a little old-fashioned about you. I would have thought you'd have come close to the altar a couple times."

Heather snorted.

"Come on," he pressed. "You're telling me you've never lost your cranky little heart to a guy?"

"No," she said slowly. "I don't know that that's for me."

"Well, would you look at that," he said with a little grin. "We have something in common."

"What, the dedicated bachelor has never been in love? I'm shocked. Shocked I say!"

"Hey, I never said I've never been in love," he corrected, "just that I don't have plans to be in the future."

"Really? When?" she asked, curious as to what sort of girl could hold the attention of a committed bachelor.

"Second grade. Her name was Robin, and she let me play her Game Boy at recess."

"However did you let her slip away from you?"

"I'm ashamed to say my eye was caught by another lady. Her name was Anna and she had a better game selection on her Game Boy."

"A player even then, huh?"

"Then and always," he said.

His voice was still teasing, but there was a slight intensity to his tone now, as though he were trying to tell her something.

Heather glanced up and locked gazes with him. "Josh Tanner, are you trying to warn me off right now? Give me fair warning not to fall in love with you because you'll never fall back?"

He laughed. "That obvious, huh?"

"Definitely," she said, shoving his legs out of her way so she could pull a spoon out of the drawer and taste her coffee cake batter.

"And in case it wasn't clear, I'm confident my poor little heart is withstanding all of your *charm* just fine."

"Glad to hear it, 4C. Because despite all your sass, you are a relationship kind of girl, and I'm not a relationship kind of guy."

"Some girl will change that," Heather said, digging her tasting spoon into the bowl.

Josh's fingers wrapped around her wrist, and she glanced up, startled by the firmness of his grip. "No," he said quietly. "That won't change."

"All right," she said with a nervous laugh. "Take it easy, no one's trying to march you toward the altar."

He smiled, but it seemed forced, and she was struck by a little stab of sadness at how resolute he was. Instinct told her this was more than just man-whore avoidance of commitment. Josh was deliberately holding himself back from the possibility of a relationship for something that went beyond a love of playing the field.

"I'm going to ask you something," he said, his thumb brushing the inside of her wrist, his voice low and dangerous.

Heather swallowed. "What?"

His gaze dropped to her mouth. "Why'd you kiss Trevor?"

She gave a nervous laugh and tried to pull her hand free, but he held tight. "Because he's hot."

Josh's eyes narrowed. "I don't think so."

"Well, I hardly think a heterosexual male is the best one to judge another guy's hotness," she countered.

Josh's gaze dropped to the spoon in her hand, and he pulled it toward his mouth, sliding it in between his lips in a gesture that was far sexier than it had a right to be.

"Delicious," he said as he licked the spoon clean, holding her gaze.

"Quit flirting," she said, trying to pull her hand back. "You *just* got done telling me how falling in love with you would be the end of life as I know it."

"Oh, I don't want you to love me, 4C. Doesn't mean I don't want you to *want* me."

"I'll try to control myself," she said, dropping the dirty spoon into the sink and shoving his legs out of the way once more to get a clean one.

He caught her chin between his thumb and forefinger, nudging her face up toward his. "I'll ask one more time. Why'd you kiss Trevor?"

"Why so curious?" she said, her voice coming out a little more breathy than she'd intended.

"Not curious," he said, his gaze locked on her mouth. "Jealous. Irrationally, crazy-out-of-my-mind jealous, 4C."

Her lips parted in surprise at the admission, and her belly flipped in excitement.

Josh's gaze held hers. Searching. Waiting.

"Oh hell," she muttered. "That's *why* I kissed him. I wanted to make you jealous."

The corner of his mouth tilted up. "I know."

Josh dipped his head toward hers, his head moving slowly, giving her time to pull back.

She met him halfway.

Their mouths collided hungrily, and it was like the Fourth of July and New Year's Eve all rolled into one. Fireworks. In her mind, her belly, her . . . other parts.

Her hands lifted to his waist, fingers tangling in the soft fabric in his shirt as his hand slipped to the back of her neck, tugging her closer as his tongue swept into her mouth, his breath minty and coffee and man.

He eased back slowly and Heather let out a little whimper of dismay, trying to pull him closer once more. Josh gave a little laugh, nipping her bottom lip in his teeth before soothing it with his tongue and releasing her. "There's someone at your door, 4C."

Heather jerked back, the sound of a knock finally breaking through her sexual haze. "Holy crap," she muttered, glancing at the clock. "How'd that happen so quickly?"

"Sorry," he said quietly, smoothing a curl away from her face before hopping down from the counter. "I meant to be gone before they got here."

Heather frowned. "What are you talking about? You're staying for brunch, moron."

"I am?" He blinked in surprise.

Heather felt something soften around her heart at the unexpected vulnerability, and she tried to ignore it. "Of course you are. You helped me shop, helped me cook . . . you have to stay."

"I don't want to intrude," he said as a louder, more insistent knock sounded at the door.

She met his eyes. "Yeah, I think we're way past that. Don't you?"

Chapter Eleven

IT TOOK JOSH ALL of five minutes of watching Heather with her coworkers to realize one thing:

Heather loved her job far more than he'd ever loved his. Or at least, she loved her coworkers.

Heather was *happy*. Radiantly so.

He wasn't sure why he was surprised. For some reason, the way she was so tightly wound all the time, he'd just sort of assumed that her stress about her job came from external pressure—a fierce demon on her back that drove her to be more, to be better.

Seeing her now though, as she animatedly described some hotel lobby she'd toured yesterday, Josh realized that it wasn't that at all. Her job had its pressures, certainly, but it was pressure Heather put on *herself*, because she cared so much.

She fiercely cared about other people's weddings—about getting them perfect.

And for a heart-stopping moment, Josh was . . . jealous.

Jealous that she'd found a calling and a career that seemed to light her up from within.

"So you're the noisy neighbor, hmm?" Josh glanced up from the stove, where he'd just dropped a pat of butter into a skillet for the eggs to find Alexis Morgan watching him.

From the second the group had walked through the door, Josh had understood what Heather had meant when she'd described Alexis as complicated. There was a duality about her. She was beautiful in an old-fashioned, composed sort of way. Wide brown eyes, slim, petite features. But just when you expected her to be quiet and sort of shy, she looked at you, and you were hit with the sense that you would never have any idea what she was thinking or feeling. Ever.

He and Heather had joked about each other having walls, and they certainly had them, but Alexis Morgan was on a whole other level. Not only did the pretty brunette construct a veritable Great Wall around her, she was aware of it—aware of how other people saw her, because she carefully cultivated what they saw.

"Noisy neighbor," Josh said, swirling the pan so that the sizzling butter coated the bottom. "Is that what she calls me?"

Alexis lifted her champagne flute to her lips and studied him. "She's mentioned being short on sleep once or twice, courtesy of your band."

Josh felt a little stab of guilt. It wasn't that he'd been completely immune to Heather's complaints, nor was he selfish enough to think it was his right to play live music at midnight in an apartment building with shared walls.

But he had enjoyed the sparring that had come with it. Hell, for all he knew, without his loud music, they might still just be two strangers who exchanged pleasantries at the mailbox the way he did with the rest of the building.

Not neighbors who kissed every bit as well as they fought.

His gaze flicked over to where Heather was refilling everyone's glasses, laughing as the blond wedding planner—Brooke—told some story about her latest client who was insistent on bacon cake.

No, he definitely didn't want to be strangers with her. He never felt quite so alive as when he was bickering with her, and these days, being alive was everything. Which was probably why he'd offered to help her with brunch this morning the instant he saw her flustered and overwhelmed. If only his mother could see him now, he thought ironically.

"You like her," Alexis said with the slightest smile.

Josh reached for the bowl of eggs he'd whisked earlier. She was a straight shooter. He liked that.

But he could be a straight shooter, too.

"I do like Heather. And you like your accountant. Logan, is it?"

Alexis's eyes narrowed. "Of course I like him. We're friends."

"Sure," Josh said with an easy smile. "That's what I meant."

It's actually not at all what he'd meant, and from

the way her eyes stayed narrowed on him, Alexis knew it.

She might think she and her accountant were just friends, but the other man had his gaze trained on her every time she wasn't looking. Josh knew a man in want, and Logan Harris was downright hungry when it came to Alexis.

Luckily, Josh was saved from having to respond to that by Logan ambling over to the kitchen as he dumped the eggs into the skillet and dug around in Heather's drawer for a spatula.

"You cook?" Logan said to Josh, his British accent doing nothing to hide his surprise.

"I know, I don't look the part," Josh said, spreading his arms to the side and glancing down at his gray Henley and jeans. "But my mother was determined I'd be able to feed myself in college and beyond, so she taught me the basics. Eggs. Chicken parmesan. That sort of thing."

"So what do you do, Josh?" Logan asked.

"I'm a musician," he said. And since he didn't particularly feel like talking about that, he shifted focus back to the other man. "You're an accountant, yeah?"

"Yep. Boring, right?" Logan said in a good-naturedly self-deprecating manner, taking a sip of his drink.

"No, actually," Josh said slowly as he dragged the spatula through the eggs. "I used to . . . I like numbers."

"Yeah?" Logan asked, his eyes lighting up.

"And, I'm out," Alexis said brightly, wandering

away to join the other women, who were interrogating Brooke's boyfriend, Seth, about some new hotel his company was opening in the Bahamas.

"I get it, you know," Logan said quietly. "I play the piano."

Josh's head snapped up, seeing from the quiet understanding in the other man's eyes that he did, in fact, get it. Which was pretty unusual: It was something that very few people in his circle seemed to understand, that music and numbers were inextricably linked. That mathematics were the very foundation of music, if you just paid attention. It was the same reason why Josh's mind always flitted to complex number problems when he was playing, and why he was never found without his earbuds in while he'd been working back when he was a hedge fund manager.

"So who do you work for?" Josh asked, dumping cheese into the nearly done eggs.

"Myself."

Josh's interest went from mildly curious to rabid. "Really?"

Logan shrugged. "I always thought I'd work for a big firm back in London, but I don't want someone else calling the shots. Running my own business isn't easy, especially in Manhattan, but it's worth the freedom and not having to answer to anyone."

"Huh." Josh flicked off the burner, but instead of calling to Heather to see how she wanted to serve up the eggs, he stayed perfectly still, lost in thought.

It was strange, but he'd never really thought about doing his own thing. For him, his work in finance had always meant the corporate world. The suits and the corner office and the life that never felt entirely like your own.

"It's okay to miss it," Logan said quietly.

Josh gave a harsh laugh. "With all due respect, dude, because you seem like a decent guy . . . you don't know me."

Logan ignored this, studying Josh with quiet brown eyes. For a man who was wearing honest-to-God tweed right now, there was a sharp shrewdness to his gaze.

"Who'd you work for?" Logan asked. "Before you tried the musician thing."

"Sullivan and Manning," Josh said, referring to his old firm.

Logan whistled. "Big time."

Josh didn't acknowledge this. He didn't have to. Sullivan and Manning was synonymous with big money. Their clients were some of the richest in the world. As a result, their employees were some of the richest in the city. But no amount of money could help you out when fate picked you as one of her victims, as she'd done to Josh.

Heather arrived at Josh's side, saving him from Logan's prying and his own dark thoughts. "You didn't have to do this," she said in surprise, looking at the eggs.

"What can I say?" he said, glancing down at her curls. "I sort of like the idea of you being in my debt. Now what am I doing with these? Do you have some fancy platter I'm supposed to put them on?"

"Not for these," she said. "Now, if you would have just let me do my quiche like I'd wanted to . . ."

Josh glanced at Logan. "You like quiche?"

"Ahh—"

"Hey, Seth," Josh called across the room to Brooke's boyfriend. "Do you like quiche?"

Seth glanced uncomfortably at his girlfriend. "Well—"

"I rest my case," Josh said, giving Heather a little pat on the cheek.

Heather rolled her eyes. "Whatever. Okay, let's just have everyone serve themselves from the stove. Guys. Grab a plate!"

"Look at you being all flexible," Josh said approvingly as the chatty group crowded into the kitchen with plates and began reaching over each other for rolls and fruit salad and eggs and bacon.

Five minutes later, they were gathered around Heather's table. He was pleased that she didn't seem to mind when he sat next to her. They were coming along quite nicely in this friendship thing, if he did say so himself.

"So, Josh," Brooke said, popping a banana slice into her mouth. "What do you think about our girl planning the wedding of one of the most famous women in the country?"

"Ah." He glanced up at the pretty blonde. "What?"

"I didn't mention it to him," Heather said quickly.

"Mention what?"

"The Belles are planning Danica Robinson's wedding," Jessie said. "As in all-the-way planning, since she's too busy to be bothered to mention her preferences. Heather's in charge."

Josh stared for a second at the redheaded receptionist before glancing at Heather's profile.

"Danica Robinson?" he said.

Heather fiddled with her fork. "Yeah. She's this big social media name. Reality TV, socialite . . . that kind of thing."

Yeah. Yeah, he was *well* aware of who Danica Robinson was.

Josh set his fork aside and leaned back. Feeling an intent gaze on him, he glanced across the table and met the light blue eyes of Seth Tyler.

Josh had actually met Tyler once or twice. They weren't best friends or anything, but back in his hedge fund days, Josh had gone to plenty of fancy fund-raisers. The Tyler family had been at most of them. Hell, they'd *hosted* half of them.

But it had been a long time ago. Surely Seth barely remembered him, much less remembered that he . . .

The sympathetic look in Seth's gaze said that the other man did remember. Just like the slight nod told Josh that Seth wasn't going to mention it.

But the silent exchange hadn't gone unnoticed. Alexis Morgan and that damn eagle eye of hers leaned forward slightly. "Boys. Anything you want to share with the group?"

Josh hesitated only for a second before realizing he had nothing to hide.

"Actually, I know Danica."

Everyone stared at him.

"You mean you know *of* her?" Heather pressed.

He glanced at her. "Ah, no. I mean I know her. Personally."

She didn't misunderstand, and her eyes bugged out. "You *boned* Danica Robinson? Are you kidding me?"

Josh barked out a laugh. "Jesus, 4C. We dated."

Heather and everyone else continued to stare at him. "You don't date."

He lifted a shoulder. "Not now. I used to."

"And back when you used to, you dated Danica Robison? How did I not know this?"

"She wasn't famous back then. Not like she is now. A few appearances on Page Six, but not a household name."

"How long did you date?"

"Two years. Give or take," he asked, reaching for the fruit salad and helping himself to another spoonful. "We met at a party, and just sort of . . . started hanging out."

He felt most of the group exchange looks.

"Two years is a legit relationship," Brooke said slowly.

Josh shrugged, trying to tamp down on his irritation, reminding himself that they had no way of knowing how much he hated talking about that part of his life. "I never said it wasn't."

"Who dumped whom?" Jessie asked in such a no-bullshit kind of way he had to smile, even as her words brought back a memory that ripped at his very core.

"She ended things," he said, picking up his mimosa.

Didn't want to get shackled with a dying man.

That wasn't exactly fair. Danica Robinson had

hardly been the love of his life, and they'd started to fizzle out even before his life had started to fall to shit.

Didn't make her abandonment any easier though. He'd never needed somebody quite so badly than at the exact moment she walked away.

Heather's fingers touched his forearm, and he glanced at her, bracing for . . . something.

"I'm sorry," she said quietly.

He shrugged. "Long time ago. Dedicated bachelor, remember?"

"Well, if it's any consolation, she seems like a real bitch," Jessie said.

Alexis let out a horrified laugh. "Jessie! She's a client! How many mimosas have you had?"

Jessie looked chagrined, but barely. "Sorry, but she is. We all think so."

Brooke sipped her own drink and patted Alexis's arm. "It's true. The woman's a nightmare. What kind of woman shows zero interest in planning her own wedding but also insists it be the event of the century?"

Josh snorted. "Sounds like Danica."

"You know her," Heather said, her voice speculative.

"That happens when you date someone, 4C," he said.

"No, I mean you *know* her. What she likes. What she doesn't like . . ."

"You're not about to get kinky on me, are you?" he asked, giving Heather a wary look.

Her smile grew wider. "You know what this

means? I no longer have to plan this wedding blind. It means that I have an inside track."

Josh dropped the spoon back into the bowl. "Tell me you're not suggesting what I think you're suggesting."

She patted his arm. "Let's just say I think we figured out how to make amends for all those sleepless nights you've caused me." Heather looked around at the other Belles' encouraging expressions and smiled almost maniacally. "You, Josh Tanner, are going to help me plan this wedding."

Josh stared at her before glancing around the table to see if anyone else was concerned that she was losing her mind. To his horror, the women were all nodding in awed agreement. Seth Tyler gave him a sympathetic look and handed him a nearly full champagne bottle.

"Yeah, that's not happening, 4C."

She sat back in her chair with a little huff. "Hardball, fine. What'll it take? Banana bread? I'll make you banana bread. Whatever you want, 4A, name it."

It was on the tip of his tongue to say that he didn't want banana bread—or anything—badly enough to help with his hideous ex-girlfriend's wedding.

But as he met Heather's hopeful green eyes, her lips pursed in a sexy little pout that made him remember exactly how sweet she'd tasted, he realized that maybe there was something he did want that badly.

He wanted Heather Fowler.

In his bed.

Chapter Twelve

LATER THAT DAY, STILL flying high from the un-questionable success of her first hosted brunch, Heather hunkered down for another treasured weekend ritual: a cup of cinnamon apple tea and her requisite Sunday-evening phone chat with her mother.

It had been Heather who'd initiated the weekly routine years ago when she'd gone away to college. She'd insisted that it was for her own sake—that she was missing being away from home. But she suspected her mother knew the truth—that Heather's weekly check-ins had been more for her mom's sake than for hers.

Not that Joan Fowler was the clingy type. Far from it, in fact. Heather had grown up with her mother working two, sometimes three jobs, which meant they'd gotten used to being apart. Heck, Heather's junior year of high school, her mom had taken the night shift at a twenty-four-hour diner, and it had seemed like they'd gone an entire year without seeing each other.

But college had been different. Although Michigan State was only an hour's drive from her hometown, the distance meant Heather hadn't been able to ensure her mom had healthy groceries stocked. Hadn't been there to move her mom's work uniform to the dryer before it started to smell mildewy.

It wasn't that her mom was flaky; it was just that the two of them had always taken care of each other. Something that had been hard to do an hour away in college, and was even harder now that Heather had followed her dreams to New York.

Her mom had never begrudged her that. Not once in Heather's entire life had her mom made her feel guilty for leaving. Quite the contrary, Joan had been her biggest cheerleader. The one who insisted that Heather not only aim high, but act on it.

When Heather's friends' moms in the trailer park had been encouraging their daughters to be realistic, Joan was telling Heather to reach for the stars.

The brightest star in Heather's case being New York City.

Her mom's blessing didn't ease the guilt though. Nothing could, although maybe the Sunday phone calls helped a tiny bit.

"Hi, honey," her mother chirped the second she picked up the phone. "How's my darling girl?"

"Wonderful," Heather said, settling into the couch and pulling her legs up to her chest, resting her mug on her knees as she made the expected response. "How's my darling mom?"

"Red."

Heather's eyebrows went up. "Hot flashes again?"

"No. Well, I mean, yes. Menopause has officially sunk its teeth in. But no, I meant red haired."

"I thought you were already red haired."

"No, I went chestnut for a while. Remember?"

"Oh right," Heather said, even though she rarely had a clue what color hair her mother had on any given day. Her mother had worked a good number of odd jobs in an effort to keep food on the table and, later, to help Heather pay for textbooks in college, but her bread and butter had always been hairdressing. The waitress gigs came and went, as did the occasional housekeeping duties, but Joan always said that she was a hairdresser through and through.

"You do it yourself?" Heather took a sip of tea.

"Nah, Sissy helped," her mother said, referring to her longtime best friend and neighbor. "I helped her go gray."

"How is Sissy not already gray? Isn't she pushing sixty?"

"Mind your tongue," Joan said without bite. "And yes, but it takes a rare skill to make the gray look intentional. Lucky for Sissy, I have that skill."

Heather smiled at her mom's complete lack of modesty.

"You'll see one day, darling. Or maybe not. You always did have exceptional hair."

Exceptional? Hardly. But then it was always people *without* the curls who wanted them.

In almost every way, Heather was a miniature of her mother. The same wide eyes, same slow-to-smile grin. Same narrow figure and sharp-winged brows.

But whereas Heather's hair was a mess (okay, tangle) of curls, Joan's hair was stick straight. The curls were the one and only thing Heather had gotten from her long-gone father. Though Heather didn't like that any physical link connected her to her good-for-nothing absentee dad, she could appreciate the irony that a hairdresser would have a daughter whose locks were virtually untamable—the shoemaker's children have no shoes, and all that.

"The girls at the shop nearly lost their minds when I told them you were doing Danica Robinson's wedding," her mother said.

"Mom! You know the Belles aren't supposed to talk about the weddings we work on. We sign confidentiality agreements."

"But *you* talked about it."

"Yes, to my *mom*," Heather said, rubbing her temple.

"And I talked to my *friends*. They won't tell a soul, don't you worry, sugar."

Heather snorted. Joan Fowler's friends were a loyal bunch, but discreet they were not. Still, she doubted the gossip in Merryville would ever make it to Danica Robinson's ears. And it's not like the wedding was top secret. Jessie said she'd been fielding calls from the media for weeks.

"Just . . . no more details for the girls, okay?" Heather asked, keeping her voice as gentle as possible.

"No, no, of course not," her mother said. "But things are going well? I know you were stressed about it last time we talked."

"Eh, I don't know about well," Heather said,

adjusting her mug atop her knees. "I toured a bunch of places yesterday and sent Danica my feedback, and she wrote back saying to pick 'the best one.'"

"Well, that's good. That she trusts you."

"I suppose. And I'm glad she's not being a total diva about it. But don't you think it's weird?" Heather asked. "I mean, she's this huge reality star, and her wedding will be everywhere, and she doesn't care enough to get involved?"

"I just watched her show the other day," Joan said. "She's busy launching her shoe line. Maybe she doesn't have time."

"For her wedding?"

"Well, not that I've ever been married," her mother said slowly. "But maybe she's smart enough to know that the wedding is just a day and that it's really about the marriage."

Heather rolled her eyes. She'd heard that before. Hell, she'd *said* that before. It was a common refrain for people trying to calm down brides-to-be. She just wasn't convinced that that was what was at work here. Danica hadn't struck her as a romantic soul in touch with what really mattered in life.

"I did have a little stroke of luck," Heather said slowly.

"Oh?"

"So, there's this guy—"

"Oh!"

"No, not that kind of guy," Heather said with a smile. Like mothers everywhere, Joan Fowler thought her daughter's life would be a little bit better if she could find a nice boy and settle down. Heather never wanted to make her mom feel bad, but she hadn't exactly had a stable picture to model her relationships off of when she was young. Joan flitted from man to man like flavors of the week, and sometimes Heather had gotten caught in the crosshairs. She'd concluded that a life without a man was a calmer, steady sort of life, just the kind she'd always wanted. "But in a crazy coincidence, the guy that lives next door actually used to date Danica."

"Huh."

"Huh what?"

"Is this the same neighbor that plays his music too loud?"

"Yes."

"The cute one."

"I don't recall saying that he was cute," Heather said warily.

"But he is, isn't he?"

Heather snorted. *Cute* wasn't the word for Josh Tanner's appearance. *Ridiculously hot*, maybe. It was almost handy, how good-looking he was. It was like a constant reminder not to fall for him, because men who looked like that were not the kind you fell in love with. They were the ones you admired from afar, sparred with occasionally, and kept at a very, very safe distance.

Even if they did seem to have a knack for planting very hot, very skilled kisses on you when you weren't expecting it.

"*Anyway*," Heather said, "Josh and Danica dated for a couple years. If anyone has a sense of what this woman wants, it's the guy who she had jumping through hoops to please her."

"And he agreed?"

"Actually, yeah," Heather said, still a little surprised by the ease with which Josh had agreed to let her run a few things by him. But then if there was one thing she'd learned to expect from Josh, it was to be surprised. "He's even agreed to go to look at a couple places with me tomorrow."

"Hmm."

"Mom."

"He likes you," Joan said gleefully.

"Well, yeah. Because we're friends." *Friends who've kissed.*

"I've had a few friends like that in my day. One of them resulted in a daughter."

"Gross," Heather muttered. She was all for the *Gilmore Girls*–type relationship she and her mom had, more friends than mother/daughter, but she drew the line at sex talk.

"You're young, honey! A little fling might be just what—"

"Nope. Not doing that," Heather said. "Subject change . . . have you thought about my offer for Thanksgiving?"

The moment of silence from her usually chatty mother was all the answer she needed, and Heather tried to ward off the stab of frustration, but it came anyway.

"The new manager at the restaurant is thinking of staying open," her mom said. "If I worked a shift, it'd be double pay."

"Mom, if you need money—"

"No," her mother said, a sharpness to her tone

that Heather was unaccustomed to hearing. "I appreciate it, I do, but I'm doing just fine. And you know I'd love to see you on Thanksgiving, if you want to come out—"

"Mom, I've been in New York for nearly five years now," Heather said quietly. "You haven't come out to visit once."

Her mom didn't respond, and Heather's frustration made the usual transition into hurt. She knew that New York was her dream, not her mother's. Knew that her mother was perfectly happy back home in her trailer in a way that Heather never could have been.

But despite repeated offers to pay for her mother to come to visit, Joan always found an excuse. It always ended up that Heather trudged back to Michigan for the holidays, falling into old habits as she and her mom crowded around the tiny kitchen table and had ham sandwiches or canned soup because her mom's grand plans of "cooking something new" had been derailed by a new TV show or a phone call from Sissy.

"New York just isn't for me," Joan said in a conciliatory tone.

"How do you know?" Heather asked with more snippiness than usual. "You've never been here."

Her mom sighed. "Honey, you know that I'm proud of all you've accomplished, but you need to accept that I'm happy here."

"I'm not asking you to move here. I don't need you to live my life. I just want you to see it," Heather said with a bit of pleading.

"I do see it. I always like everything you put on Facebook, and—"

"That isn't the same, Mom."

"What do you want from me, honey? You want me to put on high heels and come drink martinis with you?"

"You don't have to mock. That's not what I'm asking for, and you know it."

There was a long sigh on the other end. "Maybe we should both cool off a little bit," Joan said. "I hate fighting with you."

"I hate fighting, too," Heather said. "But it shouldn't be a fight just because I invite you to my home for Thanksgiving."

"I have to get going, sweetie."

For what? One of your shows? Heather said to herself, and then immediately regretted the unkind thought. Her mom worked hard, harder than almost any other woman Heather knew, and she deserved the chance to take a load off. But she couldn't help but feel like she was leaving her mother behind in a way, and the thought made her almost unbearably sad.

"All right," Heather said, forcing brightness into her voice so her mom wouldn't sense her bitterness. "No problem."

"Good luck with the wedding stuff. I can't wait to hear all about it next week!"

"Yeah, thanks."

"I love you. You know that, right? And I mean it. I'm so proud."

"I know," Heather said. "I love you, too."

They said their good-byes, and after hanging up,

Heather pulled her blue throw blanket off the back of the couch and wrapped it around her, trying to ward off the stab of loneliness.

Her mom had Sissy and her salon friends and her restaurant clients. Heck, even the noisy, sometimes-bickering trailer-park community was there for each other.

Heather had . . . no one. Sure, there was Alexis and Brooke, and they were friends as much as they were colleagues, but they also had their own things going on. Heather worked so much that she hadn't really had time to develop a social circle in New York outside of the Belles. She supposed she could call up her old Brooklyn roommates to go out, but the thought of them all catching each other up on their lives left her more exhausted than elated.

Put quite simply, in a city of millions, Heather suddenly felt very much alone.

She trailed into the kitchen to rinse out her mug. Josh had stayed to help her clean up, but there was an overstuffed garbage bag that still needed to be taken out, and Heather dragged it out into the hallway toward the garbage chute at the end of the hall.

Her footsteps faltered on her way back as she saw a familiar figure outside Josh's door. "Mrs. Tanner!"

Josh's mom turned toward her, an enormous foil-covered dish in hand and a wide smile on her face. "Heather! Honey. Don't you look lovely. And please, Sue, dear. Mrs. Tanner makes me feel old, and I already have the wrinkles to do that for me."

Heather smiled.

"I don't suppose you'd happen to know where my son is?" Sue asked hopefully.

Heather shook her head. "Haven't seen him since this morning. He's not answering?"

Sue sighed. "No. I knew I should have called first. I was just in the city visiting a friend, and I can never resist bringing him some lasagna. His favorite."

"I can keep it in my fridge for him, if you want?"

"No, no, I have a key," she said. "I was just giving him plenty of time to answer the door in case he was in there with a lady friend," Sue said with a little wink.

Heather forced a smile, even though the thought of Josh and a lady friend made her want to puke or punch something.

"Hold this for me, would you, sweetie?"

Heather obliged, taking the pan of lasagna as Josh's mom rummaged around in her purse for her keys. She felt a tiny stab of jealousy and wondered if Josh knew how lucky he was to have a mom who couldn't wait to drop by and see him, even unannounced.

Heather couldn't even pay her mom to come visit.

"Here we are," Sue said, finally pulling out a key chain with a triumphant smile before inserting it into the lock. "Bring that lasagna in here, would you, dear? Joshy, are you here? It's your mother, put some pants on!"

Good luck with that, Heather wanted to say.

But there was no sign of Josh, and Heather sent up a silent prayer that he was at the gym and not out getting laid.

"I heard it's going to snow tonight," Sue said, humming happily as she made room in Josh's fridge. "I just love the first snow, especially when it happens before Thanksgiving. It just signals that the holidays are around the corner, you know?"

Heather swallowed her bitterness, the conversation reminding her of the chat with her mom and the realization that she'd be spending Thanksgiving alone. Again.

Sue seemed to note Heather's lack of response, and glanced over, her face softening a little. "Sweetie, do you have family in town?"

Heather shook her head. "No. It's just me and my mom in Michigan."

"Ah. Are you headed back for Thanksgiving?"

Heather shook her head and opened her mouth to reply but to her utter horror, felt her eyes well with tears. "Oh, honey," Sue said, coming toward her and cupping Heather's face. "You'll come to our house."

Heather let out a little laugh and sniffled. "That's kind, but I really can't."

"Of course you can," Sue scolded. "No way am I letting a sweet girl like you spend the holiday alone."

Heather pressed her palms to the back of Sue's hands before slowly easing the other woman's away with a smile. "I appreciate it, really, but I'd feel strange intruding on a family holiday."

"Would it make a difference if I told you that you'd be a welcome buffer from my mother-in-law?"

Heather smiled but still shook her head. Sue sighed. "Okay, I won't push. Much. But promise me you'll at least consider it."

"I will," Heather lied.

It was bad enough that she was dragging Josh into the whole mess with Danica Robinson. She liked the guy far too much to crash his Thanksgiving.

Heather and Sue walked out of Josh's apartment, and Sue gave Heather a lingering, motherly hug after locking Josh's door. "I hope to see you on Thanksgiving," she whispered before pulling away and giving a happy wave.

For long moments after Josh's mom left, Heather stood perfectly still, tempted beyond reason to chase after Sue Tanner and tell her that yes, she would love to come for Thanksgiving.

Instead she turned on her heel, going back into her quiet apartment, trying desperately not to wonder where Josh was as she turned on the TV and watched a couple of mindless hours of reruns before going to get ready for bed.

As she changed into her pajamas, she got an unexpected lump in her throat—a threat of tears that came out of nowhere at the realization of just how alone she was. But just as she was on the verge of letting herself get good and deep into a pity party, the familiar sound of Josh's music hit her ears.

Just a week ago she would have already been out in the hall, banging on his door, but tonight she climbed into bed and simply *listened*.

Then she heard his voice. His voice, not the lead singer's, which meant it was a solo practice tonight.

Heather wrapped a blanket around her shoulders, curling into a ball with one ear pressed against the wall as she listened to Josh's low baritone sing something slow and moody. And even though she knew he wasn't singing to her, didn't know how much his song fit her mood, she let herself *pretend* he was singing to her. *For* her.

And as she felt some of the tension leave her shoulders and leaned back against her pillows, Heather was struck by the realization that maybe she wasn't as alone as she'd thought.

Chapter Thirteen

WHEN JOSH HAD AGREED to help Heather figure out some of the details for Danica's wedding, it had seemed simple enough. Tag along to cake tastings, maybe look at a couple of fancy hotels, maybe even suffer through some florist shops.

In other words, play along and do girly shit until he could figure out how to coax her into where they both wanted to be:

Bed.

But three hours into his first day of helping her plan Danica's wedding, he realized he'd completely underestimated the magnitude of Heather's job.

He'd thought Wall Street was nuts, but it had nothing on the warp speed with which Heather Fowler moved through the city. So far they'd been to three reception sites, a bridal shop, a tux shop, and a craft store (he'd waited outside), and it wasn't even lunchtime yet.

Speaking of lunch, he was starving. He reached out and grabbed Heather's elbow, pulling her around and interrupting her midstream as she prattled on about silk flowers versus the real thing before she could go charging down to yet another subway platform to take him out of the Meatpacking District and to God knew where.

"What's up?" she asked, glancing at her watch.

He waited until she looked up to meet his eyes before answering. He was happy to help the woman out, but he was starting to feel a bit like a dog expected to happily prance around a few steps behind her for the entire day.

"So far I've told you that Danica hates orange, loves blue, thinks roses are overrated, is self-conscious about the shape of her ass, and has zero appreciation for prewar architecture."

"Yes, and I've said thank you," she said, looking puzzled. "You were hoping for a medal?"

A blow job, actually.

"That'd be nice. All men *do* love to have a nice medal to commemorate the moment they planned their ex-girlfriend's wedding. But I'll settle for a sandwich."

"A sandwich?"

He wrapped his fingers more firmly around her elbow and dragged her out of the subway entrance and in the direction of the row of restaurants they'd just passed.

"Lunch, 4C. You need to feed me lunch."

She huffed out a breath and glanced again at her watch. "Okay, I need to get back to Midtown. There's a handful of food trucks—"

Josh ignored her as he opened the door to Pastis and ushered Heather inside.

"Josh, I don't have time for—"

"For lunch? Yes, you do," he said, before turning to the hostess and holding up two fingers.

"But—"

He put a hand on her back and not-too-gently shoved her in the direction of the hostess.

A moment later they were seated at a cozy table in the back corner, Heather was glaring at him, and the hostess was batting her eyelashes, but Josh was too busy reading the menu and salivating to care about either.

The hostess moved away, and Heather leaned forward. "Look, I appreciate you helping me, but I really—"

"This is one of Danica's favorite restaurants," Josh said, not looking up from the menu.

Heather sat back. "It is?"

"Yup. We came here at least once a week when we were dating, usually on a Friday or Saturday night, when she could see and be seen."

"And where *you* could," Heather said with a speculative note in her voice.

He glanced up. "I'm currently wearing a hoodie. Do you really think I care about that?"

"No," she said slowly. "But I think you cared about that. Why else would you date someone like Danica Robinson?"

"I already told you, she wasn't famous back then," he muttered.

"I bet she wanted to be."

"Sure," he said warily, setting the menu aside. "But I didn't."

Heather crossed both arms on the table and looked at him steadily. "So she twisted your arm, then? Dragged you in here the same way you dragged me."

Josh sighed. "Fine. You win. I *may* have been a little different back then."

Heather smiled, and damned if he wasn't getting to know the woman, because he'd come to recognize that as her victory smile. She'd never admit it, but she *loved* winning an argument.

The server came over, and after Heather ordered a boring sparkling water he got them a bottle of wine.

She blinked at him. "Seriously? I'm working."

"Fine," he said with a shrug. "But you also need to live. It's a French restaurant. Pretend you're French."

"I'm German."

"One hundred percent?" he asked, reaching for the bread basket.

She shrugged. "At least half, on my mom's side. I didn't know my dad."

"Ah," he said. There was no ire in her voice, no sadness. It told him that she'd long ago adjusted to that being her reality. As someone who was close with both parents, it bummed him out.

"You close to your mom?"

"Yeah," she said.

Her voice was confident, but she glanced down at her napkin when she said it, and even though he told himself not to press her—it was none of his business, really—the next question was out of his mouth before he could stop himself.

"Michigan, right?"

Heather nodded. "A little bit outside of Detroit."

"You see her often?" he asked, spreading a liberal amount of butter on the bread before handing it to her.

Heather didn't even hesitate before taking the bread and sinking her teeth into it. He hid his smile.

"I try to get back there at least once a year," she said, wiping her mouth with the napkin. "Thanksgiving or Christmas or whatever."

"You headed home this year?"

"This is my home," she said with emphasis. "I'm from there, but New York . . . this is home now," she repeated.

Josh leaned back in his chair and studied her as the server approached the table with the wine bottle. Josh did the whole swirl-and-taste thing, nodding at the server appreciatively and waiting until both of them had glasses before he resumed the subject.

"And no siblings, right?"

She shook her head.

"You headed back for Thanksgiving this year?"

She gave him a startled look, then shook her head.

The sadness on her face bugged the crap out of him, and he opened his mouth to invite her over to his place before he realized how odd that would be. He didn't know her that well, and inviting her would give everyone the wrong idea.

His parents.

Heather.

Himself.

Still, the thought of her spending the holiday alone . . .

"Your mom invited me over," she said, not looking at him. "For Thanksgiving."

Josh froze in surprise before letting out a resigned laugh. "Of course she did. When?"

Heather lifted a shoulder. "Last night. She brought you lasagna."

"Ah, right. Trevor and I were out grabbing a drink. So, you coming?"

Heather frowned. "Of course not."

"Why not?"

She stared at him. "Because it's a family holiday. A big one. And I'm not family."

He lifted his wineglass. "You have other plans?"

She bit her lip. "No. My mom isn't coming this year."

"Perfect." He lifted his glass. "You'll come to my folks'. The dinner will be mediocre, but the pie's magnificent."

"Well, it *is* all about the pie," she said hesitantly.

He winked. "Exactly. Speaking of baked goods, when are we making our banana bread?"

"*We* don't have a banana bread," she said, taking a small sip of her wine, and then another.

"I've dutifully followed you all around the city to plan the wedding of my ex. And let's not forget that I made your friends brunch yesterday and did your shopping. There's definitely going to be a banana bread."

And sex. Please let there be sex.

"You know what? Fine," she said, taking another sip of wine and seeming to relax slightly. "You just say the word, and we'll make the damn bread."

"I think I like this agreeable version of you. Would now be a good time to call in other favors?"

"If that's your way of negotiating more band

practice, the answer's no. Always no. Also, I noticed it's been just you playing lately. Where are the guys?"

"Listening in on me, were we?"

"Avoiding the question, are we?" she shot back.

Damn. He *was* avoiding the question.

He wasn't ashamed of canceling practices lately, although he was perhaps a little embarrassed that he'd made up a white lie about having a female companion in order to do so.

The truth was, he hadn't had female company in . . . weeks. Was that right? Hell.

As far as why he'd canceled practice—no clue other than the fact that he just wasn't feeling it. He'd wanted to play music, but not under the pretense of his group being the next Stones.

He'd wanted to play the music just for him.

And for his nosy neighbor, apparently.

"You ever just . . . need a minute?"

Heather cocked her head. "What do you mean?"

Josh rolled his shoulders, feeling foolish. "I don't know. Forget it."

She reached across the table, her fingers stopping just short of touching his hand, and he had a fierce and strange wish that she'd complete the gesture and make contact.

"You okay?" she asked.

He winked. "I'm always okay."

She merely stared back at him with a steady gaze that quietly called *bullshit*.

"I like your voice, you know."

His wineglass froze halfway to his lips. "Why, thank you, 4C."

"No, I mean . . . I *really* like it. Better than your lead singer's voice."

Josh studied her. "Trevor's voice is perfectly suited for the songs I write."

"Only some of the songs you write," she argued. "The loud, bang-the-drum noisy ones."

He laughed. "Such high praise."

"The ballads. Those are better suited to your voice."

Josh winced. "I don't write ballads."

"Well, what would you call them?" she asked softly. "The quieter ones like I heard you singing last night. They're slow. Pretty."

"Okay," he said, pointing at her with his wineglass. "We can call them ballads, but we're not calling them pretty."

She smiled. "I think you like those songs best, too."

"Jesus," he muttered, picking up his menu and holding it in front of his face to block her prying gaze.

Heather snatched it away. "Why'd you cancel band practice last night?"

"Because I had a woman come over," he snapped, the lie rolling off his tongue before he could think better of it. He instantly felt like shit. Lying to the guys about this was one thing. It was what guys did.

But lying to Heather . . . it didn't feel right.

Especially not when she blinked and looked away. Almost as though she were hurt.

Nah. Their relationship wasn't like that.

And yet, now that he thought about it, the thought of Heather bringing a guy home . . . the thought of some guy running his hands all over those slim curves, plunging his fingers into all that glorious hair . . .

Shit. *Shit!*

Their server came over, saving both of them from going any further down a path that he was positive neither wanted to. After he'd ordered a steak and she'd opted for some mussels, he gratefully let her change the topic toward safer territory:

Danica.

Never in his life would he have thought that his most toxic ex would be a safe topic, but compared to crossing a line with his neighbor, perhaps destroying the first good thing he'd had in years, it was definitely the lesser of the two evils.

"So tell me more about why you guys broke up," Heather said, helping herself to a bit more wine.

Josh shrugged. "The usual reasons, I guess. We outgrew each other. We were fighting more often than we were getting along. I found myself coming up with reasons not to pick up the phone when she called. I no longer had a clue how to make her happy, and she certainly wasn't making me happy."

He skipped the part about her telling him his sickness was "too much."

Heather fiddled with her glass. "I've met Danica. I'll admit, I'm trying to figure out—"

"What I saw in her?" he asked with a grin.

She winced. "I know I'm not supposed to talk badly about my client, but you're a . . . a friend, sort of, I guess, and I just . . . I don't get it."

"I was a different person back then," he said

quietly. "And trust me, that version of Josh Tanner was exactly the type of douche bag that would get involved with a social-climbing diva."

"Is this back when you were a hedge fund manager?" she asked.

He winced. "Not my favorite topic, 4C. You're usually pretty good about not prying."

"Well, don't get too excited, because I'm totally going to pry right now. Why did you quit?"

Tell her, his subconscious urged. *Tell her you got sick and your life turned upside down.*

But the words didn't come. He knew it was irrational, but he just didn't want to be known as the sick guy. He'd been there. Done that. Spent a year of his life being the guy who people felt sorry for, and he was just . . . over it.

He didn't want Heather looking at him with all that pity and concern, analyzing every cough and yawn.

He already had a mother for that.

"The corporate client in my old company was brutal," he said, trying to find a way to tell her the truth without telling her the whole truth. "The money was good. Really good. But the hours were long, and the lifestyle was something straight out of the movies."

"How so?"

"Drinking way too much, way too often. Recreational drugs. Workdays that transitioned straight to happy hour, and then to a late dinner, and then to a party that went all night long until you got to the office, where you kept a spare suit and did it all over again."

"This is when you and Danica were dating?" she asked.

He nodded. "Her dad was one of my company's clients. Not *my* client. I was too junior for that. But we met at some fund-raising thing, and I guess we figured we could use each other. She was new to the scene, barely out of college. I showed her the ropes, and in return, I got access to one of the richest men in the city."

Josh glanced at her, braced for censure or disdain, but instead saw only curiosity.

"You guys broke up after you quit?"

"Pretty much."

He knew he was being terse, but he didn't want to go there. Hadn't gone there in a long time.

"I know it's been a while," Heather said as she grabbed another piece of bread, "but since you knew her, don't you think it's odd the way she's so hands-off about this wedding?"

"Honestly, yeah," Josh said thoughtfully. "I suppose it's possible that she's changed, but the Danica I knew was a control freak. I still remember when she decided to redecorate her bathroom. She went through a half dozen interior designers because she was too up in their business about the precise shade of sea foam green or whatever."

Heather's fingernails tapped on the table. "That's what I expected when she hired me. I was prepared for it. So it just doesn't make sense that she'd be the most hands-off bride I ever had."

"Like I said, maybe she changed?" Josh asked.

"Perhaps," Heather said, although she didn't

sound like she believed it, and he didn't know that he did, either. Danica had always been deliberate in everything she did. Hell, conniving might be a better word for it.

"Keep your eyes open, 4C," he said, feeling the need to warn her, even though he didn't know about what. He hadn't spoken to Danica in years.

"Oh, I am," she said with a firmness to her voice. "There's definitely something going on with her, but until I figure out what it is, all I can do is plan the best wedding I know how."

"You always wanted to be a wedding planner?" he asked.

"Ah—"

His eyes narrowed at the embarrassment in her tone. "Confess."

She sighed. "Okay. Fine. But it's embarrassing."

"The good stuff always is."

Heather fiddled with her napkin. "So my mom is sort of . . . a romantic. And back when I was little, she had a boyfriend—*lots* of boyfriends—and even though they never stuck around for more than a couple months, she never stopped believing that one of them would. 'This is The One, sweetie. I'm going to marry this one,' she'd say. And back before I wisened up, knew how relationships *really* worked, I let myself dream. I let myself plan."

Josh's heart twisted a little. "You planned your mother's wedding."

"*Weddings*," she corrected with a sad smile. "There were plenty of boyfriends, and with each one, I'd come up with a new color scheme, a new theme, a new location, each one more perfect than the last."

"Did any of the weddings ever happen?" he asked gently.

"Nah," she said with a casualness that was too forced. "But hey, it was good practice, right?"

"You know, having a sister, I know that most little girls plan their own weddings."

She shrugged. "The ones who already had happily married parents, maybe."

There was no bitterness in her voice. Just tired resignation.

"You've never thought about your own?" he asked, not really sure why he was asking.

"From time to time," she said. "I just don't really see much of a point in spending that much thought on it. I get paid to think about other people's. And I love it. I really do."

"So you're living the dream."

"I am," she said, idly twisting her wineglass around on the table. "I always wanted to live in New York. I always wanted to be a wedding planner."

"And look at you now," he said.

She met his eyes and smiled. "And look at me now."

"So what's next on your bucket list now that you're on track for domination of your professional life?"

"Domination of my personal life, I guess," she said with a little shrug. "I know. It's pathetic that I have to schedule it in, but it's not happening naturally, so . . ."

"What's the plan?" he asked, feeling suddenly irritated even as he couldn't put his finger on why. "If you want, we could put together a little sign for you to wear around your neck that says 'available and looking.'"

"Actually, that's not far off," she said. "I'm thinking it's time to wade into the world of dating sites or apps, or what not."

"Oh, 4C. No."

"What!" she exclaimed. "There's nothing to be ashamed of! Plenty of people meet their soul mates that way."

"Yeah, but not *you*."

She glared. "Why not me?"

Josh opened his mouth only to realize that he didn't have a good answer for that.

"Exactly," she said with no small amount of smugness. "I don't suppose I could talk you into putting together my profile? Despite your piglike tendencies, you do seem to have a good grasp of the dating world."

"Let me get this straight," he said, leaning forward. "You've already recruited me to be your professional sidekick for Danica's wedding, and now you're wanting me to help you date as well? What's next? You want me to breathe for you, too?"

She leaned forward, matching his posture. "Well, why *not* live my life? God knows you're not living yours, are you, Tanner?"

Josh's head snapped back in surprise. That was *bullshit*. Utter bullshit. He *was* living. Hell, that's why he hadn't gone back to his old job. Why he was pursuing his dreams, why he was refusing to go back to being a destructive workaholic . . .

"I'm sorry if I overstepped," she said quietly. "Maybe I'm wrong, it just seems that beneath all the quips and winks, you seem a tiny bit . . . lost."

What the *fuck*.

His burst of temper was suppressed by the appearance of their server, and neither said a word as the obliviously cheerful man put their entrees in front of them.

Then they were alone again, and Josh took a deep breath.

"Just because *I* don't have every minute of every day mapped out as part of some grand life plan doesn't mean I'm lost," he said quietly.

"Hey!" she said, her voice wounded. "I was just trying to help you the way you've helped me."

"Well, don't," he said, gritting his teeth. "Let's just drop it."

"Josh—"

"I said drop it, Heather."

"Look, I obviously struck a nerve, and I'm sorry. I just think—"

"I don't care what you think. We clear?"

Her mouth clamped shut, and he saw from the tension in her jaw that she was gritting her teeth.

"Yeah," she said after several tense moments of silence. "We're clear."

"Good," he said quietly, picking up his knife and fork.

They began eating in awkward silence, Heather shooting him death glares from over the top of her water glass, and Josh waited for the sense of relief that she was backing off from interfering in his life.

But the relief never came.

His life was exactly as he wanted it—exactly as he'd carefully shaped it to be.

So why did it feel like it no longer fit?

Chapter Fourteen

I'M JUST SAYING, THE man stuck around for brunch with your friends. He made brunch for your friends. Are you really telling me there's nothing there?" Brooke took a demure sip of her Veuve Clicquot, nailing Heather with that dead-on look that pulled the truth out of her like magic.

It was Friday night, and they were out on the town for a belated celebration of Alexis's birthday, but in classic Alexis style, there were no shots, no nightclubs, no too-short skirts. Instead it was a quiet night at a classy Midtown champagne bar.

A handful of Alexis's nonwork friends had shown up as well, but after making the requisite small talk, Heather found herself huddled around a small table with Brooke, who, in between sexting with Seth, seemed determined to talk about the one thing Heather didn't want to talk about:

Josh Tanner.

Heather sighed and sipped the delicious sparkling rosé she'd ordered. "I'm *positive*. I'm not crazy enough to get involved with my neighbor. Then we'd break up, and I'd have to move because it'd be awkward."

"What makes you think you'd break up?" This was from the woman sitting on the other side of Brooke: Leah McHale, a stunning redhead and one of the Belles' go-to wedding photographers. Heather had known Leah and her boyfriend, fellow photographer Jason Rhodes, for years. Had actually helped them get together, if she wanted to get braggy.

Heather gave Leah a look. "You'd understand if you saw him. He is not the type of guy who sticks around. Brooke? Back me up here."

Brooke pursed her glossy lips as she pulled her long blond hair into a messy knot atop her head. "He did kind of look the part of an overgrown frat boy."

"Trust me, he acts the part, too," Heather said.

"Still doing the loud music thing, huh?"

"Yeah, although we've set up some boundaries," Heather admitted as she pulled the bowl of spiced nuts toward her, shaking it around until she found another almond.

"And he's respecting them?"

Heather lifted a shoulder. In truth, she hadn't heard Josh's music at all in the four days and nights since their near fight on Monday. Either he was playing when she wasn't around, or he wasn't playing at all.

She hoped it wasn't the latter. Any fool could see that he loved music. Needed it. Maybe she'd been imagining things when she'd thought the music wasn't enough for him, but she didn't think so. She suspected he was hiding behind his music, using it as an excuse to avoid something.

She just didn't know what that *something* was.

Should she have backed off her prying? Maybe. But damn it, she'd spilled her guts to him. She'd never told anyone where she'd gotten her interest in wedding planning, and she'd told him.

Heather had put herself out there in a way she hadn't in a very, very long time and had gotten nothing back. And she was feeling a little . . . pissed.

"How's the Robinson wedding going?" Leah asked. "Should I be offended you haven't asked me to work it?"

Heather sighed. "Trust me, I checked your and Jason's schedules first. You're all booked up, seeing as she wants this to go down in a couple months."

"Is she still clinging to the Plaza dream?" Brooke asked.

"Yup. No luck there, but I did make some headway with getting her to commit to a cake company that has an opening."

"Let me guess, she wants something huge and gaudy?"

"Pretty much. I asked her about flavors, and she told me it doesn't matter because nobody in her circle eats cake anyway."

"Her circle sounds like one of the layers of hell, then," Brooke replied.

Heather snorted. This was why she loved Brooke. The other woman looked like an adorable beach bunny in her short shimmery black dress and perfect makeup, but she knew how to appreciate a good dessert.

"I can't believe Josh dated her," Brooke said, taking another sip of her champagne. "They seem so different."

"Apparently, he was different back then," Heather said. "He used to be some big-firm hedge fund manager. I'm not even sure I know what that means."

"It means money," Brooke said.

Heather wanted to ask more questions—wanted to understand more about what Josh did and who he was back then, but Brooke wasn't the person to ask.

Brooke's ex-fiancé had been an integral part of the Wall Street scene up until he'd moved to Los Angeles and met Brooke.

And *then* the guy had been accused of just about every single white-collar crime in the book. His arrest had happened just seconds before he and Brooke had exchanged vows.

Heather supposed it was a good thing the cops had come after him before the vows rather than after, but for Brooke's sake, she couldn't help but wish they'd gotten their shit together just a little bit earlier.

The scandal had destroyed Brooke's West Coast wedding-planning career.

But it hadn't destroyed Brooke. Her friend was too strong for that. And now she'd found a man who treated her like a queen. Heather couldn't have been happier for her friend, but if she was being honest, a teeny tiny part of her was also green with envy, too. When would Heather find someone to love her so intensely and unconditionally like that? Would she ever?

"What changed?" Brooke asked.

Heather's attention snapped back to the conversation at hand. "Hmm?"

"You said he was different back then, and I believe it if he was a hedge fund manager who dated a society princess. But that's not who he is now. Right? He couldn't have seemed further from that when we all met him at brunch."

"No, definitely not," Heather said. The Josh she knew didn't seem like the type to be caught dead in a suit, and she couldn't imagine him tolerating a nine-to-five schedule.

"So what caused the change?" Leah asked gently.

"I wish I knew," Heather said, more to herself than her friends.

"Seems like you care an awful lot about a guy who's *just* a neighbor."

"He's also a friend," Heather admitted.

Brooke smirked. "Uh-huh. It's starting to sound like you're borrowing Alexis's script when she's talking about Logan."

"Um, okay, that's just insulting," Heather said. "I'm nowhere near that blind."

They all shifted their attention to the birthday girl, who was seated a little ways down the table amid a couple of her friends from college days, discussing her next champagne choice with the server. The waitress looked slightly panicked, probably having realized by now that Alexis knew far more about the menu than she did.

"Do you think she knows that Logan's in love with her?" Heather asked.

"Honestly? No. I think the man is her one blind

spot," Brooke replied. "And honey . . . trust me when I say you're going to want to down the rest of your champagne right about now."

Heather glanced back at Brooke in puzzlement. "Why?"

Brooke's eyes were locked on the front door. "Because Danica Robinson just walked in here."

Heather froze. "Seriously?"

"Yup."

"Has she seen me?"

"Yup."

"Crap," Heather muttered, smoothing a hand over her hair even as she reminded herself that it didn't matter how she looked for Danica Robinson. The woman wanted her for her wedding-planning skills, not her looks.

Still, Heather pasted on a smile all the same as Danica came into view. The other woman looked flawless in a white minidress, her long hair pulled into a high ponytail as she descended on Heather, Brooke, and Leah in a wave of designer perfume and five-inch heels.

"Heather, oh my gosh, hi, you look amazing! What are you doing here?"

Heather stood, feeling like a dork as she did the whole air-kiss thing with her most famous client. A client who'd barely managed to respond to her texts and was now hugging her like they were BFFs.

"Celebrating a friend's birthday," Heather said, gesturing at Alexis.

"Oh, Alexis, of course, happy birthday, babe," Danica said with a dismissive finger waggle at Alexis.

"Guys, of course you're all familiar with the Wedding Belles," Danica said, turning toward her group.

A couple of the girls nodded with pasted-on smiles. The guys looked like they could not care less.

Guys, Heather noted, that did not include Danica's fiancé.

"Anyway, I dragged everyone out tonight for a little break from all things wedding, you know?" Danica said with a wide smile. "But absolutely give me a call tomorrow, I want to hear all about the flowers you mentioned in your voice mail."

Heather stared at her. Was she for real?

It had been at least a dozen voice mails on the flowers, all of which were left last week before Heather had finally decided to wing it and pick them herself, courtesy of Josh's tip that Danica hated roses.

Still, what was she supposed to do? She couldn't very well call out their most famous client for being a deadbeat bride.

But she wanted to. Oh, how she wanted to.

"You guys should see my dress," Danica gushed to her friends. "It's gorge."

Heather blinked. Danica didn't have a dress. She had yet to so much as show up for a single fitting.

As though she could read Heather's mind, at that exact moment Danica caught her eye and gave her a little wink as though they were coconspirators.

Heather's temper snapped, and had it not been for Brooke's clearing of the throat and the fact that Alexis was giving her a don't-do-it look, she just might have told Danica Robinson just what she could do with her imaginary dress.

Instead Heather smiled a smile even faker than Danica's entourage. "Yes, by all means you deserve a break from all the planning," she said sweetly. "Enjoy your evening, and we can talk tomorrow?"

"Absolutely," Danica said. "I'll call you, 'kay? Can't *wait*. Ciao, darlings."

She turned on her heel, lifting a hand to signal her group to follow her before they headed toward a roped-off section in the back of the bar as half a dozen of the bar's staff scurried after them, armed with champagne buckets.

"Did that just happen?" Heather asked incredulously, gritting her teeth as her hands subconsciously balled into fists.

"Don't let her get to you, Heather," Alexis soothed, appearing by her elbow alongside Brooke as they coaxed Heather into sitting back down.

Leah rubbed her knee. "You did good. I know it sucks, but you have to respect her confidentiality."

"It just doesn't make sense," Heather said, her eyes still locked on Danica, where the other woman was sitting awfully close to one of the nameless guys in her group. "I thought maybe the whole hands-off thing was some new bizarre trend she was trying to set, but she obviously wants people to think that she's actually involved."

"It is strange," Alexis murmured, her expression speculative. "Especially with what's been going on in the tabloids."

Heather looked at her friend. "What do you mean?"

Brooke and Alexis exchanged a glance, and Heather

waved a hand between their gazes. "Uh-uh. Don't do that. Fill me in."

"There've been rumors that Danica's stepping out on Troy," Brooke said.

"Don't know how those might have gotten started," Heather said, with a subtle head nod in Danica's direction. "Still, that's nothing new, right? Everyone knows that cheating scandals sell magazines, even the ones not based on fact."

"True," Alexis said, biting her lip and looking uncharacteristically worried. "Something's just not right about all of this."

"Tell me about it," Heather muttered, rubbing her temples. "You know what? I'm not going to think about this right now. Monday morning I'll call Danica and tell her about my concerns. But right now I want a bubble bath and a very good night's sleep."

She glanced at her watch. "Or as good a night's sleep as I can get, considering it's past one."

At least there was one upside to staying out late on a Friday night; she'd miss the *thump thump twang* of Josh's band practice.

"You care if I bail on the rest of your birthday night?" she asked, turning toward Alexis.

Alexis waved this away. "Please. I'm secretly hoping we wrap up soon so I can get a little bit of work done before tomorrow morning."

Heather rolled her eyes and kissed her friend's cheek. "You're a mess. You know that, right?"

"Do either of you need help tomorrow?" Brooke asked. "I don't have anything until the small Mortin wedding tomorrow."

"No, I'm good," Heather said, standing and reaching for her jacket. "Thanks, though."

It was true. Her wedding tomorrow was an easy one. The couple had opted to keep the ceremony small, a swanky brunch reception on a yacht. All Heather had to do was make sure the appropriate vendors were on the boat on time and that the restrooms were stocked with motion-sickness meds in addition to the usual perfumes and breath mints.

Easy enough. *At least this bride had actually seemed to care about her wedding*, Heather thought sourly with one more surreptitious glance at Danica Robinson and her group.

"Honestly, you both know how much I love this business, but I'd be lying if I said I wasn't more than a little excited for the office to be closed for Thanksgiving," Alexis said, draining the last of her glass.

Thanksgiving.

Just like that, Heather's already bad mood took another dip. She loved Thanksgiving. Who didn't, really? All that glorious food and wine and excuse to have pie for breakfast the next day.

But she'd been so hoping that this was the year that would be her Thanksgiving. The one where she'd get to take her mom to the Macy's parade and then they'd come home to the delicious aroma of a cooking turkey, maybe make pumpkin pie together . . .

Instead she'd be all by herself.

And yes, it had been her choice not to go back to Michigan. Not only because she had a wedding the weekend after the holiday, but maybe because she was being a tiny bit stubborn.

Heather was always the one to travel for the holiday. Always the one to make the trek home and do Thanksgiving on her mother's terms. Which would be fine if her mom was an invalid, but Joan Fowler was active and perky and could get on a plane if she wanted to.

But she *didn't* want to. Heather loved her mother, but she was also tired of always being the one to do things her mother's way.

And as for Josh's insistence that she take his mother up on her offer—well, she was *fairly* certain that invitation was off the table. Not that she'd take him up on it if it still was, the beast.

For one tiny moment, Heather was jealous of the other Belles for having actual plans. Brooke and Seth were headed back to California to spend the holiday with Brooke's family. Alexis was . . . well, hell, nobody knew where Alexis was headed, since she refused to talk about it, but she'd announced that she was taking the rare weekend off, and everybody was too grateful for her overdue vacation to press for details.

Looked like it would be turkey and pity party for one this Thanksgiving holiday.

Heather forced a smile on her face as she said her good-byes before stepping into the brisk autumn night. It was a long walk home, but Heather needed the air. Needed to think and get herself out of her funk.

She swapped out her heels for the comfy foldable flats she kept in her oversized purse. But thirty minutes later when she got to her building, thinking had only made her thoughts muddier.

And as she trudged up the stairs, her already-simmering bad mood took a turn for the worse.

Josh's door was open, and he was standing in the doorway, one arm braced against the doorjamb, no shirt, of course.

He was saying good-bye.

To a woman.

Heather couldn't see the woman's face, but if her slim profile and long shiny brown ponytail were any indication, she was likely quite cute. The way that Josh was looking at her told Heather that.

Great. Just what she wanted. A front-row seat to the exit routine of one of Josh's flings.

His eyes flicked up to hers as she stepped into view, and she could have sworn she saw him jolt slightly in surprise.

But his eyes were bored and casual as they flicked over her, taking in the short skirt. "Hey, 4C."

"Hey," she said grimly, digging her keys out of her bag.

The woman turned to see who Josh was talking to, and Heather saw that she was right. The woman was cute. Wide brown eyes, pink lipstick, perfectly done eye shadow.

Heather smiled reflexively in greeting. The woman didn't smile back.

Okay, then.

She had bigger things to worry about than whether or not her neighbor's one-night stands liked her.

Say, like the fact that she had a weird knot in her stomach at the thought of Josh and this woman together.

Not wanting to dwell too deeply on that, at least not in front of Josh and his lady friend, she shoved the key in the lock, about to utter a terse good night, when another familiar voice called her name.

"Heather. Hey!"

She glanced over to see Trevor, Josh's band's lead singer, standing beside Josh.

Heather smiled in greeting, this time for real. She liked Trevor. Like Josh, the guy had plenty of easy charm and confidence, but unlike Josh, the guy didn't seem to have a secret side of himself that he kept hidden from the world.

"How's it going?" she asked.

"Honestly," he said, jerking a thumb at Josh, "this guy bailed on our practice to entertain Kitty here. So, feeling very third wheel."

There it was again. The knot. Tighter this time.

"In fact," Trevor said, easing by Josh with a friendly wink at Kitty, "I wouldn't mind an escape route."

"You have one," Josh said. "The stairs. Or the elevator. Your choice. Unless you want me to shove you out the window, because I'd be more than happy—"

"You want any company?" Trevor asked, interrupting Josh and directing the question at Heather.

Heather opened her mouth to say no. The entire reason she'd left the bar was to get away from people and stew on her own.

And yet, even as her brain was formulating some polite excuse about having an early morning, Heather realized that she didn't want to be alone after all.

The thought of sitting by herself in her apartment,

staring at the ceiling while picturing Josh and this girl . . .

"I'd love some company," she said with a bright smile at Trevor.

Out of the corner of her eye, she thought she saw Josh jolt again.

Trevor grinned at her, and Heather swung open her door, gesturing playfully for him to precede her.

Heather started to follow him, but at the last minute, she dragged her gaze back to Josh. It was a pull she couldn't deny—almost as though he silently *demanded* that she look at him.

He was looking right at her, his gaze unreadable, his mouth set in a firm line.

She swallowed, wishing desperately that she knew how to get rid of this bizarre tension between them. Wishing that they could have a redo of Monday's lunch, and she was torn between wanting to strike at him and soothe whatever demons he refused to talk about.

Heather opened her mouth to say something—anything—but he looked away from her, instead shifting his attention back to Kitty, rewarding her with one of his easy, charming smiles before leaning down and whispering something in her ear.

Heather's breath caught, and she felt a stab of pain.

So she clung to anger instead.

Heather stepped into her apartment with Trevor, giving Josh one last look before slowly, deliberately closing the door on him.

Chapter Fifteen

❧

Y OU'RE COMPLETELY ENORMOUS. YOU know that, right?"

Josh's sister glared at him over her cup of orange juice. "No, brother dearest. I have a bowling ball chilling on top of my bladder and ankles that feel like water balloons, but I had no idea that I'm enormous. Thanks for the public service announcement."

Josh sighed and looked at his brother-in-law. "Has she been this way for all nine months?"

Kevin scratched his cheek. "I'm going to get pizza. Who wants pizza?"

Jamie's hand shot in the air. "I want *all* the pizza."

Josh reached over and patted his twin's protruding belly. "You are eating for two, after all."

His sister snorted. "Please. The kid can get by on the umbilical cord. The pizza's mine, all mine."

"Speaking as someone who shared your umbilical cord, I'm pretty sure that's not how it worked."

"Don't get me started on that. I know you were

in there figuring out how to give yourself the fit gene while I got the chubby gene."

"I forgot how good you were at science," Josh mused.

Jamie started to lean forward to swat him but leaned back with a tired sigh. "Forget it. Once the kid's out, I *will* be kicking the shit out of you, but for right now I'm too grateful that you made the trek down here. I'm getting sick of Kevin."

"And that's my cue to go get pizza," Kevin said, standing and placing a kiss on his wife's head. "Canadian bacon and pineapple, same as last time?"

Jamie made a gagging motion. "What are you trying to do, kill me? Who eats fruit on a pizza?"

"You did, just last week," Kevin said, searching around on the messy desk until he came up with the car keys.

"Well, the baby's cravings have shifted. Now she wants sausage and mushroom."

"I thought you said the baby didn't get any pizza," Josh said.

"Don't do it, man," Kevin muttered. "Just don't do it. Be back in a bit. Don't kill each other."

Josh lifted a hand to wave good-bye to his brother-in-law before frowning. "Do they not have delivery here?"

"Easy there, New York, this is Nashville, not rural Wyoming. Of course we have delivery. He just needs any excuse to get away from me these days."

"I can't imagine why," he teased, standing up from the kitchen table and going to refill her orange juice glass.

"I know, I'm a monster," she said, leaning back in her chair and rubbing her belly. "I'm just grumpy I can't be with the family for Thanksgiving. Stupid third-trimester flight limitations."

"You know we could have come to you," he said, placing the orange juice in front of her and sitting back down.

"I know, but Dad has to work on Monday, and Mom's got that charity thing she does on Friday. And honestly, it's probably better. I'm so dang pissy these days, because I feel fat and cranky and my back hurts."

He leaned forward and grabbed her hand. "You'll get through it. Just a couple more weeks, right?"

Jamie sat up a little straighter. "Oh my God. Josh. I'm sorry, you must think I'm the worst, complaining about a little back pain and swollen feet. I didn't think. I'm sorry."

He shook his head. "Don't do that. My experiences don't make yours any less valid."

The miserable expression on her face didn't fade, and Josh squeezed her hand. "Jamie. I thought we were over this."

"The guilt?" she muttered. "No, not really."

Josh dipped his head forward and tried to think of the right thing to say. Nobody was closer to him than Jamie—they'd been best friends and worst enemies growing up, as siblings often were, and by the time they got into adulthood, only the friendship was left behind.

But then he'd gotten sick, and in ways that only a twin could understand, Jamie had blamed herself when she hadn't been able to fix him.

"You want another pep talk?" he teased. "The one where I tell you all the reasons it wasn't your fault, and talk *realllllly* slow like Dad when he's disappointed?"

Jamie smiled, but it was tight and forced, and his gut tightened when he saw her eyes were watering. "I'm just really glad you're okay," she whispered.

"You and me both," he said. "But it's your turn to let people fuss over you. Why do you think I came down here to visit?"

"Actually, I'm glad you brought that up," she said, wiping at her eyes. "I'm glad to see you. So glad. But don't think for one minute that I missed the fact that you have your escape face on."

Josh blinked. "Am I going to need a drink for this?"

Jamie waved behind her. "Beer in the fridge, booze above the fridge."

"Shit, so that's a yes, then," Josh muttered, going to their liquor cabinet and rummaging around until he came up with some Maker's Mark bourbon. He poured him himself a healthy serving, added a splash of water, and joined his sister once more at the table.

"I know you're not going to shut up until you say your piece, so have at it."

"You're running from something, and I want to know what."

"I'm not," he replied, taking a sip of the strong, bracing drink.

"Please. You know that time you wanted to dump Kelly Nicholson because you liked Valerie what's her name better, but couldn't figure out how to tell

Kelly? Escape face. Or that time you took Dad's Cal Ripken–signed baseball to school for show-and-tell and lost it, or the time you broke Grandma's jewelry box—"

"Jamie. The point."

"Right, anyway . . . whenever you're avoiding someone or something, you get this look on your face."

"A look."

She nodded. "Yep, like your mouth is kind of tight at the corner and your nose is all flat and your eyes are shifty."

He could only stare at her. "Is it cool if I record this so later when you're not pregnant, I can play it back and laugh at you?"

"*Oh*, did I mention?" she asked, pointing at him. "You also try to change the subject."

"Yeah well, I can't imagine why. Having my past faults described in great detail is definitely my idea of a good time."

"Fair enough," she said, nodding her head graciously. "Let's not talk about your past mistakes. Let's talk about your *current* ones. I'm sensing a female is involved?"

Josh pretended to look around the kitchen. "Don't you need your crystal ball for this?"

"Josh!" she said, finally snapping. "Would you talk to me. Please."

He sighed and took another sip of his drink, hating that she was right, the way that she usually was.

He was avoiding something.

And it was a female.

Josh sighed. "Okay. There's this girl."

Jamie smirked but managed to withhold the *I knew it.*

"She moved in next door a few weeks ago, and we've been . . . hanging out."

"You know, I'm thirty-three just like you. You don't have to apply a euphemism for sex."

"Actually it's not really like that," he muttered.

"*Really*," she said, her interest seeming to increase tenfold as she sat forward, hand resting on her stomach. "This just got interesting."

"Not interesting so much as frustrating. The attraction is mutual. We both know it. But she's all wrapped up in her job, and then she's got this thing with Trevor, and she asks all these annoying questions all the time . . ."

Jamie put a hand to her mouth, but not before he saw the smile.

"Don't," he muttered.

"I'm sorry," she said, reaching out a hand toward him. "It's just that you're so cute when you're falling for a girl who's not falling back."

"I'm not falling for her," he muttered. "We're just friends, and I wouldn't mind adding benefits to the arrangement."

"And how does she feel about that?"

"Good question. One minute she's kissing me like she wants to have her way with me, the next she's dragging me around the botanical gardens and talking about peonies, and the minute after that she's making sexy eyes at Trevor."

Jamie's eyes were wide with fascination. "So. Many. Questions. I don't even know where to start."

"Here's another one for you," he muttered. "Mom invited her to Thanksgiving."

Jamie barked out a laugh and slapped her hand on the table. "Oh my God, it keeps getting better. Oh, what I wouldn't give to be there."

"Yeah well, you might not be missing much. Pretty sure she's not coming."

Jamie's smile dropped. "Josh. Tell me you didn't uninvite her."

"No. Of course I didn't. It's just . . . we had a thing, and she's not exactly pleased with me."

Her eyes narrowed. "What'd you do?"

"How do you know it was me that did something?"

She pointed downward. "Ovaries."

Josh winced. "Gross. Don't. Anyway, I didn't do anything, precisely, I just sort of . . . snapped at her to stay out of my business."

Jamie's smile was all the way gone now. "Josh . . . does this girl—"

"Heather."

"Does Heather know you were sick?"

He took a sip of his drink. Then another. "Nope."

She gave a little sigh. "Josh."

"It's not relevant," he snapped. "That's my past."

"Sure, but it's shaped your present. And your future. And if you want this woman to be a part of either . . ."

Jamie broke off, and Josh rubbed his forehead. What did he want from Heather? He couldn't think about her as part of his future. He didn't let himself think about anyone in terms of his future. He wasn't sure he had one.

But the thought of her not being a part of his life had him all sorts of irritable.

Josh sighed and glared at his sister. "Any chance we can skip the bit where you laugh at me and call me names, and just go straight to the advice?"

"Absolutely," she said, surprising him by reaching across the table and patting his hand. "Okay, so here's the thing. Did Heather say yes to Thanksgiving?"

He shrugged. "I think she feels awkward."

"But she has nowhere else to go? Otherwise she wouldn't even be considering it."

Josh felt tense at the thought of Heather being alone. "Her mom's out of state. I feel like there's a story there, but I don't know what it is."

"So I've never met the woman, so this is a guess," Jamie said, pursing her lips, "but is it possible she's feeling as vulnerable as you?"

"Hey, who said anything about vulnerable?"

"Right, right, because you're a big man," his sister soothed. "But my point is, maybe this girl needs something different from your sexy smile and your crooning and your biceps."

His eyes narrowed. "I'm not buying her flowers."

Jamie smiled. "I think it might be even simpler than flowers. Cheaper, too. This woman's on the verge of spending the holidays alone. Is it possible that what she wants more than anything from you . . . is just a little bit of kindness? To not be alone?"

Josh blew out a breath and sat back, irritated by

how easily his sister had cut straight to the heart of the issue, when he'd been gnawing on it for days. "So what do I do?"

"Be her friend. Trust me when I say that for some women, there's no better seduction technique. And, Josh?"

He rolled his eyes. "What?"

Jamie squeezed his hand and waited until he met her gaze. "I think maybe you need a friend, too. A real friend. One that knows everything."

Chapter Sixteen

HEATHER HAD EXACTLY ONE plan for Thanksgiving: Sleeping in.

She'd even bought a sleeping mask for the occasion. A fuzzy leopard-print affair to block out the morning light so that she could finally—*finally*—catch up on some sleep.

The sleep mask did an excellent job blocking out the sunlight.

It did not, however, stand a chance against a thirty-something male rummaging around in her closet.

At first Heather thought she was dreaming. Or hallucinating.

But a full minute after she'd shoved her mask up onto her forehead and blinked sleepily in the direction of the ruckus, it became painfully clear that this was no dream.

Josh Tanner was in her bedroom, rifling through her clothes like he owned the place.

What. The actual. Fuck.

"Seriously?" she managed, her voice still croaky with sleep.

He glanced over his shoulder with a cocky grin. "Morning, 4C. Aren't you pretty in the morning. And by pretty I mean your hair is *enormous*."

Heather sat up. "How did you get in here?"

"Key," he said simply, as though it were obvious, turning his attention back to her closet and pulling out a blue-and-white-striped dress. "Is this a tent?"

"What do you mean *key*?" she asked, lifting a hand to smooth her hair and then realizing it would be futile. She'd slept with it wet last night. His description of *enormous* was probably phrasing it politely.

"Mrs. Calvin had one made for me a while back." Of course.

"And I'm just learning about this now, because . . . ?" she asked.

He shot her another of those cocky grins. "Been saving it for a special occasion. Happy Thanksgiving, 4C."

"Hang on," she said, lifting a hand and frowning as the last remnants of her sleep fog drifted away. "You're talking to me now?"

"What do you mean?" he put the maxi dress back in the closet. Not where he'd found it, but in the very back corner, as though hoping she'd forget about its existence.

"Oh, I don't know, how about the fact that you've been giving me the silent treatment ever since I pried into your personal life last week? Hell, Josh, I haven't even seen you in days." Or at least not since that horribly awkward scene outside their apartments the other night, with Kitty and Trevor.

Heather knew that nothing had happened with her and Trevor. They'd talked, watched a movie. She'd fallen asleep, and when she'd woken up the next morning, he was gone.

But as far as what happened with Josh and Kitty, she didn't have a clue. And if the truth wasn't the one she wanted, she wasn't sure she needed to know.

"That's because I've been out of town," he said, tossing a black sweater on the bed. "You should wear that."

"Out of town where?"

"Nashville. To see my sister."

"Since when do you have a sister?" she muttered, reaching for her hair band on the nightstand and pulling her hair into a knot on top of her head.

"Since always. Jamie."

"Older? Younger?"

"Twin."

Heather stared at him as he pulled out a pair of black pants and tossed them on top of the sweater. "Yup. Lives in Nashville. She couldn't come home for Thanksgiving because she's a hundred pounds pregnant, so I went down to visit her for a couple days."

"Well, what about before that," Heather said. "You were barely speaking to me."

"I was brooding."

"You mean sulking," Heather corrected.

"No, *you* were sulking. I was brooding."

"Why the distinction?"

He pointed at her breasts, then her crotch. "Tits. And, ah—"

Her eyebrows lifted. "Yes? What charming word for the female anatomy do you want to throw out there, big guy?"

Josh merely grinned. "Coffee's almost done. Get thy ass to the shower."

"Um, why?"

"Because it's Thanksgiving. We're supposed to be at my parents' house in a couple hours, and I'm supposed to pick up some flowers for my mom's damn centerpiece on the way."

"*We're* supposed to be at your parents' house?"

"Did you forget that I invited you?"

"No, I guess I just thought that what with the brooding and all that the invitation was off the table."

"Quit being such a girl. You going to shower, or you want to go like that, all drooly and crazy haired?"

She lifted a hand to her cheek to wipe away any drool marks. "Are you sure about this?"

He pointed to her bathroom. "Go. Or I won't share any of the coffee I brought over."

"I have my own coffee."

"I know. Decent stuff. Mine's better."

"Josh, I appreciate the offer, but I really don't think—"

He pulled his cell phone out of his back pocket. "No problem. Just give my mom a quick ring and tell her you're not coming. She's already set a place for you at the table and has been talking about it for days, but I'm sure she'll only cry a little—"

Heather groaned. "You're evil. Also, you're the one who screwed this up. Remember your whole beastly 'I am man, I no talk' routine? You were a jerk, Josh."

He surprised her by giving her a steady look, sliding his phone back into his back pocket. "I know. I'm sorry. Really. Let me make it up to you."

"How?" she asked, with narrowed gaze.

"Well, okay, I didn't really have a plan beyond bringing you coffee," he admitted with a sheepish grin.

Heather gave a fake-weary sigh. "Coffee'll do."

"You're easy, Heather Fowler. Way too easy."

"Says the guy who's never gotten near my lady bits."

Heather meant the comment as a joke, but his gaze seemed to darken, and his eyes drifted downward slightly.

"Hey," she said, holding up a warning finger. "Don't do that. I'm not becoming one of your women."

"We'll see, 4C."

Heather rolled her eyes and reached for the covers, then paused as she waited for him to leave. He didn't budge. He'd traded his usual Henley and jeans for a button-down dress shirt and slacks, and he looked good. Really good.

"Privacy, please?" she asked when he still hadn't moved.

He grinned. "I knew it. That tiny little tank top doesn't have any bottoms, does it?"

"I'm wearing underwear," she muttered.

"Thong?"

She snorted, but actually, it *was* a thong. Not her favorite to sleep in, but she was a little behind in laundry. And she hadn't slept in pants or shorts since she'd gotten her own place after college.

"*Out,*" she ordered.

"Prude." But he left, closing the door behind him.

Once he was gone, Heather couldn't hide the huge, happy smile as she flung back the covers and hopped out of bed.

She'd been surprised by how much she'd missed his presence in her life. And if he wanted to keep their friendship all flirty and on the surface, she could do that. Better than not being friends at all.

And hell, maybe if they got back to being friends, she'd stop having the naughty dreams about him that had been plaguing her sleep for weeks. Dreams of him pulling off her thong with his teeth, dreams of dragging her nails down his back as she lay pinned beneath him—

"Wow," Heather muttered as she jerked open her dresser drawer. "So a *cold* shower then."

"Why's that?"

Heather squeaked in surprise, and spun around, clutching her bra to her chest as she glared at her neighbor.

"Josh!"

He gave her a lazy grin and held out one of the two mugs in his hands. "Coffee?"

For two seconds, her modesty demanded she order him out, but . . . what the hell. He'd already gotten an eyeful of her ass, and she really did want the coffee.

She marched toward him and accepted the coffee, ignoring his smug smile. "For someone who complains about his mother's lack of boundaries, you're definitely crossing some of your own."

"What can I say, a chip off the old block. Also, 4C, can we talk about your bra choice?" he asked, nodding to the bra in her hand.

"No," she said, taking a sip of the still-too-hot coffee.

"Because I've got to tell you, if we're going to do the deed, I'd like to request something other than that light brown thing in your hand." He wrinkled his nose. "It looks like something my grandma would wear."

Heather choked on her coffee. "First of all, it's a nude bra, not light brown."

"It's brown," he said, sipping his own coffee.

"Second of all," she continued, "where on earth did you get the idea that we were going to *do the deed*?"

He shrugged. "You were muttering about needing a cold shower, and I can assure you that scratching the itch is a better solution than trying to stifle it."

"Gross."

"Also," he said, "I just saw your ass, and . . . well-done, 4C. From the day I met you, I knew you had sweet buns, and we just confirmed it."

Heather laughed and put a hand on his chest, shoving him backward. "Out. For real this time."

"Fine," he called after she shut the door in his face. "But don't think I didn't notice that you just copped a feel of my pecs!"

She was still smiling by the time she got out of the shower and got dressed, purposefully wearing the nude bra just to spite him, even though he'd never know it, she reminded herself firmly.

The sweater he'd set out was one of her favorites, so she put that on, and then spent a little extra time with her makeup, just because it was a holiday and all.

"How much time do we have?" she called through the door as she added another coat of mascara.

"Dry your hair," he called back. "I don't want you dying from exposure on me."

She opened the door and found him sitting on her kitchen counter, flipping through something on his phone. "How'd you know that's why I was asking?"

"Twin sister, remember?" he asked, not glancing up from the screen.

"Yeah, about that," she said, leaning a shoulder on the doorjamb of her bedroom door and studying him. "How is it that you've never mentioned Jamie?"

"We have time for you to dry your hair, not chitchat," he said.

"Right. Heaven forbid we talk in between arguments." She shut the door again, disappointed to be shut down, but not surprised.

Still, odd that he'd never mentioned a twin. It implied they weren't close, but then, he'd flown out to see her the week of Thanksgiving, when travel was a nightmare. They had to have at least a somewhat stable relationship.

Thirty minutes later, Heather's hair was mostly dry, courtesy of the expensive diffuser attachment on her dryer that kept her curls from frizzing up (much), and Josh was standing at the front door holding out her coat and purse for her.

"I feel weird going to someone's house empty-handed," she said, slipping her arms into the coat as he held it for her.

"We're not. Flowers, remember? Mom's also invited her neighbors *and* my dad's parents over, and even after thirty-four years of marriage, she's hell-bent on winning over my grandma. She's pretty sure the perfect centerpiece will do it."

"And that has what to do with me?"

"Are you or are you not a wedding planner?"

"Sure, but I hire the florists. I'm not one myself," she said as he all but shoved her out of her front door.

"You've got a leg up on me. I brought her yellow carnations last year when she'd invited her priest to dinner, and she nearly disowned me."

"Yellow carnations? Jesus. It's a good thing you're pretty," Heather said.

As it turned out, Josh wasn't *bad* at selecting flowers so much as disinterested, opting to flirt with the cute young assistant working the cash register as Heather talked shop with the owner.

Truth be told, Josh had been right. Heather was in her element, and she loved this. And if she was being even more honest, she was secretly thrilled to put her skills to use for someone who'd appreciate them.

Heather loved her mom to death. She really did. But she'd long given up showing off any of her skills when she went home. Her mom insisted that fake flowers were a better investment than real ones, that she'd rather have her trusty Nutter Butters than the delicate macaroons that Heather had carefully carried onto the plane in lieu of carry-on luggage.

She knew her mother didn't mean to belittle Heather's career, but she'd be lying if she didn't secretly wish her mom got it. Just a little. Maybe was even a bit proud of her daughter for all that she'd accomplished.

Heather shook her head to rid herself of the negative energy invading her Zen as she carefully selected from the different buckets, putting together a fully formed arrangement that she admired as she twirled it around for effect. It was Thanksgiving, and she was going to be with a family. So what if it wasn't hers? It sure as hell beat tofurkey for one.

A dorky smile on her face, Heather crept up behind Josh and bonked him on the head with the bouquet she'd assembled, effectively severing whatever he'd had going on with the jailbait.

"Come on, moron. Let's go."

"Oh, Heather, honey. They're beautiful!" Sue gushed, holding out her arms and making grabby fingers for the flowers. An hour and change later Heather and Josh were standing in his family's foyer in New Jersey, putting the artfully designed bouquet into Sue's arms.

"How do you know I'm not the one that picked them out?" Josh grumbled as he handed them over.

"Yellow carnations, dear. You remember," Sue said as she turned her cheek up so Josh could kiss it.

"It's a wonder you still call me your son," he said. Then he wrapped both arms around his mother, flowers and all. "Hi, Ma. Happy Thanksgiving."

Heather's heart melted just a little. Or a lot. A man who was good to his mother. Was there any better kind?

"Hi, dear," Sue said as she patted Josh's cheek and gave him a smile.

Heather could have sworn Josh's mom's eyes were watering just a little, and she looked away, suddenly very aware that she was a stranger intruding on a family holiday.

But then Sue shifted her attention back to Heather, reaching out her free hand as she shifted the flowers to her other side. "Heather, honey, it's so good to see you again. Josh was so excited you could join us, and trust me when I say we share his enthusiasm."

"Yup. I wrote all about it in my diary," Josh said sarcastically.

Sue rolled her eyes. "Josh, go help your father."

"Help him what, find the remote?"

"Oh, I didn't tell you. We're deep-frying the turkey this year. You can guess whose idea that was."

"So the diet's going well, then?" Josh said.

"Shoo," Sue said, waving her hand. "He's out back. Your grandparents aren't here yet, thank God. I'll need a mimosa or five before that happens. How about it, Heather?" Sue turned to Heather and winked conspiratorially.

Heather nodded gratefully. "A mimosa would be great."

"Josh, honey, make us a couple mimosas, would you? There's stuff set up on the sideboard in the dining room."

"I thought I was supposed to help with the turkey."

"Champagne first, always," Sue said, linking her arm in Heather's as Josh rolled his eyes but dutifully headed toward what Heather supposed was the dining room.

"I'm so glad you're here," Sue said, giving Heather's arm a little squeeze.

"I really appreciate you inviting me."

"Josh said you don't have any family in the area?"

Heather shook her head. "My mom's from Michigan, and she doesn't love New York."

Not that she'd ever been here to know.

"It took us a while to get used to it as well. Not that Jersey is quite Manhattan, but it's an adjustment from Bozeman, Montana."

"That's where you're from?" Heather asked in surprise.

She and Josh had never talked about where he was from, but somehow she'd assumed that he was local. He seemed so very at home in New York.

"How long have you lived here?" Heather asked, as she paused to peek at the numerous photos on the wall.

"We moved out here a few years ago," Sue said, stopping with Heather as her eyes roved over the pictures. "To be closer to Josh."

There was something in the older woman's tone then. A sadness, and Heather glanced at her out of the corner of her eye and wondered why the sadness on Sue's face matched her tone. This must be one tight-knit family, if the parents had missed their son enough to move to an entirely new state to be closer to him. She felt a sting of bitterness, thinking of her own mother, who couldn't even be bothered to hop on a plane to come visit.

Heather glanced back at the wall, leaning forward to look at a picture of Josh and a pretty, plump blonde with a happy smile. "Is this Jamie?"

Sue smiled. "Yes. She lives in Nashville with her husband. Usually she comes up for Thanksgiving, but she's due with my first grandbaby in just a couple weeks."

"Yeah, Josh mentioned that he went down to visit her."

"He's a good boy."

"They're close?" Heather asked.

Sue hesitated before answering. "They're working on it. They used to be inseparable, but after . . . Jamie pulled back a little bit. Josh is working on her though, and I'd like to think they're close to being back to normal."

After *what*? It was the second strange reference Sue had made in as many minutes, and Heather felt her curiosity getting the better of her. But before she could ask more, Josh reappeared with two mimosas. "My ladies," he said, handing them each a crystal champagne flute.

His eyes flicked to the pictures on the wall before narrowing slightly on his mother, but Sue had banished all traces of sadness and had another of those big smiles pasted on her face.

"Where are my manners? Heather, honey, come out of our hallway. You'll have to help me arrange these lovely flowers while the boys add a zillion calories to our turkey. Off with you, Josh, honey."

"And miss the girl talk?" he said.

His voice was casual, but Heather could have sworn there was a note of warning in his voice as he looked at his mother. Sue reached out and squeezed his forearm before moving into the kitchen.

Josh's shoulders relaxed slightly at whatever silent communication had just passed between mother and son, and he shifted his attention back to Heather. "You good?"

She smiled. "Yeah. I really am."

"Good."

He started to leave, but Heather said his name, and he turned back around.

"What's up?"

"Thanks," she said, holding his gaze.

"For?" His eyebrows lifted.

"For this," she said, gesturing to his parents' home. "For including me. I would have . . . I would have been alone today. And I was pretending that's what I wanted. But this is nice. It's better."

He smiled. "Nobody wants to be alone, 4C."

He walked away, whistling a premature Christmas song, and Heather stared after him.

Nobody wants to be alone, he'd said.

Strange words from a man who she suspected was more *alone* than any of them.

Chapter Seventeen

I LIKE HER."

Josh accepted the dripping platter his mother held out and dried it. "Yes, so you've said about a hundred times."

"You like her, too. Otherwise you wouldn't have brought her here," his mom said pointedly, giving him a knowing look as she added another dirty plate to the soapy sink.

"We're friends, Mom."

"Mmm-hmm. You've never brought a friend around for a holiday dinner before."

"That's because the rest of my friends have family," he said, glancing toward the living room, where Heather sat next to the fire with his father, laughing as they looked through an old photo album that probably had no shortage of pictures of his bare toddler butt.

"She mentioned her mom's from Michigan?" Sue asked.

"Yeah," Josh said, accepting another plate to dry.

"But they're not close."

"No, I think they are," Josh said, setting the plate on the clean stack. "They talk every Sunday. But her mom didn't want to come to New York, and I get the impression it bothers Heather."

"Of course it does. This is her home. I'm sure she wants to share that with her. A pity her mom can't understand that."

"Not everyone's so lucky," he said, bending down to kiss his mother's cheek.

Sue rolled her eyes. "You're buttering me up so that I'll quit prying into your and Heather's relationship."

"Friendship. It's a friendship," he corrected, thinking of his sister's advice.

And the more Josh had thought about it, the more he wondered if friendship is exactly where he should leave it with Heather. He still wanted her—rather desperately. But he also liked her too damn much to leave her. And if he slept with her, there's no way he could *not* leave her.

But that didn't solve the not-so-small problem of him not being able to get the visual of her ass out of his mind. He'd been playing around when he'd barged into her bedroom this morning, wanting to get under her skin because it was fun and it was what they did. And wanting to make nice and apologize for being an ass the other day at the restaurant.

But then she'd been standing there, all messy hair and tiny tank top with only a small red thong, and he'd felt a shot of lust so intense he'd thought he was going to pass out.

It needed to stop. Now. Especially since Trevor seemed to be hung up on the woman, and he didn't want to cock-block his best friend. For the hundredth time in the past week, he wondered if anything had happened between them that night when Trevor had gone into her apartment.

He hadn't asked Trevor, knowing that his friend would see right through him and not wanting to give his lead singer the wrong idea. He didn't want Heather for himself, he just wanted . . .

Hell if he knew.

He had no idea what he wanted.

"She doesn't know about what happened with you," his mom said casually, handing him another dish. Good Lord, did the pile never end?

"What do you mean?"

His mom turned and gave him a steady look. "You know what I mean."

He swallowed and glanced again in the direction of Heather. She'd shifted her attention to his grandmother, nodding and smiling politely at what was likely a lecture on her posture. Josh was lucky enough to have all four grandparents alive, but his father's parents were from the South and could be a bit formal.

"I don't see a reason to mention it," he said. "I'm not that guy anymore."

"No, you're not that guy in the sense that you're no longer a Wall Street hotshot. And in the sense that you're no longer sick."

He gave her a sharp look.

"But, Josh, honey, that past . . . it's a part of you.

If she's really your friend, she'd want to know. How is it that it's never come up?"

"It has," he grumbled.

"And?"

"I shut her down," he said quietly.

Sue looked at him sadly and sighed. "Oh, Josh."

"Look, I'm not proud of it," he said. "I only sulked for a couple days before I came to my senses and realized I was being an ass."

"And you apologized."

"Of sorts."

His mom snorted. "Said like a man. What time is it? I wanted to Skype with your sister before it gets too late."

He glanced at his watch. "Half past six."

"How is she?"

"Huge," Josh replied. "But good. Really good."

"I'm glad things are . . . mended between you."

"I just hate that they were ever broken in the first place," he said quietly. Though he'd never admit it to her now, he'd been devastated when Jamie had pulled away from him back when things were really rough, and even though they were better now, up until his most recent visit, a part of him was still holding her at arm's length so she couldn't come quite close enough to hurt him again.

"It was hard for her. Seeing her twin, thinking she should have been the one to help and not being able to."

"Absurd," he muttered, setting a plate on the growing pile of clean dishes.

"I know you think so. But put yourself in her

shoes. If she was the one who'd needed a bone marrow transplant, and you'd been told that you weren't
a match . . ."

Josh was silent for several moments. "I'd have
been destroyed."

"As was Jamie."

Josh blew out a long breath. He hated that his
family had had to see him be sick, but he knew it had
been especially hard on his sister. Siblings were the
most likely match for bone marrow, and Jamie had
gotten it into her head that as a twin, she'd be a sure
thing.

Alas, that was only true of identical twins.

Jamie hadn't been a match, and she'd just . . .
retreated. Not physically. She'd still been there, and
held his hand, and brought him brownies, the *good*
kind, while he was on chemo. But she'd held herself
back from him, and when her husband had gotten a
job offer in Nashville, she'd gone with him the second
Josh was in remission.

"We talked about it," he told his mom. "During
this trip."

"That's good," his mother said in delight. "I'm so
glad. Any breakthroughs?"

Josh shrugged. "Not really. It was about what we
expected. The guilt nearly ate her alive, but I think
she's finally coming around. Realizing there's nothing
she could have done. That it wasn't her fault, all that
good stuff."

"I knew it would just take some time. It was her
own battle. Nothing you or any of us could have
done but give her a bit of space."

"I know," he said quietly.

He'd never blamed his sister. Obviously. Yes, he along with the rest of them had hoped that she might be a match. And yes, his own heart had sunk a full foot when news came back that she wasn't.

But he'd gone on a donor list. And he'd gotten lucky. Jamie hadn't been a match, but someone else had.

Josh's new reality was remission, and as far as his family knew, a relapse was near impossible. The truth was between Josh and his doctors.

His own private reality, and one he wouldn't wish on any other person he cared about.

"Can I recruit Dad to take over on drying duty?" Josh asked. "I'm thinking maybe I should rescue Heather. Grandma just started a sentence with, 'in my day.' I think maybe we've subjected her to plenty of Tanner time for her first visit."

"Her first visit, huh? So there will be others?" his mom asked slyly.

"Yup, it's official," he said, tossing the towel on the counter. "I'm off dish duty."

She laughed. "Okay, fine. Let me at least send some pie home with you two."

By the time he and Heather were saying their good-byes at the front door, they had a hell of a lot more than pie. Turkey, white for him, dark meat for Heather. Mashed potatoes, stuffing, extra gravy, and his grandmother's reminder that they should both learn to take smaller bites while they ate to ease their digestion.

Josh hugged his family, and Heather did the same.

He noted it was a genuine, full-body hug, rather than the stilted, formal hug of a stranger. She'd gotten comfortable with his family rather quickly, and it made him . . . glad.

He liked seeing her like this. Easy. Relaxed. Happy.

"You want me to carry something?" Heather asked as they finally managed to escape his family and were walking down the quiet street toward the train station.

"I didn't hear that offer when I was hauling your mountain of flowers on the way over."

"If you think flowers and pie are the same thing, you're nuts. Hand it over."

"But you're a wedding planner," he said, keeping both stuffed paper bags out of her reach. "You're supposed to love flowers."

"And I do. But I love pie more. I'm a woman first, wedding planner second, after all."

Josh grunted as he begrudgingly handed over one of the bags.

"I love your family," she said, tilting her head back and looking up at the clear night sky. "You're lucky."

"I am," he said in agreement. He was no fool. He knew he had it good. Yes, his mom was meddling and his dad's deep-fried turkey had been a semi-disaster, and his grandparents could be a little uptight, and his sister had sort of lost her shit when he'd gotten sick.

But they loved each other. Were there for each other, messy drama and all.

"You want to call your mom?" he asked as they climbed the stairs to the train platform.

She looked at him in surprise. "How'd you know that's what I was thinking?"

"It's a holiday. She's your only family member. Not a stretch."

"Do you mind?" she asked.

"Not at all. We've got a few minutes until the train gets here."

Josh set the bags on a bench and sat down as Heather wandered away. Her mom must have picked up on the first ring. He noted Heather's voice went up a full octave when she talked to her mom, full of enthusiasm that was . . . not false, exactly. The smile on her face was genuine as she chatted.

But there as a purposefulness about her happy tone, as though she didn't want to let her mom know how much it stung that they hadn't spent the holiday together.

Josh was willing to bet that Heather's mother was a nice enough lady, but that maybe the older woman didn't quite realize how important her recognition of Heather's success was to Heather.

As he watched her roam around the platform, laughing at something her mom said, he itched to hug her and tell her that she was enough, just as she was.

No, not enough.

That she was exceptional. Successful and driven and funny and bright.

And hot.

The thought of keeping his hands to himself where she was concerned was growing less and less appealing than it had been yesterday when he'd come up with the dumb plan.

The train approached, and Heather dropped her phone in her purse and came to join him as he picked up the bags.

"Everything good?" he asked.

Heather shrugged. "Yeah. I thought she had to work today, but I guess she opted to take it off after all, so that's good. She and a friend hung out, watched Julia Roberts movies."

Josh nodded in silent acknowledgment, wondering if it stung to know that her mom had used work as an excuse for why she couldn't come to New York, and then hadn't even ended up working.

But she seemed in a happy enough mood as they found two seats together on the train, both content to wallow in the silent joy of full bellies and a long weekend ahead.

It was enough, he thought as he settled more comfortably in his seat. Enough to be her friend.

And then he felt something nudge his shoulder.

It was Heather's head. She'd fallen asleep.

He smiled, shifting slightly to be at a better height for her, carefully cupping her cheek and positioning her head more firmly against his shoulder so it didn't do that awkward lolling around thing.

She let out a happy little sigh, and Josh let his hand linger on her face, just for a second.

It was enough, he thought again.

It had to be.

Chapter Eighteen

I TOLD YOU, YOU were drooly," he said, wiping at his shoulder as they climbed the steps toward their respective apartments. "I have dried spit on my shoulder."

"You do not," Heather retorted, not looking back.

He probably did.

She would have felt awkward about waking up with her head nestled under his chin, her arm looped over his waist, with his around her shoulder.

But since this was Josh, he'd quickly made a joke about her snoring and was now complaining about her drool.

Two topics that definitely ensured any intimacy between them was purely platonic and wildly unsexy. And although a part of her wanted him to see her as a woman, she was too high on the warm fuzzies of the day to let his indifference to her lady bits get to her.

Heather felt horribly disloyal to her mom for having the thought, but today's Thanksgiving had been the type of holiday she'd dreamed about on the

Thanksgivings spent at the diner when her mom had to work, picking at green beans from a can and gravy that had congealed on the plate long before it had been set in front of her.

The family element had been exactly right, too. The gentle bickering, the exasperation, and the love. So much love. It had been everywhere, from the way Josh had gently coaxed smiles from his grumpy grandma to the way Josh's parents had snuck gooey, lovesick looks across the table.

The Tanners would likely never know the gift they'd given her, but she was grateful all the same.

When they reached their respective front doors, Heather made a grab for one of the bags and peeked inside. "Is this the one with pie in it?"

He glanced down into his own bag and gave her a victorious grin. "Nope. You've got the carrots and potatoes. I've got the pie."

She held out the bag to him. "Trade."

"Hell no. I want a piece of this pie just as badly as you do. Maybe with a cup of really excellent coffee."

She groaned. "You know I can't handle it when you talk dirty."

Josh stepped closer and wiggled his eyebrows, lowering his voice to a husky tone. "Can you smell it? All those dark roast beans? A hit of smoke, a little bit of chocolate. The way its rich bitterness rolls over your tongue, mingling with the sweetness of the pumpkin pie."

"So this is how you coax women into your apartment? Because it's totally working," Heather said with a whimper.

Something flickered in his gaze, but then he smiled and it was gone. "Actually, I'm inviting myself into *your* apartment. My coffee stash is still in your place from this morning."

"Even more impressive," Heather said as she shoved her key into the lock. "You've managed to get yourself an invitation into my apartment."

"Ah, but will it get me into your thong?"

She rolled her eyes and ignored him, stepping into her apartment and knowing he would follow.

"Speaking of this morning, are you still wearing a thong?" he asked, shutting her front door.

"Speaking of this morning, how about you hand over that spare key?" she shot back as she hoisted the bag onto the counter and began putting leftovers in her fridge.

"I see you're helping yourself to my family's leftovers," he said.

"Okay, fine, keep the key in the short term," she said, shoving aside a carton of milk to make room for a Tupperware of gravy. "We'll have joint custody of the leftovers."

Heather pulled down two plates for their pie as Josh went about the process of heating water and scooping coffee into her French press, trying to ignore the little sense of contentment she felt at how easily he fit into her apartment.

Almost as though he belonged there.

"Pecan or pumpkin?" she asked.

"Really?"

"Both it is," she said, cutting two enormous slices of pie for him and two smaller ones for herself.

Heather waited patiently for the coffee to finish before taking a bite. Josh did not, and he was already on his second slice of pumpkin as they settled at her table with two steaming cups of coffee and plates of pie.

"Can I ask you something without you freaking out?" she said. His chewing slowed and his gaze went wary, and Heather lifted her fork in reassurance. "Don't worry, you don't have to answer."

"Okay," he said hesitantly.

She put a piece of creamy pumpkin pie in her mouth, slowly withdrawing the fork as she studied him, wondering at the wisdom in asking.

What the hell.

"I'm missing something, aren't I?" she said.

"Huh?"

"About your past. You don't have to tell me what it is if you don't want to, and I promise never to ask specifics, but there's a piece missing, right? Something I don't know about you? Something you don't like talking about? That's why you got all mad at lunch the other day. It's why your entire family will talk endlessly about your childhood and yesterday, but anything a few years back is off-limits."

Josh stared at his coffee for a long moment, and for a second she thought—hoped—he might actually confide in her.

Instead he merely nodded. That was it. A nod.

Heather swallowed her disappointment.

"Okay!" she said with false brightness. "I won't mention it again. Really. I know you don't want to talk about it, I just sort of wanted to make sure I wasn't crazy, you know? And I—"

"4C. Heather. Stop."

His voice was quiet. Steady.

She clamped her mouth shut. "Sorry."

"No, don't apologize," he said, starting to reach across the table, and then stopping, as though thinking better of it. "I'm sorry. It's not you that I don't want to talk to. I just don't like talking about it with anyone. My family knows what went down because they were there, as do some of the friends who stuck around. But trust me when I say I sometimes wish I could erase their memories."

"It was that bad?" she asked quietly.

"Not so much." He fiddled with his fork. "It's just that I don't want to be defined by something that happened in the past. I want to be defined by who I am now, not something that happened a couple years ago."

"But I wouldn't—"

"Yes," he interrupted kindly but firmly. "You would. You wouldn't want to think of me differently, or act differently around me, but you would. And I don't want that."

She sighed into her coffee, knowing a lost cause when she saw one. "Okay."

"I like us as we are," he said. "I like the way you act around me *now*."

A corner of her mouth lifted at that. "What, slightly bitchy?"

He smiled back. "Not bitchy. More . . . unabashed."

She snorted. "Just how every woman wants to be described by a man she . . ."

Josh's gaze sharpened. "A man she what?"

Heather froze, as every swear word in the book ran through her head at warp speed.

"Nothing. I don't know," she said, dropping her fork onto her plate and carrying it to her sink even though she hadn't finished her pie. Didn't matter. Her appetite was long gone.

Josh followed her, his own plate in hand, although his was empty. He set it beside hers on the counter, and when Heather tried to move away to put more distance between them, he lifted his arm, resting one hand on the counter so that she couldn't move forward without touching his arm.

And touching him was really not on the agenda right now.

"A man you what, 4C?"

She shook her head. "I don't know."

"Yes you do."

She lifted her chin and met his eyes. "I really don't. Really. I don't know what I was going to say."

It was true. Even now she wasn't sure what word her brain was trying to come up with. It was as though the sentence had come from the deep, forbidden part of herself that she kept on lockdown.

"Take a guess," he said, coming infinitesimally closer. Not enough to touch, just enough for her to feel his body warmth. Smell his cologne. See the dark gold of his five o'clock shadow.

"You're not the only one who thinks some things are better left unsaid, Josh."

His eyes narrowed just slightly. "No?"

She shook her head and took a step backward so she could move around him the other way, but he lifted his other arm, slowly lowering his hand to the countertop so that she was good and truly caged by his arms.

And they were good arms.

Even beneath his dress shirt she could see the curve of the biceps, see the way the fabric stretched across his chest and shoulder. Her eyes dropped to where the top button lay open, just enough to perfectly frame his Adam's apple and give a glimpse of the smooth skin beneath.

And suddenly Heather knew exactly what word her subconscious had been trying to say:

Want.

This was a man she wanted.

Rather desperately.

All of the swear words sounded in her head again, louder this time.

She might want him, but she didn't want *this.* Didn't want to be another of his flings, another in a long line of Josh Tanner's conquests. Hell, not a week ago she'd watched that Kitty girl slink into his apartment all trim and sexy and shiny haired.

And tomorrow there'd be another Kitty, and the night after that yet another, and—

"Heather."

"What?" This time she wasn't brave enough to meet his eyes.

"Look at me."

She shook her head.

"You're sure you don't want to finish that sentence?"

"*Positive*," she blurted out.

His laugh was startled, maybe a little hurt, but more likely it was just his ego that was stinging. She suspected not very many women rejected him.

But then not that many women had to live next door to him, either.

Lucky for them.

"A couple minutes ago, you asked if you could ask me something," he said. "My turn."

"I already told you, I don't know how I was going to finish the sentence," she lied.

"That's not my question."

"Fine. And then you'll move?" she said.

Josh smiled, the warmth of it making her hot. "Sure. And then I'll move."

She gestured impatiently with her hand for him to continue.

"Did you sleep with Trevor?"

Her eyes flew to his. "*What?*"

His face was unreadable now, his smile gone. "That night when Trevor came into your apartment. Did you sleep with him? Or any night after?"

She laughed disbelievingly. "You don't get to ask me that. Not with your constant string of women coming in and out."

Josh inched closer, and Heather shifted backward until her butt hit the counter, her hips now just inches from his thumbs. "Did. You. Sleep. With. Trevor."

Heather frowned in confusion and shook her head. "No. Why?"

"Because I needed to know if you belong to someone else before I do this."

His mouth dropped to hers.

And just like that, Heather was kissing Josh Tanner with everything she had.

Chapter Nineteen

JOSH WAS A GOOD KISSER.

She'd kind of hoped she'd been imagining that the last couple times, but nope. The man was really, truly good at this.

She'd known from the very second he'd opened the door with no shirt the first time they'd met that she would enjoy it. The *real* surprise came from the fact that this kiss wasn't just skilled, wasn't just *hot* like the others had been, although it was both of those—the surprise was that it was *perfect*.

As though their mouths had been meant for each other.

He started off slow, his lips lightly brushing over hers. No tongue, just his lips against hers as they explored each other, trying to see how they fit—if they fit.

And they definitely did.

His tongue caressed the center of her bottom lip. *Open.*

She obeyed, and then his tongue was sliding

against hers. Heather whimpered and lifted her hands to his face, her palm cupping his jaw as the other hand slid around to the back of his neck, keeping his head bent to hers lest he come to his senses and pull away.

Josh's hands found her waist, his fingers curving around to her lower back as he pressed forward until they were chest-to-chest and she was pinned between him and the kitchen counter.

He tasted like nutmeg and coffee and *Josh*, and it was the last one that was the most potent of all.

His hands slid up her sides, his thumbs idly moving over her rib cage, stopping just beneath her breasts, which were now full and heavy and wanting.

Heather made a whimpering noise of need and he groaned in response, his arms winding all the way around her now, drawing her to him as he tilted his head and took the kiss deeper, hotter.

It was the sort of kiss that was better than sex. Unless, of course, one was talking about sex with Josh, in which case she was pretty sure this was just the appetizer.

When they pulled back to breathe, he rested his forehead against hers with a soft laugh. "Well, what are we going to do about this, 4C?"

In response, she lifted her eyes to his and slowly brought her hands to the front of his shirt, her fingers toying with the second button before flicking it open.

His eyes flickered. "Heather—"

She leaned forward and pressed her mouth to the V of his throat, teeth scraping against his warm skin before she soothed it with her tongue.

His breath hitched even as he lifted his hands to her head as though to pull her away, and in a last-ditch effort to persuade him otherwise, she tilted her hips forward, rubbing rather shamelessly against the unmistakable bulge of his erection. But she didn't care. Now that she'd had a taste of him, she knew she wanted—no, needed—to see this through, even if it was only for tonight.

His body went still as his fingers tangled in her hair. "You seducing me, 4C?"

"Is it working?"

His breath was hot against her cheek. "I want you. Obviously. But—"

"No but," she said quickly, lifting her head and brushing her mouth against his. "We don't have to make a thing of it. It can just be sex."

His eyes flickered in doubt, and she lifted her eyebrows in challenge. "Unless, of course, you're in danger of falling madly in love with me. It's okay if you are, it happens."

She smiled in response as she met his eyes. "Oh, that's not what you're worried about, is it? It's my poor little heart you think is at risk."

Josh winced. "It sounds so condescending when you say it like that."

Her eyebrows lifted. "It does, doesn't it?"

He opened his mouth, and she rested her fingers lightly against his lips. "Josh. Hear me out. I like you. You like me. We're friends. We're neighbors. But with all due respect, I'm way too smart to fall in love with you."

He smiled. "Should I be insulted?"

"How about you just be naked instead? I'm getting impatient."

"Will you hate yourself tomorrow morning? Or me?"

"No. Not once I've had my coffee," she retorted.

Josh's laugh was swift and genuine. "Well, you were right about one thing, 4C. I do like you."

"I know," she said before she pulled his mouth down to hers once more. "But Josh. No more talking. Tonight I don't want to be bickering Josh and Heather, I want to be—I want—"

Josh's mouth brushed softly over hers. "I know. I want, too. Heather."

Heather. Not 4C.

His kiss was gentle as he coaxed her lips open, his mouth making love to hers in sweet, hot caresses, his tongue lingering and seductive.

In the very back of her mind she knew that he'd kissed dozens of women. Perhaps even more. But tonight he was kissing *her*, and it felt . . . significant.

His hands slid up her sides, reminding her of her naughty dreams, and she smiled. He pulled back. "Tickle?"

She shook her head. "No. Just really, really good."

They undressed each other in leisurely, slow movements, taking time to explore every inch of skin revealed.

She gave back as good as she got, her fingers making quick work of the remainder of his buttons as she shoved the dress shirt over his shoulders and down his arms.

Heather froze a little in nervousness when he

tugged her upward to unsnap the back of her bra, and he stilled. "Want me to stop?"

Her eyes closed. "I'm not good at this like you are."

Josh pulled back slightly, touching a knuckle to her lip. "Trust me. It's already very, very good because it's you."

Her eyes closed and her breath caught.

It was the right thing to say as he'd likely known it was. This time when he reached for her bra, she didn't freeze. And when his palms came around to cup her, she arched into him, biting her lip as his thumbs brushed over the sensitive peaks. He smiled at her whimper as his fingers continued their slow perusal, circling and flicking until her nipples were hard and begging.

"You like that," he whispered.

She nodded.

"Me too," he whispered. He dipped his knees so his mouth was even with her breasts, and her breathing quickened in anticipation.

But his touch didn't come.

Wild with need, she glanced down, saw him watching her. Only when their eyes met did he give her what she needed, his mouth slowly closing around one nipple and pulling it into his warm wet mouth.

"Josh." Her fingers dug into his hair.

In response he moved to her other breast, giving them both equal worship time before he straightened and took her hand, leading her into the bedroom.

"A bed? How conventional," she quipped, trying to ward off some of the embarrassment of being mostly naked, her nipples damp and cold from his mouth.

"Yeah, well, thought I'd spoil you, what with it being a holiday and all," he said.

"What happens when it's not a holiday? Kitchen sex?"

Josh turned once he reached the bed and tugged her toward him, her bare breasts brushing the hard planes of his chest and sending her already-simmering lust up another notch. "Kitchen sex. Shower sex. Couch sex, taxi sex—"

"*Taxi* sex?"

He smiled wickedly against her mouth as he kissed her slow and deep as she tried to figure out whether he was joking.

In the end, it didn't matter. Because when he gently lowered her to the bed and lowered himself on top of her, there was only *this* moment.

He removed her pants and then his own, before glancing down her body and running a single finger along the top edge of her panties, just below her belly button.

"You never answered my question," he said, his voice quiet as his finger roamed lower.

"What question?" Her voice was breathy.

"Are you still wearing a thong?"

In response, Heather merely lifted her eyebrows. "I thought we agreed no more talking."

His gaze narrowed, and he slowly pushed her onto her stomach, groaning as he got the answer to his question.

"Why am I so obsessed with your ass?" he asked,

his fingers trailing down her back until they reached the tiny fabric of the thong.

He hooked a finger beneath it teasingly, and Heather folded her arms under her head, biting the back of her hand to keep herself from begging him to touch her.

She didn't have to beg.

He was already touching, his palm molding the shape of her butt as he planted hot kisses on the back of her neck.

His hand trailed lower, snaking under the fabric of her underwear as he slid a finger into her wetness without preamble. They both moaned.

Josh shifted, pulling his hand away only to reach under her, sliding his hand into her panties once more, this time using two fingers to circle her slowly and she bucked against him in need.

Heather tried to roll to her back, but he wouldn't let her, his body weight holding her still as he trapped her against the bed—against his relentless fingers, probing and teasing until she exploded in his hand, muffling her cries against her arms.

He let her recover, brushing kisses over her shoulder until her cries turned into heavy breaths, before flipping her over.

Josh's mouth dropped to hers, kissing her wild and hot before pulling back slightly. "Tell me you have a condom."

Heather managed to move her lethargic limbs to get at her nightstand, pulling out a box of condoms that hadn't seen action in a very, very long time.

Josh pulled the condom from her hand before

slowly pulling her toward him once more, his hand tangling in her hair as he kissed her thoroughly, lowering her slowly to her back.

"You're so beautiful," he whispered against her neck. "And I've wanted this so damn long."

Heather pulled his mouth to hers. "Then let's not wait any longer."

She opened to him as he settled above her, waiting until she gave him her eyes before he slid inside her, slow and thick and hard.

"Jesus," he whispered into her neck. "Jesus, 4C."

He pulled his hips back slowly, and this time when he pushed forward, she arched to meet him, their bodies sliding together in perfect rhythm.

"Again," she whispered. "More."

He gave her more. He gave her everything, one arm hooked behind her neck, the other finding her center, two fingers rubbing over her clit until she was there, shattering against him, around him.

"Yes," he said. "Heather—"

He let out a hoarse cry against her hair, his body bucking into hers, her hands on his ass, urging him on until he collapsed on top of her, a heavy, welcome weight.

And even in her postcoital bliss, Heather had the annoying realization that Josh Tanner was the best sex she'd ever had.

Her eyes flew open when she realized she'd said it aloud, but before embarrassment could sink in, he pressed his lips gently to hers. "Right back at you, 4C."

She smiled happily, her fingers drifting over his

shoulder as he settled his head beside hers on the pillow.

But as postorgasmic bliss slowly faded and reality crept in, Heather realized that far from scratching the itch, she had never wanted him more.

Dangerous territory for a man who made it very clear he wasn't playing for keeps.

Chapter Twenty

HEATHER WOKE UP TO a large male hand on her breast and a large male penis against her butt.

Even before sleep had totally faded, she rolled her eyes and turned toward Josh, but he scooted closer, keeping her back to him.

"Stay," he ordered. "I don't want you to start fussing about morning breath and early-morning details."

"The only early-morning detail I'm caring about at the moment is coffee," she grumbled.

His thumb flicked over her nipple, and she sucked in a breath.

"Coffee first," she said, wrapping her fingers around his wrist and trying to pull his hand away.

His hand slid down her body, a finger sliding between her legs.

In about ten seconds, she was wet and squirming against him.

"Coffee first, or . . ."

"Coffee second," she said on a gasp as two fingers slipped inside her. "Coffee second."

Josh reached over her head and grabbed a condom—their fourth—and put it on, before hooking a hand behind her knee.

He lifted her leg slightly and positioned himself, pausing for a heartbeat before plunging inside her.

It was good. Always so good.

"Damn you," she said on a gasp.

"Touch yourself for me," he ordered, lifting onto his elbow as he looked over her shoulder and down the length of her.

Heather bit her lip. She wasn't unadventurous in bed, but she usually felt a hell of a lot braver when it wasn't the early morning with sunlight displaying imperfections and all.

Josh's mouth dropped to the sensitive spot where her shoulder met her neck, and he licked her lightly. "You're beautiful," he whispered.

It was all the encouragement she needed. Her hand slid down her stomach, hesitating only briefly before she let her fingers rub over her sensitive flesh.

Josh groaned and quickened his pace as he levered himself up once more, watching her hand. Watching them.

She couldn't help it. She looked down, too, at the sight of him plunging in and out of her while her own fingers circled and stroked. It was so blatantly sexy, so unapologetically carnal that her orgasm was upon her far faster than it had any right to be.

"Josh—"

"Come."

She did. And he came with her, his groan low and growly and pure man.

They both slumped back into the pillows, his arm heavy on her waist, his breath ruffling the hair that she knew had to be, in his word, enormous.

Eventually, she rolled onto her back and glanced toward him, holding a hand over her mouth. He was right about the morning breath thing. Sure, it was just Josh, but she still had standards.

"Coffee," she said, the world muffled by her fingers.

"I'd love some," he said, not opening his eyes.

She reached out and slapped his stomach, which probably hurt her more than it did him considering he had an honest-to-God six-pack.

He grunted and rolled off the bed into a standing position in one motion, pulling off the condom before ambling toward her bathroom. She heard the flush, and then he ambled back into the room for his pants, putting them on commando as he studied her.

"You look hot like that."

"Hot mess," she corrected.

"Nope. Just hot. Don't let it go to your head though, you're already insufferable enough with that big ego."

She gaped at him. "*I* have the big ego?"

"You do."

Then he was singing "Deck the Halls," a favorite of his, apparently, and banging around in her kitchen.

A second later his head poked into the bedroom. "I just realized we never made our banana bread."

"For the hundredth time, quit acting like that's a thing that we do."

"Okay," he said agreeably. "But only because I've

discovered another thing that we do that's slightly more interesting than banana bread."

She lifted her head and narrowed her eyes. "*Slightly?* Exactly where does sex rank next to your precious banana bread?"

"Depends. Does the banana bread have nuts?"

Heather reached behind her, picking up a candle she kept on the nightstand and lifting it like one might throw a football. "Speaking of nuts, you'd better watch yours."

"I forgot what you were like without coffee," he said. "Put the weapon down, 4C. I've got some Italian roast with your name on it."

He disappeared again, and Heather smiled as she went to the dresser, pulling on underwear—nonthong this time, since he had a weakness for them, and her lady bits needed a break—and then tugged on gray sweatpants and a tank top.

Ordinarily she might have combed her hair, but this was Josh. And wasn't this the entire point of having sex with someone that would never turn into something romantic? She didn't have to worry about things like frizz.

She walked into the kitchen just as he was pouring them each a mug.

"And you thought I would hate you in the morning," she said, greedily grabbing at the cup he held out.

"So you don't, then?"

"Don't what?" she asked, taking her coffee into the living room and sitting on the couch.

"Hate me." His voice was casual, but his eyes

were just the slightest bit wary as he searched her face.

She shrugged. "This doesn't feel awkward-morning-after to me. Does it to you?"

"No," he said. "But how do I know you're not waiting until I leave to start your shame cycle."

"Shame cycle? What the heck is that?"

"You know, when you women start overthinking things, wondering why I didn't ask for your number, wondering if you made a mistake, wondering which notch on my bedpost you were . . ."

"Yeah, I'm not going to do that," she promised, taking a sip of the coffee. "Although out of curiosity, how many women have you slept with?"

"A lot," he said without apology as he plopped into a chair across from her.

That didn't surprise her. Heck, she'd seen plenty of them. And speaking of . . .

Heather glanced at the clock on her wall. "Hey, how long until your mom gets here to make pancakes? That's what she does for your one-night stands, right?"

Josh groaned. "Trust me when I say that is not how I was hoping that morning was going to go."

"What, your mom catching you in the act?"

"She just caught the aftermath, thank God."

"So the pancakes aren't typical."

"God, no. Usually I just offer cereal only to tell them that I'm out of milk if they say yes."

"Are you *actually* out of milk?"

"Hardly ever."

Heather shook her head. "Josh."

"What? It's not like I promised them breakfast in bed when I invited them over. They know the score."

Heather wondered if there was a hidden message there. A gentle reminder that Heather too should know the score and not expect anything more than he wanted to give.

Heather leaned forward, cupping her mug in both hands as she waited for him to meet her eyes.

He did so, warily. "You look like you're about to give a speech."

"I am, so listen up and take notes if you need to. I meant what I said last night. I'm not reading too much into what happened. I didn't wake up in the middle of the night to watch you sleep. I didn't punch holes in all the condoms in hopes of having your love baby—"

Josh laughed. "Jesus, 4C."

She leveled him with a look. "I am, however, hungry. Your mom's not here to make us pancakes, I'm not making pancakes, and I don't want your stupid cereal."

"Pie?" he asked hopefully.

"I was thinking more like brunch," she said. "I hardly ever get to go out to brunch. The wedding business almost never provides a free weekend, and the Belles have an event-free day today before all post-holiday hell breaks loose tomorrow."

He said nothing, and she felt a flicker of disappointment. "It's okay if you don't want to," she said quietly. "I'm perfectly happy going to brunch on my own. I have zero qualms about drinking mimosas by myself."

"You'll do no such thing," he said, taking a sip of coffee. "I know just the place. The hash browns are straight from heaven, and the French toast is stuffed with mascarpone, if that's your thing."

"Really?" She didn't bother to hide her happiness. "You want to go with me?"

"Of course," he said, standing and finishing the last bit of his coffee. "What better way to listen to you talk about how I was the best sex you ever had?"

Heather pursed her lips as she watched him amble into the kitchen, all broad shoulders and trim waist.

"I don't hear any denials," he said.

"I'm not going to feed your voracious ego," she said climbing to her feet. "So don't hold your breath."

"I don't suppose you'd let me go to the gym before brunch?" he asked hopefully.

"You watch your mouth," she said as she headed toward the bathroom to shower. "I'm leaving in thirty minutes. You'll have to decide what you want more, to bench-press or that French toast."

"What about sex?" he called after her. "Is that on the table?"

"Seriously? We went at it, like, four times." She tugged the tank top over her head, unsurprised to see him watching her.

"How about five?" he said, his eyes locked on her bare breasts.

"Seriously?"

"Absolutely," he said, giving her a crooked smile as he ambled toward her, hooking a hand behind her neck and forcing her to look up.

His eyes dropped to her mouth. "You're the best I've ever had, too, you know."

Heather's heart flipped, and her lust-addled brain clung to the hope that it wasn't a line. "I never confirmed you were the best," she teased.

Josh rubbed a thumb over her lip. "If you're still unsure, I think I know a way I can convince you."

"How's that?"

Josh backed her into the bathroom. "Time to make good on my threat of shower sex."

"Okay, but I meant what I said about leaving in thirty minutes."

"Not a problem, 4C. I'll only need five for what I'm about to do to you, but I'm happy to stretch it to ten if you find you want more time."

Turned out she wanted fifteen. And then some.

Chapter Twenty-One

D UDE, YOU DO THIS every time," Trevor said as he flipped open the pizza box and started picking at the pie. "You know I hate olives."

"Sorry, forgot," Josh lied. He knew perfectly well his friends hated them, but he loved them, and Trevor had turned the process of picking them off into an art form. It was Wednesday evening, and Heather had a rare weekday evening wedding to work, so he'd invited Trevor over to watch the Rangers game. It was his first Heather-free night in quite some time, and damn if he didn't miss her despite having just seen her the evening before.

He was really up shit creek with this one.

Trevor shoved the olive-free piece in his mouth and shot Josh the finger as he took an enormous bite, then flopped back on the couch. "How you been, man?"

Josh flipped the lids off two beers, setting them on the table before dropping onto the opposite side of the sectional. "Good."

Trevor smirked. "You've been better than good. You've been practically strutting. And you canceled band practice on Sunday night."

"Holiday weekend."

"Sex weekend, I'd wager," Trevor countered. "A hot broad's the only reason you'd ever cancel practice."

Guilt flickered, and Josh leaned forward for a slice of pizza so he had an excuse to break eye contact with his best friend. "Were the guys upset?"

"Nah," Trevor said, taking another big bite of pizza. "It's just a hobby for them. Something to do. They don't care about it like we do."

Josh glanced up in surprise. "Do you care about it that much?"

"Of course," Trevor said, his attention still locked on the TV.

"Trev."

His friend looked at him in surprise. "What?"

"Where do you see the band going?"

Trevor stuffed the rest of the crust in his mouth and leaned forward for his beer. "I don't know. I guess getting a few more gigs would be a start. We really haven't done anything since the summer when we played at a couple of those random weddings."

"What about beyond then?"

Trevor took a sip of beer and studied him. "How about you spit out whatever you're thinking?"

Josh took a bite of his own slice and shrugged. "I don't know. Just been thinking lately."

"'Bout?"

"The band." *Life. And what the hell I should be doing with mine.*

"And?"

Josh rolled his shoulders and reached for another piece of pizza. "I don't know. Never mind."

"You want to break up the band?"

"I didn't say that," Josh said quickly.

Trevor's smile was fleeting. "But you didn't not say it, either."

"I don't know that I see us going big places," he admitted.

Trevor sighed and set his beer aside, pulling the box of pizza toward him as he started dismembering another slice. "I don't know that I see it, either."

Josh's chewing slowed for a second. "Yeah?"

"We're good. Maybe even really good. Your songs are awesome, man. But to make it in a way that would enable us all to quit our day-job things and really just go for it, we've got to be better than awesome, you know?"

Josh nodded. He did know. And he didn't take offense. He had a talent, he knew that. So did Trevor, and the other guys. But it took more than talent to make it in music. It took drive and sacrifice and a sort of soul-deep *want*, and he wasn't sure they had that.

He knew that he didn't.

"I'll probably always sing," Trevor said, flinging an olive onto a spare plate. "And you'll always write and sing and play, being the triple-threat bastard that you are. That's what I meant when I said we want it more than the other guys. I don't know that they'd keep playing if it wasn't easy and they didn't have someone else supplying the space and the time and the motive. But is it lame to say that I like my day job?"

"No, of course not, man."

Guilt flickered again, because Josh didn't know exactly what Trevor did for a living. A project manager at some big web design firm, whatever that meant. But Trevor had always seemed to like it. He didn't bitch about *work* the way most people did.

"What about you?" Trevor asked after a few minutes' pause.

"What about me?"

"I know that you've got a shit-ton of money stashed away. I'm guessing enough to not have to work again if you don't want to, considering you live like an eighteen-year-old kid."

Josh tipped back his beer and didn't confirm what Trevor had said. He didn't have to. Trevor was one of the few friends from before. One of the friends who'd been there before he was sick, after he was sick, and most important, while he was sick.

"I also know you're bored," Trevor continued.

Josh shrugged.

"Your old bosses won't take you back?"

"They offered. I passed."

"I don't blame you. That place nearly ate you alive. But, man, you've got to do *something*. You're too smart to spend your days working out and writing music you don't care about selling and flirting with the neighbor."

Josh stilled as he remembered the real reason he'd invited Trevor over tonight. "Ah, about said neighbor—"

"You're boning her. I know," Trevor said distractedly as he glanced back at the TV.

Josh scratched his forehead. "Not the word I'd use, but, yeah, we've crossed that line."

"The naked line."

Josh nodded, watching his friend's profile for any trace of tension or resentment. Instead Trevor took another bite of his pizza, reaching across the couch with his other hand in a fist bump, all without glancing away from the hockey game.

Josh returned the hand gesture and laughed. "You're not pissed."

"Why would I be pissed?"

"You seemed . . . interested."

Trevor turned and grinned. "I did, didn't I?"

"But then why . . ." Josh's eyes narrowed, and this time when he offered Trevor his fist, it was with a punch to the shoulder. Hard. "You bastard."

"What? It was obvious you were hung up on her. Thought a little jealousy might get the ball rolling."

Josh didn't want to admit to his friend just how well his asshole plan had worked. "I am not hung up on her. I just like her."

"Dude, that's what being hung up means."

"What, you're telling me you don't have female friends that you like?"

"Sure."

"And you don't have women you sleep with that you also like?" Josh said.

"Yup."

"Are you *hung up* on all of them?" Josh asked smugly.

Trevor sighed and rested his head back against the cushion. "Man, you're dumb."

"What?"

Trevor turned his head and met Josh's annoyed gaze. "Yes, I like my female friends. Yes, I like some of the women I sleep with. But, dude, it's the overlap that's the *gotcha*. She's a female friend *and* you're sleeping with her. That's dangerous territory."

"It's not," Josh said automatically. "It's just . . ."

Trevor's eyebrows lifted. "Yeah?"

"Fuck," Josh said, slumping on the couch. "Never mind, I don't know. Shut up. I don't know why I mentioned it."

"Sure you do. You needed to make sure that you weren't falling for your buddy's girl."

"Oh my God, can we stop with the womanly talk?" Josh muttered. "I'm not falling for anyone. Heather and I are just having fun."

"Fine," Trevor said, holding up his hands in surrender. "Whatever. You want another beer?"

Josh nodded, and for several blissful minutes, there was silence, just two dudes watching a game and drinking beer while polishing off an entire pizza.

"Where is Heather tonight?" Trevor asked casually.

"Wedding," Josh said, not glancing up from his phone. No text from Heather yet. She must still be working.

"Huh," Trevor said with a smirk.

Josh ignored him, setting his phone aside.

He picked it up again two minutes later. Just to text her that he'd be up late if she wanted to come over later.

This time his friend's silent laughter was too much to ignore. Josh reached into the pizza box and threw an olive at him, but Trevor only brushed it off.

"It's cool, dude, it's cool. But, hey, I'm just curious . . . do you think she's going to plan your wedding for free, or will you have to pay the fee of her fancy wedding-planning company?"

This time it was a handful of olives that hit Trevor's smirking face.

"We're just having fun," Josh repeated.

Then he forced himself not to check his phone the rest of the time Trevor was there.

But he wanted to.

And damn if that didn't freak him out, just a little.

Chapter Twenty-Two

"SHIT. *SHIT*." HEATHER RAPIDLY pressed the delete button on her laptop, deleting the entire insipid paragraph she'd written on the benefits of serving eggs Benedict at a bridal brunch. She tried for a deep, cleansing breath as she refocused and began pecking at the keys again. A little after nine o'clock on Monday morning, and Heather was a bundle of nerves.

On the one hand, she had finally gotten what she wanted:

Danica Robinson was on her calendar for an in-person meeting.

On the other hand . . .

Danica Robinson was on her calendar for an in-person meeting.

As in, the first one since their initial consultation, because their strange run-in at the bar absolutely didn't count.

Which meant that Heather had exactly thirty minutes—it was all Danica would commit to—to run through an entire wedding plan, from rehearsal dinner to bridal brunch.

And she still needed to deliver the not-so-minor bomb that the Plaza was still very much *not* on the books. She had several other very viable options cued up to try to defuse this bombshell, but she had a very strong sense that Danica wouldn't give a crap.

Heather had left her office door open, as they were all likely to do except when on the phone, and she was completely unsurprised when her boss appeared in her doorway. She'd certainly been making enough noise.

"You good?" Alexis asked, getting straight to the point.

"Yeah," Heather said, her eyes remaining fixated on her iPad. "Or no. I don't know. This whole thing is just not what I dreamed of with my first celebrity wedding, you know? I wasn't expecting to be Danica's BFF or anything, but somehow I thought it would be more . . . fun. Hard work, sure. But fun."

"If it makes you feel any better, you're not overreacting," Alexis said, coming into Heather's small office and sitting in the small side chair beside Heather's desk. "I've been doing this a lot longer than you, and I've never seen anything quite like it."

"Well, hopefully my little come-to-Jesus talk won't lose us a client," Heather said with a sigh.

Alexis shrugged. "Maybe it wouldn't be so bad if it did."

Heather looked up, her mouth dropping open. "I'm sorry. Have you seen Alexis Morgan anywhere?

There seems to be a very chill, whatever type of woman lurking inside Alexis's type A body."

"Everybody has limits, and Danica is very close to breaching mine," Alexis said. "I expect my planners to work hard, even put up with some pretty outrageous behavior, but something's not right here. Danica doesn't get to be hands-off *and* demand the Plaza. It's one or the other. Either all in or all out."

"Great," Heather said with a toothy smile. "Let me know how it goes when you tell her that in"—she glanced at her watch—"twenty minutes."

Alexis gave a slight smile. "You've got this. Just keep your voice calm and tell her you want to continue working with her, but you need to better understand what she's looking for if she wants to get her money's worth."

"She's a gazillionaire," Heather said. "What if money doesn't work with her?"

"Then appeal to her ego. The whole 'help me help you look good,' and all that. Maybe imply that the dress you've picked out that she hasn't bothered to see might make her look hippy."

Heather laughed around a sip of her latte. "Yeah. That should go over great."

Alexis stood. "You've got this. Let me know how it goes."

Heather nodded distractedly, turning attention back to her iPad.

Her boss hovered at the doorway. "Heather."

"Yeah?" She looked up.

"Sex looks good on you."

Heather's mouth fell open. "Um—"

Alexis held up a hand. "No need to explain. You just look happy. Even with the Danica stress. You'll have to thank Josh for me."

"Yeah, I'm pretty sure the last thing he needs is me thanking him for sexing me on someone else's behalf. You've met him, right? His ego barely fits into our apartment building as it is."

"Well, judging from your downright dewy complexion, I'd say maybe that ego is earned?"

You have no idea.

She and Josh had spent most of the past week and a half, well . . . *doing it*. Mostly just the evenings, but the nights had gone on and on and on, and for the first time since she met the guy, she didn't mind quite so much that he was keeping her up at night.

"I thought so," Alexis said smugly. "Good for you."

It was on the tip of Heather's tongue to suggest that maybe Alexis find a little sexing for herself. Maybe with a certain sexy British accountant. But Alexis was already gone, leaving Heather to count the minutes until her showdown with Danica.

Heather was fully expecting her client to be late, but to her surprise, Danica showed up five minutes early, and even more pleasantly, without her mother.

"Hi, thanks for coming," Heather said with a polite smile as she gestured for Danica to enter the consultation room. "Can I get you anything? Coffee? Water?"

Danica smiled. "Last time you offered me champagne."

"Which you didn't like," Heather pointed out, before she could think better of it.

The other woman gave a startled laugh.

"But yes, of course, if you'd like some champagne," Heather quickly added.

"No, I'm fine," Danica said.

They both sat down, in the same spots they'd sat last time Danica had come. As with before, Heather felt the other woman studying her, but this time, Heather studied Danica right back.

The woman was gorgeous as ever. Her hair was in a long, flowing blowout today, one that Heather bet serious money came from a salon. Her nails were a deep, trendy black without a hint of a chip anywhere. Her outfit, completely on point.

But Heather was feeling pretty darn good about her own appearance today. Her hair was doing the sexy wave thing instead of the frizzy ringlet routine, thanks to a bout of dry, crisp winter weather. She wore a simple white camisole with a black blazer that made her feel sort of badass. She'd even rediscovered a pair of gray slacks in the back of her closet that she was pretty sure made her butt look just a tad perkier than it actually was.

Josh, at least, had been a fan as he'd handed her a to-go mug on her way out the door and swatted her butt with a lingering caress.

And speaking of Josh, it was strange to think of him dating the creature before her. Danica seemed so cold and calculating, and Josh was anything but.

"So. You asked to see me?" Danica said with a passive smile.

"Right. Yes, I've got some things I'd like to run by you," Heather said, setting her fingers on the iPad. "But first there's something I'd like to discuss."

Danica's perfect eyebrows lifted. "Yes?"

Here goes nothing.

"I respect your hands-off approach to this wedding, but I'm becoming increasingly concerned that without a bit more guidance from you, this wedding might not be at all what you're expecting."

Danica blinked, obviously surprised that she was being called out, but she didn't look immediately pissed, so that was something.

"I told you up front that I was giving you free rein. I'd think that would be a wedding planner's dream."

"Yes," Heather said slowly. "And no. To be honest, this isn't just any wedding. As I'm sure you can imagine, every wedding magazine on the planet is anxious to feature you. Even non-wedding magazines have been calling, hoping for an exclusive."

"And that's a bad thing?"

"Honestly? It's my dream," Heather said, deciding to go for broke. "It probably sounds dorky to you, but I've been dreaming of being a wedding planner for most of my life, and with that dream comes fame. I'm not ashamed of it."

"Of course not," Danica murmured.

"But the thing is, I always imagined that when I finally made it . . . when I finally got to plan that big, gorgeous wedding that everyone looked at, that every other bride pointed at and said, 'That one, I want *that* one' . . . I imagined that my success would be because I planned the *bride's* dream wedding. Not my own."

"Based on what I've seen so far, you're representing me just fine," Danica said with a wave of her hand.

"I want to do better than fine. I'd also like to ask you point-blank if there's something I need to know. A specific reason that you're disinterested in your own wedding."

"I'm not disinterested."

Heather merely leveled the other woman with a stare.

To her surprise, Danica's face crumbled for a second before she lifted both hands and plunged her fingers into her perfect hair. "Crap. Okay, *fine*. This has to stay between us."

"Of course," Heather said with calm she didn't feel. She was right. There *was* something weird going on here.

Danica looked up, her eyes miserable, and not at all the confident woman who usually stared back at Heather from the glossy magazine pages.

"Of course I have a dream wedding," Danica said quietly. "Like most little girls, I thought about it constantly. The details would change, of course, considering my favorite color changed about every other week. But I thought about it. Every time I've gone to a friend's wedding, I've made mental notes. I want this, but not that. Oh, I love the cake, but not the flowers . . ."

She broke off and Heather stayed silent. Waiting.

"Once Troy proposed, I went a little . . . crazy. In

fact, I found the ring before he proposed and put the announcement in the paper before he'd popped the question."

Heather's eyes widened slightly, and Danica gave a grim smile. "I know. Trust me, I know. I was just so excited, you know? And I apologized, and it was fine, and he proposed the way he wanted to with the champagne and all that. But I got a little . . . crazy. Totally crazy. It was all I could talk about, and I started bringing wedding magazines to the dinner table and demanding he pick his wedding party."

Danica sighed and dropped her hands to the table, staring blindly at her manicure.

"The truth was, I went full-on bridezilla before I even came to you guys. I wasn't even sure I wanted a wedding planner, because I wanted to do it all myself. *My* way. And it drove a rift between me and Troy. He's older. All he's wanted is a quiet wedding, and fast, hence the January date. But *I* wanted . . ."

"The big white wedding," Heather supplied.

"Yes. That. So . . . I quit cold turkey. Almost. I found you guys, and promised Troy that I wouldn't so much as talk about the wedding except for what was needed logistically. He's happy. I'm happy—"

"Are you?" Heather asked quietly.

Danica bit her lip. "I'm trying really hard not to care about the details, and for the most part I'm succeeding. There's just one part of the dream that I can't quite let go of. The one part of my wedding fantasy that's never faded."

"The Plaza," Heather said slowly.

Danica nodded.

Well . . . crap.

"It was our compromise," Danica said with a sad little smile. "He got to have the wedding in three months if I got to have it at the Plaza."

Heather sat back, overwhelmed at the unexpected information dump. Truth be told, she was feeling a little guilty about assuming the worst about Danica. Yes, the woman was a bit self-absorbed and oblivious, but Heather had been assuming the Plaza obsession was about competing for Page Six dominance.

Apparently, it was more than that, and Heather could understand. Every bride she'd ever talked to had that one thing. The piece of jewelry, the type of flowers, the cake flavor, the favorite song that was nonnegotiable.

Heather had even managed to coordinate a midnight delivery of actual Philly cheesesteak sandwiches for a bride and groom who'd met at Geno's in Philadelphia.

But there were some things that money couldn't buy.

A free Saturday at the Plaza was one of them.

"It's all right," Danica said glumly. "You can tell me. It's not going to happen, is it?"

Heather felt another flutter of surprise at Danica's perceptiveness. "I'm not going to lie to you; it's very, very unlikely," she said quietly. "I've been calling a couple times a week. They're sick of me over there. But the best I've been able to get is that we're first on the waiting list. And if something does open up, you have to understand that we're not likely to have much notice, and we definitely won't have control over the date."

Danica glanced again at her nails. "And you said that we need to send out the save-the-date cards soon."

Um, like, yesterday, Heather thought.

"We do, yes. Here are our options. We can send out the save-the-date cards and hold off until the very last minute to send the invitations, hoping that by some miracle, the Plaza might become available on that date. Or, we can skip the save-the-date and official invitation process and instead keep this wedding very small and spontaneous. If and when the Plaza does open up, we can gather close friends and family members for a quiet, intimate affair."

Danica bit her lip. "So basically, it's the slim possibility of tiny and last-minute at the Plaza, or I drop the Plaza and plan for something else."

Heather nodded. "Yes. That, or we push the date out to when the Plaza *is* available."

"Not an option," Danica said. "I promised Troy."

Heather pulled the iPad back toward her, knowing now wasn't the time to start showing Danica bridesmaid dress patterns and fondant colors. Not when they didn't even have a date and location.

"Why don't you take some time to think about it," she said gently. "Let me know by the end of the week which direction you want to head."

Danica nodded and swallowed. "Okay. And also . . . I guess I want to say thank you. I know I can be sort of . . . I'm used to getting what I want. Sometimes it doesn't occur to me that I can't have it."

Heather stifled a smile. Danica was absurdly pampered, but at least there was a sliver of self-awareness there. Somehow divas were more tolerable when they realized they were divas.

"Touch base whenever you're ready," Heather said as they both stood. "And in the meantime, I'm here for anything you might need."

Danica gave a distracted smile. "Thanks. I appreciate your patience with this. I'm sorry if I seemed flippant before. I've been pretty determined to be nonchalant about the wedding, and I may have gone overboard."

"It's fine," Heather said smoothly, as though it hadn't been the cause of several migraines over the past few weeks. "My only goal is to get you your dream wedding. I just need a bit more help in understanding what that is."

"Understood. I appreciate your patience. I really do."

After Danica left, Heather headed back to her office feeling a fierce sense of relief that the conversation was over, and maybe a bit embarrassed that she'd expended so much energy freaking out about the Robinson wedding instead of addressing the problem with Danica head-on.

Had she been more assertive weeks ago, she'd have saved herself a few huge headaches.

Still, she supposed maybe this was part of the learning curve. If she wanted to be like Alexis and Brooke, she had to make her own mistakes. Learn when to roll with the punches, when to deliver the punches.

Today had been a deliver-the-punch day. Gently, of course.

Heather reached for her cell phone, brought up Josh's number, and tapped out a message about her mini-accomplishment, only to hesitate before hitting send.

Just days ago, she would have sent it without thinking twice. She'd be telling her friend—the one who was helping her with the wedding—that she'd made some progress.

But now that they'd slept together, she was telling him what, exactly? He wasn't her boyfriend. Lord knew he'd made that clear. Nor did she want him to be. Heartache that way lay.

She put her phone down, tapping her fingernails on the desk as she considered. Then before she could overthink it further, she picked up her phone and hit send.

Any other guy she'd been sleeping with for a week, no way. He'd likely freak out that his new bed conquest was getting all personal and sharey.

But this was Josh. He hadn't started treating her differently once he'd started seeing her naked, and she wouldn't treat him differently, either.

They were still friends, after all. And he was still Danica's ex—gross. All the rules for why she could share with him still applied.

She was pretty sure.

Josh texted back almost immediately. Hell yes. Did you tell her you were shagging her ex? Was there a cat fight? Did you take pics?

Heather rolled her eyes as she replied. Yes. Because this is obviously about you.

Speaking of me and everything that I am, want to make banana bread later? I bought more bananas

after you let the other ones get rotten. They're
perfect for baking.

I can't handle you and your banana bread fetish
right now. I have to work.

Go get 'em. Don't forget to send me the cat fight
pictures. You both were naked right?

Heather was still smiling as she put her phone
back in her purse and turned back to her work.

"Someone's in a good mood."

Heather spun around, smiling in surprise when
she saw Logan Harris standing in her doorway.

"Logan! Come in! What are you doing here? I
thought you and Alexis only had your super-secret
meetings early in the mornings."

He smiled his slow, sexy smile and came in, settling himself in her guest chair. "You realize that
sounds like a double entendre, right?"

"I think you wish it had a double meaning," she
quipped.

He blinked in surprise behind his horn-rimmed
glasses, and Heather felt color flood her cheeks as
she realized what she'd said. She and Logan were friends,
but not *that* good of friends.

"*Well*," he said, sitting back, the simple word
sounding crisp and precise in his lovely accent.

"Sorry," she said. "I don't know why I said that,
I'm all frazzled today—"

Logan held up a hand. "Heather. Please. It's okay."

"I'm sorry," she said again, miserably.

"Don't apologize for being observant."

Her mouth dropped open. "Wait, so you do . . . you want . . ."

"Alexis? Yes, of course. I should think it's been quite obvious these many years. Your comment assures me that it is."

"Well, to me, I guess. And Brooke."

"And Alexis?" he asked. "Does she know?"

Heather blew out a breath, wishing she had better news for the guy. "I don't know. Maybe? We've teased her about it before. You two are just so . . . right. But she's always insisted that you're just friends."

His smile was fleeting. "Just friends. Yes. We are most certainly that."

"Why don't you ask her out?" Heather said, leaning forward and resting her arms on her legs, hands clasped between her knees.

"You know Alexis as well as anyone. How do you suppose that would go?" Logan asked.

Heather sat back, picturing exactly how it would go and feeling bad for the guy sitting opposite her.

"Exactly," he said. "The woman doesn't do anything she doesn't want to do. Doesn't embark on any venture that's not her idea."

"Ah," Heather said, as his strategy clicked into place. "You're waiting. For her to come to her senses."

"I am," he confirmed. "And I'd request that you do the same."

"In other words, you've been waiting too long for me to go mucking things up?" Heather asked.

He winked, quick and sexy. "Let's just say I'm playing the long game."

"You are a patient man, Logan Harris."

"A curse, to be sure." He shifted in his seat and immediately his face was back to implacable, business-minded Logan. "But actually, Alexis isn't the reason I stopped by."

"Hit me," she said.

Logan adjusted his glasses, and Heather nearly smiled because the shift from a besotted man to an accountant with a mission was visible.

"Your friend. Mr. Tanner. You're close?"

Heather smirked. Boy, was that a loaded question. "We're . . . we're on good terms," she finished lamely.

"He's a musician," Logan stated.

"Yeah," Heather said, puzzled.

"But he hasn't always been. He said he was a hedge fund manager?"

Heather lifted her shoulders. "Yeah. I don't know much about it. To say that he doesn't like talking about that stage of his life is an understatement."

"Interesting," Logan said. "Because I got the impression that he missed it."

Huh.

Heather got that impression sometimes, too. But if he did miss it, why didn't he go back?

"I think he loves music," she said slowly.

"Oh, I'm positive he does," Logan said. "I love music, too. But I don't think the music is enough for someone like Josh."

"By all means, feel free to tell him that," she said. "Might I suggest Kevlar for the conversation?"

"You've spoken with him about it?"

"Not about going back to Wall Street, specifically.

But I've sort of suggested that he seemed . . . lost. He didn't speak to me for days after. That is apparently off-limits."

"Well," Logan said with a small sigh. "That is most disappointing."

"Why?" Heather asked, curious why someone who'd met Josh once, talked to him for all of five minutes, was so interested in him.

"I'm thinking about expanding my practice," Logan said. "Actually, perhaps *expand* isn't the right word, although I do need another person to help me achieve my vision."

"Which is . . ."

"I want to create an app."

"An app? Like . . ." Heather lifted her iPhone in question.

He nodded. "Yes, precisely. I won't bore you with the details, but short version: Accounting is and always will be a necessity for businesses, and yet we as a group have failed to evolve in any meaningful way. From ledgers to calculators, yes, and eventually to spreadsheets, and so on, but while that makes my work easier, it doesn't change the fact that the clients are, in fact, reliant on me."

"Isn't that a good thing? For you, I mean. Job security and all that."

"Yes. And no. I spend significant amount of time on tiny, basic functions. Over and over and over."

Heather studied him. "You're bored."

"I'd like to stretch."

"A British way of saying you're bored?"

Logan laughed. "Sure. Anyway, I want to create

a new model. One that allows customers to balance their books on their own. One that has a large database of information on FAQs, because trust me when I say that the questions I get are frequent. And repetitive. I envision a subscription-based model. They sign up with my company and get access to all my knowledge."

Heather nodded, understanding why something like this could potentially be huge. "But how does Josh fit into this?" she asked.

"I need a partner. It's just me, currently. And there simply aren't enough hours in the day for me to support my current customers and undertake this new venture. I'll need to hire developers and build a website and a business plan. I need help."

"Why not find another accountant?"

"Because I liked your friend," Logan said simply. "We accountants can be a stodgy lot, and Josh is anything but. He already understands the basics of what I do. He thinks in numbers, I know he does. I can tell. Plus, there's a . . . youth, about him."

"I'm pretty sure he's your age," Heather said.

"Yes, but does he wear elbow patches?" Logan said, lifting his arms and revealing that his tweed blazer did, in fact, have elbow patches.

Heather burst out laughing. "Point taken."

"It may not work out," Logan said. "It's a long shot. I just wanted to feel you out. See if it would even be worth speaking with him. If I ever decide to return to England, I'll need someone here that I can trust."

He looked at her expectantly, and Heather bit her

lip. "I don't know what to tell you. I really don't. I think your idea's brilliant. I think you're right that Josh probably would have plenty to contribute. I also think he'd love it. The trouble is . . . well, heck, I don't know what the trouble is. Like I said, he's weird when it comes to his life's purpose, or whatever."

Logan nodded and stood, lifting the modern-style briefcase that was slightly at odds with his elbow patches. "Understood. If you decide not to bring it up, I won't mention it again. No hard feelings, all right?"

"Logan?" she asked before he could leave.

He turned back.

"I know you don't know Josh, not really, but when you spoke to him at brunch, did he seem . . . happy?"

Logan was silent for several moments as he considered. "I wouldn't say he was unhappy, but no, happy isn't the word I'd first use to describe Mr. Tanner."

"What is?"

Logan's smile was a little sad. "Scared. I'd say Mr. Tanner is terrified of something."

"But what?" Heather asked.

Logan lifted a shoulder. "I dare say that's perhaps for you to find out."

Chapter Twenty-Three

~

"OKAY, WHICH OF THESE do you think Danica would like best?" Heather said, sliding the iPad across the table to Josh before refilling both of their wineglasses.

He pulled the tablet toward him and looked at the screen for a long moment before lifting his head and looking at her. "You are joking right? I'm looking at pink, pink, and pink?"

"No." She leaned forward and tapped her nail against the swatches. "You're looking at dusty rose, heaven's mauve, and winter blush."

Josh made a gun motion with his hand and held it under his chin. "Can we order dinner yet?"

"After we pick the bridesmaid dress color."

"That one," he said, pointing to the screen without glancing.

She tilted her head. "Really? You don't think that's a bit dark?"

"Heather. I *will* kill you."

"Fine, fine. Winter blush it is." She pulled the iPad

back toward her and switched back to her notebook, where she typed it in.

"Why can't Danica pick her own ugly bridesmaid dress color? I thought you guys were besties ever since your little powwow?"

"I wouldn't go that far," Heather said, sitting back and picking up her wineglass. "Things are definitely better. But I'm still trying to shield her from some of the more mundane details."

"Right. By all means, don't bother the bride, but harass the bride's ex."

"I didn't see you complaining when I brought home the chocolate turtle cake to taste-test."

Josh stretched his arms over his head, his shirt lifting to reveal a tiny sliver of abs that made her mouth water.

Work first, play later.

"So you're willing to help with the food portion of the wedding but not the color scheme," she said.

"Honestly, I don't know why you sound surprised. How many dudes do you know who want to sit and discuss various shades of pink dresses?"

"Actually, I'm good on the dresses. I do, however, need to figure out whether we want to go with ivory or white candles. The white will better match her dress, the ivory will work better with the pale-pink color scheme I'm putting together. Thoughts?"

"Is there any cake left?"

Heather sighed and turned her iPad off. "Okay. You win. No more wedding talk."

"You can talk. I'm just fresh out of things to say on the subject," he said, reaching across the table and taking her hand, rubbing his thumb across her wrist.

"Nah, I think I've given enough of my week to Danica Robinson."

"But you've made progress, right? Picked the place and all that?"

Heather nodded.

Danica had called her today—called, not texted, shock of all shocks—and said that she'd decided to forgo the Plaza. She'd even agreed to tour Heather's top-two backups tomorrow, both gorgeous hotels with the same classy elegance of the Plaza, and the not-so-minor perk of *being available*.

Josh's phone rang, and he pulled it out of his pocket, only to silence it and set it on the table.

"You can pick up if you need to."

He shrugged. "It's not a big deal."

Heather fiddled with the corner of her iPad. Most of the time, she was pretty content with whatever it was she and Josh were doing. The sex. The companionship. They hung out most nights, working, eating. Watching a movie.

And then there was the sex. Lots and lots of sex.

But sometimes it was as though there was this extra layer between them. A line that Josh wouldn't cross. When it came to her job, her life, her issues, he was always there to listen and advise. He could tease or seduce her out of a bad mood like nobody she'd ever met.

But it was a one-way street. His life remained strictly off-limits. She could barely get him to talk about his day at the gym or his latest song, much less anything deeper that had to do with his life.

And yet, her conversation with Logan Harris earlier in the week was still lingering. Instinct told her that Josh was the perfect man for the job—it also told her that he would enjoy it.

The question was whether or not he'd let himself enjoy it.

"It's Trevor," he blurted out. "That's who's calling."

"Oh," Heather said, blinking in surprise. "You don't want to get it?"

"He thinks he found someone to buy my drum set."

Heather blinked. "What do you mean? That drum set is yours? I thought it was what's his name's?'

Josh shook his head. "Nope. Mine. Everything in the practice room is mine; the guys just play it."

"Ah. Are you thinking of replacing the set with something newer?" She tried to keep her voice casual, even though she was secretly thrilled he was opening up, even a little bit.

Instead of responding, he held up his phone. "You care if I order Thai?"

She bit back her disappointment. "No. Go for it."

"Pad thai with shrimp, right? And spring rolls."

"Yup, that's great." She pulled her iPad toward her, flicking it back on. "Hey, how's your sister? She's due about now, right?"

"Past due. Baby Josh is past due, but no sign yet."

"Baby Josh?"

"It's a girl, but I'm still holding out hope they'll name her after her uncle. If the kid's at all lucky, she'll look like me."

"Yes, that's what all little girls dream of. To resemble an overgrown frat boy."

He glanced up. "Overgrown frat boy?"

"Who's good at sex. Really good. Did I not mention that bit?" she asked teasingly.

Josh didn't smile back.

"Hey," she said, reaching toward him, but he stood up abruptly, moving away from her.

"Would it be better if I wore suits all day? Walked around with my phone plastered to my face, rambling about shit that doesn't matter?"

Heather blinked. "Um. Where is this coming from?"

"I'm thirty-three years old. Guess being called a boy isn't exactly every adult male's dream."

"I didn't mean it like that," she said quietly.

"How did you mean it?"

Uh-oh.

"I just meant you're not on a typical path," she said gently. "It's not a bad thing."

"I broke up the band."

Whoa. What?

She shook her head. "Sorry, I'm getting conversational whiplash. Back up. What now?"

"It's not a big deal. Trev and I talked about it a few nights ago. It's just a hobby for the other guys, and we just don't see it going anywhere unless we're really going to give it our all, which we're not. So . . ." He lifted his shoulders in a shrug. "*Finito.*"

"What about for you?" she asked. "I always got the impression you were pretty passionate about it."

"I am. That won't change. I just . . . I don't know. It just felt right."

Heather nodded. "As long as you're happy with the decision."

"Happy's a stretch," he said, tossing his phone on the table with a sigh. "It feels right, I just don't know . . ."

He trailed off and Heather swallowed, deciding to take a risk. "You don't know what to replace it with?"

His blue-green eyes snapped to hers. "Yeah. Something like that."

"Well, what do you want to do?" she asked.

"I don't know, 4C. Not all of us had our dream job lined up at the age of twelve, or whatever."

"Fine," she snapped, losing patience. "You want to have another of your sulking episodes, have at it, but do me a favor, and don't bring up things you don't want to talk about."

She grabbed her wineglass and stormed toward his kitchen sink. She couldn't quite bring herself to dump it, but neither was she going to sit there and try to make small talk with a guy who ran hot and cold every time she tried to connect with him on a remotely human level.

"Don't get pissed," he muttered, coming up behind her.

"Well, I am, a little," she said, grabbing her iPad. "Sometimes it's like you want to have a conversation, you start it, then decide you don't want to talk after all, and you blame me."

He rubbed at his forehead. "And *this* is why I don't have a girlfriend."

Ouch.

Her mouth dropped open. "Seriously? You don't have a girlfriend because you're an *ass*."

"Heather."

But she was done. He wanted to keep things light, fine, but she was *not* going to sit around and serve as his emotional punching bag.

"This goes both ways, you know." She threw the words out at him as she headed for the door. "Conversations—sorry, *non*-conversations—like this one are exactly why *I* don't have a boyfriend."

"Hey, would you hold up a minute?" he asked, coming after her.

Heather spun around. "Why, so you can sit here and dangle all sorts of conversation starters and then get pissy when I respond? You're selling your drum set, but don't want to tell me why. You're dismantling the band, but don't want to talk about that, either. And God forbid we talk about what you might want to do *instead* of the band, because you totally lose your shit."

His nostrils flared in irritation, his eyes turned flat and cold, and she suddenly had a very good sense of what the old Josh might have looked like before he decided to be all devil-may-care. The aura he must have given off when he was striding around in expensively tailored suits, barking orders at lowly peons, and going out for $400 power lunches.

But although it was becoming increasingly clear that while there was an old Josh and a new Josh, nowhere to be seen was the *real* Josh.

"Can we just hold on a second?" he said.

"How about you come up with a list of safe topics,

and then we'll talk," she snapped, reaching for the door handle and jerking it open. "I'm not in the mood to walk on eggshells tonight. I've got work to do."

"You always have work to do," he muttered.

"Well, that makes one of us," she shot back, stepping out into the hallway and slamming the door behind her. She didn't wait to see if he'd follow her before she stormed into her apartment and slammed that door, too.

It felt . . . good.

A little petty, sure, maybe a touch immature. But sometimes a good old door slam was exactly what one needed.

She threw herself on the couch, determined to get some work done. Because that's what adults did. They worked.

You always have work to do.

Heather scowled as she thought back over Josh's words. She didn't always have work to do. Well, she did. The wedding-planner business wasn't exactly nine-to-five. But she didn't let it rule her life.

Did she?

Sure, she brought her work home with her sometimes. Often.

But she also loved it.

Maybe it had been a touch unfair to make him look at color schemes tonight—she hadn't really needed his opinion. But talking about Danica's wedding gave her an excuse to see him without seeming clingy, and—

Heather sat up straighter. Well, *crap*.

Her mind flitted back to the week that had just

passed in a flurry of sex and laughter, realizing that almost always, it had been her seeking him out. He'd always seemed amenable to hanging out, sure, but wasn't it her who usually called first?

In fact, after they'd first slept together on Thanksgiving night, he hadn't been to her place once. It was always the other way around. He hadn't used his key, hadn't so much as knocked on the door.

Heather groaned and slumped back on the couch, tossing her iPad aside.

Had she been that girl? The one who wouldn't go away? He hadn't seemed to mind. He'd always smiled when she'd knocked at the door, never seemed to be trying to get rid of her, and yet that was what Josh did. He was polite to the women he slept with. Hell, how many women had she watched him say good-bye to with a smile and a wink and a flirt?

Her eyes flew open. For that matter, how many women had there been since they'd started sleeping together?

And even if there hadn't been any, there likely would be now. She wouldn't be the least bit surprised if he was calling another one up right this very minute. A woman who wouldn't overstay her welcome, who wouldn't ask pesky questions, who wouldn't be distracted by something as mundane as her career.

The thought made her sick, considering the guy wasn't her boyfriend.

And she didn't want him to be.

Did she?

No.

He was mercurial and immature, and half the time she felt like she didn't even *know* him.

But the other half of the time she suspected he might very well be the best man she'd ever met.

"Tricky," Heather muttered to herself. "Very tricky."

There was really only one thing to do in these situations, and Heather headed toward the kitchen, grabbing a spoon even before she opened the freezer door to contemplate her emergency supply of ice cream.

Heather's brow furrowed as she surveyed the variety of options. Was getting in a fight with your booty-call neighbor a cookie-dough situation? Mint chocolate chip? What she really wanted was the special-edition pumpkin pie ice cream she'd picked up last week, but pumpkin pie reminded her of Thanksgiving, which made her think her of Josh . . .

She reached for the plain vanilla. To punish herself.

Heather had just pulled the lid off, spoon ready for demolition, when there was a knock at the door.

Her eyes narrowed as she glanced at it.

She dug her spoon into the ice cream, scooped out an enormous mouthful of vanilla, and shoved it in her mouth, trying to ignore the second knock.

By the third mouthful, the knocking hadn't stopped. In fact, it was growing louder.

"Go away," she called. "I'm in a mood."

To her surprise, the knocking stopped. For once, the man had listened to her. Heather told herself she wasn't disappointed at how easily he'd given up on her.

But then, how hard did a guy like Josh fight for

an easy lay, really? He likely had dozens of others a phone call away, and it wasn't like he couldn't pick up fresh meat in a bar in two point four seconds.

She'd just inhaled another giant mouthful of vanilla when an awful banging started up. One couldn't call it music coming from the other side of her bedroom wall. This was no band practice, no solo playing.

This was someone banging on a drum set as loudly as he could with no perceptible rhythm.

"You've got to be kidding me," she said around a mouthful of ice cream.

The banging persisted. No, it got louder. And louder.

Heather's hand clenched around the spoon so hard she thought she might actually bend the metal. What a jerk. No big deal. She could ignore it. Could ignore him.

She made it about three minutes before she barged into his apartment, still wielding her spoon and temper.

As expected, she found him seated by the drum set, not even pretending to do anything other than bang it over and over.

"What the hell is your problem?" she yelled over the banging.

His hand paused only briefly when he saw and heard her, but he crashed the drumstick down onto the drum one more time for good measure before tossing it aside and storming toward her.

Heather held her ground, and they were toe-to-toe, glare-to-glare.

She spread her arms to the side. "You happy? You get what you want?"

Josh shook his head. "Not even fucking close."

His mouth slammed down on hers a half second before his hands closed greedily around her head as he took her in the hottest kiss of her life.

Heather's spoon dropped to the floor as her fingers found his waist, clawing at his shirt.

His lips were possessive, his tongue insistent, and his fingers punishing as they tugged at her hair.

Heather had never had makeup sex before, had never quite understood the big deal, but she got it now. Oh, did she ever.

Josh had them both out of their clothes in seconds, but Heather didn't have time to be impressed because she was too busy being turned on at the feel of his hands on her breasts before he dipped his head and sucked a nipple into his hot and greedy mouth.

She moaned something that might have been his name or might have been a wanton plea as his hand slid down her stomach, this thumb circling her as his middle finger slid inside. Even more erotic was the way he watched her as he played with her, his eyes never leaving hers as he touched her everywhere she needed him.

Josh had never been stingy with the orgasms, but tonight he pulled away just as she was on the crest, and she let out a moan of protest and leaned forward and bit his shoulder in revenge. He growled, spinning her around and pushing her upper body onto the small console table where he kept his sheet music and notebooks, paper scattering as he bent her over.

"Stay," he commanded, swatting her ass with just enough force to sting as he went to his discarded jeans, fumbling through the pockets until he came up with a condom.

"You just carry those around?" she asked huskily, watching him over her shoulder. Even still, she stayed put, her breathing heavy as she waited. Wanted.

He didn't respond, for once, not willing to engage in flirtation as he walked back toward her, ripping the condom wrapper open with his teeth before rolling it on as he positioned himself behind her.

There was no warning. His hands closed around her hips at the same moment he plunged inside her. She cried out at the unexpected invasion, arching her back in pleasure.

He gathered her hair in one hand, winding it around his fist, holding her captive as he slammed into her over and over again. There was no gentleness tonight, but she didn't want it. She wanted this—this unapologetic carnality that had come out of nowhere and somehow was exactly what she needed.

His other hand slid around to her front, his fingers stroking her in light teasing flicks until she was practically sobbing for a release he kept just out of reach.

"Please," she whispered.

He grunted in gratification, stroking her harder still, his motions growing smaller and more precise until she shattered against him.

He'd been waiting for her, and the second she clenched around him and cried out, he came with a low groan, one hand on her hip, clenching and unclenching in a helpless surrender that mimicked her own.

Her knees buckled, and he wrapped an arm around her waist, lowering them both gracelessly to the ground.

Josh rolled to his back, his chest still heaving with exertion, and Heather did the same, so they lay shoulder-to-shoulder, basking in the aftermath of the hottest, most intense sex of her life.

"What was that?" she asked several minutes later, still splayed out on the floor next to him, when she finally stopped panting.

"Fantastic," he said, his voice raspy as though his throat was dry.

"Well, yes, that. But why?"

"Hell if I know," he said. "I just saw you there, wielding your little spoon, and I just wanted. So I took."

His words sent a shockwave of forbidden want through her. Nobody had ever wanted her this way. And she had never wanted anyone else.

Maybe it was okay that this was all they were. Friends and neighbors who could make each other lose their minds in the most raunchy, unapologetic kind of way.

"So do we talk about it?" he asked quietly.

"Talk about what?" she replied, keeping her voice light.

He turned his head slightly and looked at her. She looked back. For a moment his expression seemed almost tender, and she could have sworn she saw a thank-you in his gaze. Maybe a sorry somewhere in there, too.

But then he reached down by his side, picked something up, and flicked it against her bare thigh.

"Ouch," she yelped, realizing she'd just been slapped with her own spoon.

"Come on, 4C. Let's make banana bread."

Heather groaned, but let him help her to her feet. "Not that again."

As usual the banana bread never happened.

But round two *definitely* did.

Chapter Twenty-Four

I KNEW IT. SHE looks just like me," Josh said as he gazed down at his days-old niece, and felt his heart lurch as one of her tiny arms flopped outside of her tight pink swaddle blanket, her features peaceful as she slept.

"Sure, if you look like an adorable Craisin," his sister said, coming to peer over his shoulder at her infant daughter. Jamie leaned forward and pressed a kiss to the baby's forehead, then each of her cheeks.

"Did you just compare this lovely lady to a dried cranberry?"

"I did. She's all sorts of wrinkly pink goodness, and the most beautiful thing I've ever seen."

Josh didn't disagree. Marian Margaret Clyde was pretty much perfection in his eyes. His niece had come into the world hearty and healthy, if a bit late by her mother's preferences, and Josh had been on the first flight down to Nashville once his brother-in-law had given him the go-ahead.

Kevin was off fetching BBQ to satisfy his wife's

post-pregnancy craving, which meant it was just the twins and new baby hanging out in his sister's comfortable suburban home. He supposed he'd have to give Marian back eventually, but not anytime soon. At least, not until she started crying.

"I never really pictured you as the baby-swooning kind of guy," Jamie said, giving him a thoughtful look as she leaned back and resumed folding the mountain of towels on the couch beside her.

He snorted. "Just because I don't go up and coo at strange children on the subway doesn't mean I'm not completely enamored with this little princess."

"If you and Kev keep talking like that, you're going to turn her into a spoiled brat," Jamie said fondly.

He glanced up. "Oh, so is now not a good time to bring in the pink pony I brought her along with an IOU for a Porsche on her sixteenth birthday?"

His twin merely rolled her eyes as she moved the stack of clean laundry to the side. "How are you, anyway?"

"'Bout the same as I was last time you saw me a few weeks ago," he said.

Jamie shook her head. "I don't think so. There's something different about you."

Oh great. Not this.

"You're my twin," he deflected. "Aren't you just supposed to *know*?"

"All right, then, if that's how you want to play it," she said, leaning back. "I think there's a woman in your life. I think that's why you're down here twice in one month. Not just to see me, not even to see the baby, but because you're running."

"Yes, there are women in my life," he said, dodging the last part of her accusation. The part that hit way too close to home. "Lots, actually. You. Mom. Your little Craisin. Two grandmothers, both of whom have deemed me their favorite. A handful of aunts. Also who insist I'm their favorite."

"Who is she?" Jamie asked, refusing to be sidetracked. "The girl you took to Thanksgiving?"

He glanced up sharply, and his twin shrugged. "Mom told me how you brought her and how you both fell all over each other insisting you were just friends, but she's never seen you so happy."

"Mom sees what she wants to see. You know that."

"Well that's what I figured . . . that you were just taking pity on a lonely neighbor. I know how you like to take care of sad creatures. Cats, dogs, even that weird turtle."

"Agatha wasn't weird."

"She bit me."

"Probably because you called her weird," Josh said.

"Seriously though, tell me about the girl."

He opened his mouth to tell her to mind her own damn business when he caught a whiff of something less than fresh. "Ah, I think we have a cleanup on aisle baby."

Jamie sighed. "Yeah. She does that. A lot."

His sister didn't seem too bugged though as she pushed up from the couch and came to gather the now-waking infant in her arms. "I'd make you change her, but you'll probably withhold information to get back at me," she said over her shoulder as she headed upstairs.

"I'll withhold information anyway," he called after her.

His sister disappeared upstairs, and Josh started to take out his phone to text Heather, just to check in, but decided against it. As much as he'd teased her about not reading his mind, the truth was, Jamie was as good at it as anybody. Even more annoying, his twin had a tendency to figure things out about Josh before he'd had a chance to figure them out.

He was having a hard enough time keeping his own thoughts off Heather—he didn't need Jamie's weird twin juju to make a mess of things he was struggling to keep under control.

They'd emerged mostly unscathed from their fight-and-fuck the other day. Both were doing a damn good job of pretending it hadn't happened. And while he was grateful, he was also feeling like something was missing.

It made no sense. The sex was great, both the makeup sex and the not-makeup sex.

He liked Heather. She liked him.

They were enjoying each other, which is all he'd wanted from the very beginning.

And now that he had what he wanted, it was somehow not enough?

What the fuck was that about?

Maybe it was just the guilt talking. He still bit her head off anytime she tried to talk to him about something real. Things with Heather were starting to feel a good deal more complicated than he'd been prepared for, and not because she wanted to know about his personal life.

But because he wanted to tell her.

A small, fragile part of Josh wanted Heather to know the whole him, the risks and the danger of who he really was, what life with him would be like. But he was too terrified that in letting her know about his past, she'd also have to discover what life *without* him would be like.

He wouldn't do that to someone he . . . liked.

"Okay, she's asleep again," Jamie said, coming back into the room and fiddling with her baby monitor, disrupting Josh's rather disturbing train of thought. "I'm pretty sure it's not supposed to be this easy. Do you think I'm going to pay for this later?"

"Probably when she's a teenager."

"Ugh, I don't even want to think about that." Jamie resumed her spot on the couch. "Okay, so, seriously, I want to know what's going on with you and this Heather girl. You might as well start talking, you know I'm not going to relent until you tell me what's going on."

Josh grunted. He did know. His mom won the award for meddling, but his sister took first prize for persistence.

"You already know the important parts. Her name is Heather, she's my neighbor and my friend. End of story."

"And you're sleeping with her," Jamie added helpfully.

"Ah—"

"Right. End of story, my ass. Is she your girlfriend now? Mom said she seemed like your girlfriend."

Maybe. "No," he said out loud, annoyed by how defensive he sounded.

"So let me get this straight. You like her. She's your friend. You live next door to each other. You're having sex. But she's not your girlfriend."

It sounded as ridiculous coming out of her mouth as it had Trevor's, but Josh held firm. "Right."

"Okaaaaay," Jamie said in a skeptical tone. "And what would make her your girlfriend?"

"Nothing."

"So you're a pig."

Josh laughed and rubbed at the back of his neck. "It's not like that. She knows the score. She's not exactly dragging me to meet her parents."

"And yet you dragged her to meet *your* parents," Jamie said smugly.

Shit. He'd walked right into that one.

Josh took out his phone and pretended to scroll through his sports app, affecting a casual tone. "I'm not interested in a relationship."

"Why not?"

He glanced up and gave her a steady look. *You know why.*

Her look was a mixture of sadness and exasperation. "J. You're not sick anymore."

But I could be at any time. I could relapse in an instant, and I don't need yet another person I care about mourning me.

He said none of this. Josh knew it was wrong to

keep his family in the dark, but they'd already been through so much—his parents and sister, even his brother-in-law, had all lost years worrying about him already. The least he could do in return was to give them peace of mind now, however false it might be.

"You're not sick, right?" she said, her voice a little bit higher than usual.

"No, I'm fine," he said quietly. It was the truth. His last regular doctor's appointment had confirmed that he was still in remission. "But think about what not being able to help me did to you. That almost killed you, and in turn almost killed me. I can't put someone else through that. I won't."

"Because you care about her," Jamie said.

Josh lifted his shoulders. No use denying it. He *did* care about Heather, which is why he wouldn't do either of them the disservice of falling in love with her. Or letting her fall in love with him.

"You're not doing that thing, are you?" Jamie asked with narrowed eyes.

"What thing?"

"That guy thing. Where you push her away for her own good, or some shit?"

"I'm a cancer survivor, Jamie. Not an egomaniac with a playboy complex."

"Exactly, you're a *survivor*," she shot back. "Meaning you're not sick anymore, and you should get married and have babies and be happy."

"I am happy," he said automatically.

"No. You aren't. You're content, and you smile a lot, and you've still got the best sense of humor of anyone I know, but you're not happy, Josh. You want everyone to think you're living life to the fullest with the music and the laissez-faire 'tude you've got going on, but you're really living a half life because you're too scared of having *no* life."

"That's deep, sis. Also, bullshit."

She threw her hands up. "I should have listened to Kevin. He told me not to get into it with you."

"Smart man," Josh said. "Speaking of, was that the garage door opening?"

"Saved by the BBQ," she muttered as they both stood. "Hey, Josh," she said, touching his arm as he started to walk past her toward the kitchen.

He tensed but turned toward her. "What's up?"

"I love you."

His throat tightened. "I love you, too."

"I also think you're an idiot."

Josh smiled. "Noted."

"Heather's not coming for Christmas, right?"

He shook his head. "Nope. She's going back home to Michigan to spend it with her mom."

"Ah. Maybe next year, then," she said, patting his arm with a smile.

It was on the tip of his tongue to tell his sister that in no universe would his and Heather's fling last an entire year to next Christmas.

But the words never made it out.

Because somehow, the thought of him and Heather parting ways just seemed . . .

Wrong.

Chapter Twenty-Five

CHRISTMAS HAD NEVER BEEN one of Heather's favorite holidays.

She didn't *dislike* it. She enjoyed the lights and the carols and the general festivities as much as the next person.

But when it came to the actual day, Christmas always felt a bit like a letdown. After a month of parties and selecting the perfect gift and ogling the window displays on Fifth Avenue, you were left with a strange sense of disappointment, knowing that you have to wait a whole other year to do it again.

But Christmas *did* mean spending time with her mom. And even though once again Heather found herself back in Michigan, in the same tired trailer at the same tired table, Christmas meant family.

And family was Joan Fowler.

"I'm sorry it wasn't fancier," Joan said, nudging her plate away with the base of her wineglass.

"If I ever choose fancy over homemade mac and cheese, just put me out to pasture," Heather said, picking up her own glass and leaning back in her chair with a contented sigh.

Her mom was right. Dinner hadn't been fancy. Macaroni and cheese with bacon. But they'd grated the four kinds of cheeses together, stressed over how much salt to add to the water together, and eaten half the bacon together before it ever made it to the pasta dish.

The perfect Christmas.

"I still can't get over cooking bacon in the oven," her mother mused. "That's going to be very dangerous to my waistline. Who'd you say taught you that trick again?"

Heather gave her mom a look. "Mother. You're fishing."

"Guilty," Joan said with a wide grin. "It's just that you've been here for three days and have told me next to nothing about your young man."

Heather shifted in the uncomfortable chair. "I've told you, there's just . . . not much to tell. I like him, we're having fun, but he's told me in no uncertain terms that he doesn't want anything serious, and I'm trying to respect that."

"What about you? What do you want?"

Heather groaned and stood before flopping on the ugly old couch directly behind the kitchen table. "I don't know. Are the brownies cooled yet?"

Her mom didn't let her off the hook. "If you want something more, you should tell him. Men appreciate honesty."

"Respectfully, Mom, I'm not sure they do," Heather said, closing her eyes and laying her head back. It was times like this that she appreciated her mom's casual lifestyle. Christmas was so much better in yoga pants.

The couch sagged as Joan sat beside her. "He must think you're more than a piece of ass if he took you home with him for Thanksgiving."

Heather let out a horrified laugh. "'Piece of ass,' Mom? We're going there?"

Joan didn't say anything, and Heather opened her eyes and turned her head toward her mom, surprised to see a sad expression on her face.

Her mother was one of those chronically happy people; always determined to see the bright side, quick to lose her temper, but even quicker to forgive and forget.

"I want to talk to you about Thanksgiving," Joan said.

Heather stilled. "Okay?"

"I know you were upset with me."

"I was," Heather said slowly. "But I got over it. Really."

She was like her mom in that way. Had never really gotten into the whole "holding a grudge" thing. Way too exhausting.

"May I speak frankly, dear?" Joan asked.

Heather blinked. "Depends. May I have more wine?"

Her mom smiled, reaching for the bottle of merlot on the table behind her and topping them both off. "Okay, here we go. This is going to come out a little tough love, but I've been thinking about it for a while, and I love you, so it needs to be said."

Heather took a sip of wine and waited, more curious than she was tense. Her mom had never been the tough-love type. More the free-love, really.

"I worry that you rely too much on external validation."

Heather blinked in surprise. External validation? Not her mom's usual MO, and she wondered if she'd seen it on *Oprah*.

"Explain," Heather said slowly.

Her mom reached out and took Heather's hand. "I love you to death. I love that you love New York, I love that you chased your dreams. But, Heather, sweetie, New York has always been your dream. Not mine."

"I know that," Heather said slowly. "But I don't think it's unreasonable to want to share those dreams with people we care about."

"Of course not," Joan said. "But I don't think that's why you want me to come to New York so badly. You want me to come to New York so I can tell you that you're doing the right thing, that you've made the right choices. So that I can reassure you that the goal you've been chasing all this time is the right one, and that you have everything you need to make you happy."

"You don't think I'm happy?" Heather asked.

"I think you're on your way," Joan said carefully. "But I think you know there's a piece missing, and you're hoping that I, or your boss, will assure you that you're wrong."

"Whoa. What does Alexis have to do with this?" Heather asked.

"You're looking for the same thing from her as you are from me. Validation."

"Well, yeah, I kind of need her validation to get the promotion," Heather countered.

"And this promotion will get you what, exactly?" Joan asked gently. "More money, and that's good. Prestige, and that's good, too. But I don't think that's why you want it so badly."

Heather started to take another sip of wine, only to realize she didn't really want it. She set her glass aside. "Okay, Mom. Help me out here. Why do I want the promotion, then?"

"I know why you became a wedding planner, sweetheart, and it's not because you love churches and carrying around safety pins for emergencies or because you love bossing people around, although you've always been startling good at that. I know the real reason."

Heather looked away, and her mom squeezed her hand. "I know you planned weddings for me and the men I dated. I know you wanted a father, and a family. I know you wanted the white wedding, not because of the wedding itself, but because of what it represented. Stability. Happiness."

"I was happy with you, Mom," Heather said, her eyes watering.

"And I with you, but you wanted more for yourself. As well you should."

"So why do I feel like I'm being scolded for wanting more?" Heather asked.

Her mom smoothed a hand over Heather's hair, shoving the curls back. "I just worry you're wanting the wrong thing. I worry you think happiness is your address and your job, and while those are important factors, you've pursued them at the expense of other things."

"Like what?" Heather sniffed.

Although she already knew, really.

Boyfriends.

Relationships.

Love.

Heather had been telling herself that she hadn't fallen in love because the time hadn't been right, that she hadn't had serious relationships because she'd been focusing on her career.

But the truth was, Heather had been focusing on the Manhattan zip code and the promotion because they were easier. Not easier to achieve necessarily, but less painful if she failed.

But if she tried for love and failed—if she tried for her own wedding, and it didn't happen—it wouldn't just be her pride that was broken.

It would be Heather.

She started to cry harder, although she couldn't quite put her finger on why. She only knew that some tiny, unidentified part of her was being brought forward, and it was as painful as it was necessary.

"Oh, sweetie," her mom soothed. "Should I not have brought this up now?"

Heather let out a mangled laugh. "Well, it is Christmas, Mom. Couldn't have hit me with this to-morrow?"

"Perhaps I should have," Joan said, playing with Heather's curls. "Are you mad?"

Heather shook her head and rested her head on her mom's shoulder. "No. Not mad. Confused as heck though."

"Yes, love can be that way sometimes," her mom said with a sigh.

Heather frowned. "Who said anything about *love*?"

Her mom pressed her lips to Heather's forehead and smiled. "Your phone's ringing."

Heather lifted her head and listened. Sure enough, her phone was ringing on the small table by the front door. "Who'd be calling me on Christmas?"

She picked it up, her hand faltering a little as she saw the caller ID. She picked up. "Josh?"

"Hey, 4C. Calling to wish you a merry Christmas. Are you as fat and full as I am?"

"More so," Heather said with a smile.

"Really? Come back to New York so we can compare belly bulges. We can make it sexy."

Heather laughed. "That's one thing even *you* can't make sexy."

"You're just saying that because your mom's around. Tell her I say *hi*, Mrs. 4C."

"What makes you think I've told her about you?"

"Oh, 4C. You're so cute when you try to play coy. Put on your coat and go outside so I can talk dirty to you about the pie my mom made. And then you can talk dirty back by telling me about the banana bread you're going to make me when you get home on Wednesday."

"Not happening," Heather said as she shrugged on her coat. "Not now, not ever."

She put her hand over the mouthpiece. "Mom, I'll be right back. Just going to talk in privacy for a while."

"You take your time," Joan said as she took another sip of wine. "I'll just be here gloating."

Heather's eyes narrowed. "Gloating about what?"

Her mom gave a secret smile. "I'm confident you'll let me know when you figure it out."

Chapter Twenty-Six

⌒

Does this seem weird to you?"

"The fact that I'm willingly wearing a suit right now? Yes. Yes it does," Josh said, tugging at the collar of his shirt.

"Please," Heather said with a wave of her hand. "You look like you came out of the womb in that thing."

It was true. Josh Tanner in his usual T-shirts and low-slung jeans was mouthwatering. But Josh Tanner in a charcoal suit, sans the tie, the white dress shirt open at the collar lending the ensemble just the slightest casual touch, was downright breathtaking.

Josh caught her hands, which had been fiddling with her clutch, cradling both her hands and the small gold clutch between his own. "Talk to me, 4C. What's weird? Why are you all fussy?"

She bit her lip, tasting the sparkly lip gloss she'd applied on the cab ride over to Seth and Brooke's place.

"This," she said, jerking her head toward Hamilton

House, the quiet building in front of them, the entire top floor of which Seth had purchased and turned into a gorgeous home for him and Brooke.

"Going to your friend's party on New Year's Eve?"

She resisted the urge to kick him with her pointy stiletto—*also* sparkly, given that it was New Year's Eve, and she'd busted out every glittery, shimmering item in her possession for the occasion. "You're being deliberately obtuse. I mean us going to a New Year's Eve party. Together."

He pretended to take a shuddering breath as though on the verge of tears. "Don't cry, Tanner. Don't cry. She doesn't mean it."

Heather laughed and stepped closer. "You know what I mean. People might get the wrong idea about us."

I *might get the wrong idea about us.*

Heather had been doing a lot of thinking in the days since her conversation with her mom on Christmas, and although she didn't have any answers, one thing was becoming abundantly clear.

She wanted a hell of a lot more than what Josh Tanner was offering, and didn't have the faintest clue about what to do with it.

In fact, Heather had decided on her New Year's resolution:

Winning Josh Tanner's heart.

A huge task, to be sure, but an important one. Perhaps the most important one of her life.

And one she'd deal with. *Tomorrow.*

But tonight she wasn't going to worry about anything other than enjoying herself and enjoying him.

Seth and Brooke had decided to host a big party, complete with expensive invitations and a top-notch caterer and cocktail attire. Of course, Brooke had insisted that Heather extend the invitation to Josh on her and Seth's behalf. Heather knew what her friend was up to—giving Heather a reason to invite Josh without having to ask Josh as her *date*.

Clever, sneaky Brooke.

But when Heather had straightened his collar earlier that evening, and when he'd zipped up her little black dress and helped her with her necklace and kissed her shoulder and told her she looked beautiful . . . well, it felt like a date.

And as they stood out here in the winter night, her hands cradled in his, they felt like a couple.

"Think of it this way," he said, pressing his lips to her forehead in a casual display of affection that she'd been noticing more and more of lately. "You can pay me back for all the sex by serving me your friends' fancy champagne."

"Uh-uh," she said, tapping a nail against his chest. "I pay you back for all the sex with *sex*."

"That you do," he said, glancing down at her low-cut dress. "Have I told you how hot you look tonight?"

She smiled. "Several times. Just like I've told you several times that this is absolutely not the night that I endeavor to try your taxi sex."

"Damn," he muttered, releasing her hands so that he could touch a strand of her hair. "I still don't understand how you got it like this."

"I didn't 'get it' like anything. The salon that I

forked over triple digits to blow it out got it like that," she said, batting his hand away. "Don't touch it. You'll make it frizz."

In honor of the holiday, Heather had treated herself to a lengthy hair appointment, complete with a rare blowout. Her stylist had undertaken the impressive feat of wrestling her curls into smooth, flowing straightness.

Heather wasn't turning her back on her curls, but the change was nice. It was emboldening to feel a little different. Reckless, almost.

"Come on, sexy," he said, putting a hand on her back and guiding her toward the front door. "Let me show you off."

But as what? she wanted to ask. *Your girlfriend? Your lover? The neighbor who lets you into her pants most nights?*

She pasted a smile on her face, and by the time the elevator opened into the top-floor apartment, the hum of tipsy partygoers and big band music luring her in, she felt herself relax slightly.

Brooke swept upon them, as bubbly and golden as the champagne she pushed into their hands. "You're here! Heather, honey, you look amazing in that dress, and I'm digging the hair! Josh, you're passable. A little puny in the shoulders, maybe."

Josh laughed and bent to kiss Brooke's cheek. "Thanks for having us. You look beautiful."

Brooke laughed. "Damn, you're pretty and good with the compliments. You're lucky I'm taken. Heck, for that matter you're lucky that *you're* taken."

Josh stiffened a little, and Heather gave Brooke

an eyes-wide *seriously?!* look, which Brooke either missed or pretended not to see, linking her arm in Heather's and pulling her away.

"Josh, you mind if I steal her for just a sec? My best friend's visiting from California, and I want to introduce her to this one. Seth is hiding out in the kitchen, if you're interested in a bromance."

He waved them off. "Go. But you bring her back to me," he called after Brooke.

His tone was joking, as it usually was, but Heather felt a distinct little thrill at the slight possessiveness in his voice. Maybe she'd imagined the way he'd freaked out when Brooke suggested he was taken.

"Do I even need to tell you how right you guys look together?" Brooke said loudly into Heather's ear, raising her voice to be heard over the music.

Heather shook her head and sipped her wine. "I can't even deal with that right now. Neither can he. That's next year's problem."

"Got it," Brooke said, squeezing her hand. "Tomorrow we'll scheme, tonight you celebrate the fact that you're gorgeous and here with a delicious man."

"Speaking of gorgeous, can we please talk about this dress," Heather said, stepping back and giving her friend a once-over.

"What, this old thing?" Brooke said on a laugh, running a hand over the short, shimmery silver dress. "Is it too slutty?"

"It's fabulous. Where the heck have you been hiding those legs?"

"Under three layers of leggings and pants, trying to survive this monstrosity you guys call winter. Oh look, Alexis is here. With *Logan*," she added in a sing-song voice.

Sure enough, their boss and Logan had arrived at the same time, although Heather wasn't entirely sure that Alexis was even aware of it. Alexis was dressed to kill in a short white dress, her dark hair down around her shoulders instead of wrapped up in its usual chignon.

No doubt about it. Her boss looked hot.

As did Logan. No sign of tweed or elbow patches tonight, just a light gray suit and a skinny black tie. He'd opted for contacts, apparently, which made his brown eyes even more piercing than when they were hidden behind his glasses.

Yummy.

Alexis, as usual, hadn't seemed to notice that Logan was nearby, much less that he looked like an even sexier version of James Bond.

Poor Logan.

Or maybe not, Heather thought, as a striking black-haired woman walked up and wound an arm around Logan's neck and pulled his head down for a kiss that lasted just a bit longer than the standard greeting smooch.

Heather's gaze flicked back to Alexis, and her boss didn't look quite so oblivious now. Nor did she look happy as the curvy dark-haired woman led Logan away by the hand.

"Speaking of New Year's resolutions, you think those two will get their act together?" Brooke said.

"Beats me." Heather took a sip of champagne. "I can barely figure out my own love life, much less theirs."

Brooke grinned. "Aha, so you do admit you have a love life."

"Sex life," Heather quickly amended.

"*Riiiiight*," Brooke said, raising one perfectly arched eyebrow.

Luckily, Heather didn't have time to dwell on her accidental use of the *L* word. Soon she was swept up in introductions with Brooke's California friend, then a couple of people from Seth's work. She was especially delighted to run into Maya Tyler, Seth's younger sister, the one who'd actually been a client of the Belles last year, up until she'd learned her fiancé was planning to use her inheritance to settle a gambling debt. It was hard to feel *too* bad for the pretty blonde though, given the fact that she'd found what seemed to be a very happily ever after with a longtime family friend.

Heather lost count of how much time had passed or how many times she refilled her champagne. Instead she let herself have fun, catching up with friends she hadn't made nearly enough time for this fall, even connecting with a handful of old clients who had become friends of the Belles one way or another. There was nothing quite like seeing the bride and groom whose wedding you'd killed yourself over as a happy, content husband and wife.

This is why she did what she did.

The happiness. The forever kind of love. That was everything.

And it might have been the reason she kept avoiding Josh throughout the evening. Just a tiny bit.

She'd caught glimpses of him a handful of times, making sure he wasn't feeling abandoned, but this was Josh. As far as she could tell, he'd become the best friend of just about every person he talked to.

Still, even as he laughed and charmed his way through a roomful of strangers, he seemed to sense whenever her gaze was on him, and his eyes would seek out hers, locking onto them from across the crowded loft, following with a wink, or a chin lift, or even a small two-fingered wave.

Mine, she thought every time, without fail. *He's mine.*

Damn. She was definitely going to have to figure out what to do about that. Tomorrow. She'd figure it out tomorrow.

Heather tilted her champagne glass to her lips, only to realize it was empty. She headed toward the makeshift bar for a refill, but her footsteps faltered when she sought Josh out in the crowd once more and saw him talking to a stunning brunette.

His hand was on the other woman's back, his head bent down toward hers.

Heather's fingers tightened on the glass. Just two seconds ago, she'd admired the way he could work a crowd, but this felt different. The way the woman looked at him was different, the way they stood close was different.

She felt jealousy, hot and stabbing, rush over her.

She knew then. The woman Josh was talking with was an ex-lover. It was written all over their body language.

Which . . . fine. She knew he'd slept with other women. Lots of them. It was just *seeing* one of them . . .

She closed her eyes and counted to five, but the suffocating misery didn't fade.

Air.

Heather needed air.

She opened her eyes and stepped backward, only to back into a very firm, very close male body.

Josh. She didn't have to turn around to know it was him. She knew his touch. His smell. His taste.

But she didn't know *him*. Not really.

His hands closed around her elbows, but she jerked free and headed toward the exit.

"Heather." She heard Josh call her name, but didn't turn around.

He caught up with her just as she was about to punch the down button on the elevator.

His fingers wrapped gently around her elbow, pulling her back around. "Would you wait up a second? What's going on?"

"Nothing." Her eyes filled, and she tried to turn away again, but he reached for her other arm with his free hand, drawing her to him. "Heather."

"That woman," she said, her voice wobbling a little. Darn champagne. "Seeing her . . . seeing someone you've slept with. I mean, I know that's who you are. It's what you *do*. It's just a reminder, you know? Of what I am to you. Which is nothing—"

She broke off, looking upward and blinking quickly, hoping to keep the tears at bay so they didn't ruin her smoky makeup.

"Heather. I'm sleeping with you now. *Only* you."

She lifted her eyes to his. "Since when?"

"A while," he said quietly. "There's been no one

but you since I kissed you that day before your brunch."

She didn't believe him. She hated that she didn't believe him, but she didn't. Couldn't.

"But I *saw* you," she said. "That night when Trevor came to my place—I only did that because you were with that girl. Kitty."

"For God's sake, I didn't sleep with Kitty. I thought you knew." His eyes were dark green as he pulled her closer. "I was playing the same game as you, 4C. I wanted you to see me with her, but I didn't want to *be* with her. And yes, I do actually hear what an ass that makes me," he said sheepishly.

He frowned and searched her face. "I thought you knew," he said again.

"How would I know that, Josh? You sleep with everyone."

"Ouch, 4C."

"It's true. I mean, I've always known that about you, it's just . . . that woman tonight."

"Was looking for a repeat of last time we hooked up, yes. I'm not going to lie to you. So you'll have to trust me when I told her I wasn't interested. Okay?"

Heather wanted to believe him. So desperately. It was just . . .

"Heather, I—" His fingers tightened on her arms, and his eyes stared into hers as though trying to tell her something. Begging her to understand.

But she *didn't* understand. Didn't understand any of this.

"You think I've been sleeping around on you?" he asked, not finishing his sentence.

She looked away. "I wasn't sure. I didn't want to ask, because you've been so clear that it's just sex."

"As have you," he challenged.

Yes, but that's changing, her heart cried.

"Fine, you want to do this?" he said, resting his forehead on hers. "I didn't sleep with Kitty that night. I swear it. Not any woman since I kissed you at that fussy brunch of yours. I don't know when I stopped bringing them home, but I do know that it had everything to do with you. It was annoying, but I couldn't quite seem to stop thinking about the girl in 4C."

Heather's heart leapt, and she slowly lifted her hands to his wrists, wrapping her fingers around his warm, firm flesh, feeling his pulse steady and strong.

Steady like him.

More so than she'd given him credit for.

The truth of the matter was, she loved him, plain and simple.

She loved the annoying neighbor in 4A, who made her laugh and was better for her, and who took her home with him on Thanksgiving so she wouldn't be alone, and who helped her plan a wedding, and not just any wedding, but the wedding of his ex.

He was good.

He was the best.

He was everything.

"Josh—"

"Ten! Nine! Eight . . ."

She jolted a little at the sudden chorus of drunken shouting coming from behind them. The countdown to midnight. She'd all but forgotten that they were at a crowded party, much less that it was New Year's Eve.

"What is it?" he asked, his voice urgent. Maybe a little bit desperate.

"Four, three—"

She shook her head. A reprieve. She had a reprieve from telling him how she felt.

"Two, one. Happy New Year!"

There was a barrage of the noisemakers Seth and Brooke had supplied as "Auld Lang Syne" blared from the sound system, but Heather didn't hear any of it.

Because Josh's mouth was on hers, his lips sweet and tender as they poured a world of meaning into the kiss. Heather didn't know how long they stood there, her arms wrapped around his neck, his around her waist, and it took her several seconds to register that someone was saying her name.

She slowly pulled away from Josh, relishing the warmth in his eyes before she turned to Jessie, who was now tugging on her arm like an impatient child.

"Sorry," Jessie said, her eyes bright with excitement. "But you two will have to finish that later. Did you hear? Brooke and Seth are engaged."

Heather's mouth dropped open. "What?"

Jessie nodded happily, orange curls bouncing all over the place. "Seth pulled her into their bedroom at midnight. Nobody noticed they disappeared, but when they came out . . . bling city! I need to get myself a billionaire hotel tycoon, that's for sure."

Heather was already scanning the room for her friend, catching a glimpse of Brooke's blond hair and happy smile in a break in the crowd, before Brooke got swallowed by the well-wishers.

She glanced back at Josh. "I have to—"

He winked. "Go. I'll be around."

Heather and Jessie fought their way through the crowd to get to their friend, and though Heather's heart was bursting with happiness for her friend, she couldn't resist a quick glance over her shoulder at Josh.

He was watching her, and grinned when she met his gaze. But her own smile faltered, because she could have sworn that amid the crowd and the festive mood and the celebration, Josh Tanner suddenly looked rather alone.

And very, very sad.

Chapter Twenty-Seven

D O YOU THINK WE even want to mentally add up the cost of these bottles?" Logan asked, holding up three empty champagne bottles in each hand as Josh held open a garbage bag.

"I doubt it," Josh said, eyeing the label. "That shit's the good stuff. Seth certainly goes all out for New Year's Eve."

"Correction," came a low voice from behind them. "I go all out for the night I'm planning to propose."

Josh turned and grinned as Seth Tyler joined them in the kitchen, and then because he was that kind of guy, went in for a man-hug. "Congrats, dude."

Seth ran a hand over his head. "Thanks. Thanks. I thought . . . I hoped . . . let's just say I haven't slept in weeks. Maybe months."

"Drink?" Logan asked, holding up a bottle of champagne that wasn't yet drained.

"Yeah, but not that," Seth said, moving to open a cupboard and rummaging around until he came up with a bottle of Pappy Van Winkle. "Join me?"

"Twist my arm," Josh said as Logan nodded enthusiastically.

Seth pulled out three crystal tumblers, pouring them each a liberal amount before lifting his glass. "Thanks for sticking around. To help with the cleanup."

"Are you toasting to us right now?" Logan asked in puzzlement.

Seth's smile was slight and embarrassed. "I don't really know what a guy's supposed to say right now."

"Nothing. You are supposed to stand there and gloat, and we're supposed to say well-done," Josh said, clinking his glass with Seth's, then Logan's.

The majority of the guests had left or were stumbling around by the foyer, searching for coats and purses. The Belles were gathered in the living room, sprawled out on the white couch. Heather hadn't left Brooke's side since news of Seth and Brooke's engagement had broken, and it made him smile to see that she looked almost as happy as Brooke herself.

Seth let out a small snort. "You realize, right, that of the three of us, I'm the one that just got engaged, and yet I have the least whipped expression on my face."

Logan and Josh glanced at each other before looking away in embarrassment, and Josh made a big show of clearing his throat before taking another sip of the exceptional bourbon Seth had shared. The drink was excellent, but the burn of the whisky seemed worse than he expected, aggravating his throat, which come to think of it, had been a bit raw all day.

"So you and Heather are sleeping together," Seth said to Josh, taking a sip of his own whisky as he turned to Logan. "What's your story, Harris?"

"A lot of sleeping alone," Logan said in his clipped, precise voice.

"Sucks," Seth said quietly. "I don't know Alexis well, but she's good people. She's also—"

"Difficult, stubborn, and mostly blind?" Logan asked. "Yeah, got that. Thanks."

"Tell me you at least got a kiss at midnight," Josh said with a grin.

Logan scowled. "Couldn't find her. Had an ex-fling wrapped around me all night, and Alexis was cozied up to some wannabe bassist. No offense," he said, with a nod at Josh.

He shrugged. "None taken. Not a bassist. Also no longer pursuing the music thing."

Logan looked at him in surprise, opening his mouth as though he wanted to say something but instead shaking his head and shrugging.

"What?" Josh asked.

"Nothing." Logan sipped his drink. "Just assumed you turned down my offer because you'd decided to make a go of it in the music scene after all."

Josh frowned. "What offer?"

"Ah—" Logan glanced in the direction of the women. "Damn. Well, okay, I suppose we're doing this. I'd mentioned to Heather a couple weeks back that I'd like to hire you."

What. The Fuck.

"You told Heather you wanted to hire me."

Logan nodded. "Now's not the time for the details,

but I thought she was the best one to broach the topic, since you two are . . . close."

Seth snickered.

Josh turned his head and glanced at Heather, who seemed oblivious to him at the moment. For about half a second he was angry with her, mad that she hadn't even bothered to bring it up, given him the choice to say no. Josh's head throbbed at the thought, a dull ache in both temples, the slight headache that had been plaguing him all day worsening.

But he was self-aware enough to know this wasn't about Heather.

This was about *him*.

He'd been keeping her at arm's length from the very beginning, and this is what he got for it. A woman who dodged anything that might cause him to push her away.

Even more surprising was that Josh was intrigued. He liked Logan. And even without knowing what the job offer entailed, he knew he was interested. His instincts were humming, and a man learned to trust that.

"I'd like to talk next week," Josh said quietly. "If you're still amenable."

Logan studied his face. "I am."

"Hey, boys, come over here," Brooke called. "I need fresh meat to admire my ring."

"Delicate angel you've got there," Josh said to Seth as they picked up their drinks and headed into the living room, where the women sat gathered around the fire.

"Don't I know it," Seth said in his quiet rumble.

But a quick glance at the man showed a softness about his features as he stared at Brooke—a look in his eyes that went beyond lust. Beyond friendship, even.

Damn. *Damn.*

The truth hit Josh hard. *He* wanted that. He wanted that stability, that faith that the other person would be there.

He wanted it with Heather. Badly.

But wanting it would never make it so. Not for him.

Chapter Twenty-Eight

HEATHER WAS EXHAUSTED. BONE tired in that way that came from too little sleep, too much champagne, and a very late night complete with very big news.

But despite having spent the entire quiet cab ride back to their building fantasizing about removing her tight dress and stilettos and crawling into bed, Heather was a little surprised to find a surge of energy returning as she and Josh tiredly trudged up the stairs.

Not just any energy.

A certain . . . lustful energy.

They paused outside their respective doors. Usually there was a playful your place or mine dialogue, but either they were too tired or their emotions too raw, because neither one said a word tonight.

In fact, Josh suddenly looked exhausted, and Heather had a moment of fear that he might be tired of *her*.

She stepped toward him, seeing his eyes cloud in surprise before she rested both hands on his cheeks and pulled his face down to hers, pausing when their lips were just inches apart.

"I want you," she whispered.

His smile was slow and deliberate. "Yeah?"

She slowly leaned forward, pulling his bottom lip between her teeth and biting. "Yeah."

Josh groaned, turning her around so that her back was against her door, his mouth finding her neck as he caught a bit of skin between his lips and sucked hard before soothing the spot with his tongue.

There were things to be said. Things to be addressed. But Heather clung to the same mantra she'd been chanting all day. *Tomorrow.* She'd deal with it tomorrow.

"Come inside?" she said, pulling back and trailing her lips down his neck.

Josh didn't respond, and Heather pulled back to look at him.

"You okay?"

He forced a smile, but it was obvious he wasn't okay. He looked pale, his eyes a little glassy.

"Are you okay?" she asked, setting her palm against his cheek.

His eyes closed, and she got the sense he wanted to lean on her. Just a little. Instead he turned his head, pressing his lips to her palm. "I'm about to do something that no man should ever have to do. Ever."

She snorted. "Turn down sex?"

He put a hand on the door behind her, pushing himself upright as he nodded. "I'm thinking it's better to quit now than find out halfway through that I can't perform to my usual sex-god status."

"You're not feeling well?"

He lifted his shoulders. "Just a sore throat. A little tired."

He didn't meet her eyes as he said it, and Heather internally snickered. What was it with dudes? Either they became huge babies at the first sign of a cold or they were ashamed of it and had to puff up their chest and dismiss it entirely.

Heather opened her clutch and pulled out her keys, turning toward the door and unlocking it before she grabbed his hand and tugged him into her apartment.

"Hey, 4C, I should really get some—"

"Sleep, I know," she interrupted. "You're going to do it here."

"At your place?"

"We both know my bed is more comfortable. My sheets are better *and* they're clean."

Josh opened his mouth and she turned back to him, putting her hands on his face as she had in the hallway, but this time with tenderness instead of lust.

"Let me take care of you," she said quietly.

Let me love you.

She knew he was tired then, because there was no protest. No snappy comeback. No dirty joke. Josh merely nodded.

In the bedroom, Josh removed his suit, but it was Heather who hung it up for him. Heather who turned down the bed, fluffing the pillow.

He sat on the bed wearing only his boxer briefs, catching her by the waist as she passed by him, lifting her hand and pressing a kiss to the inside of her wrist.

"It kills me. Going to sleep instead of taking you up on your . . . offer. Especially when you look as smoking as you do tonight."

She ran her fingers through his hair. "Tell you what. In a few days when you're feeling better, we can have a redo. I'll straighten my hair and repurpose the dress and shoes."

"Thong?" he asked hopefully.

Heather rolled her eyes. Obviously he wasn't feeling that sick if he was still obsessed with tiny underwear.

"Yes. And the thong."

"The little red one," he said, lying back on the bed. "It's my favorite."

"The little red one," she soothed as she tugged the sheets and blankets up around him.

Josh's eyes closed the second his head hit the pillow.

By the time Heather finished hanging up her dress, taking off her makeup, and brushing her teeth, it was past three and Josh was sound asleep. She quietly eased into bed beside him, her eyes studying his profile as he slept.

It was rare that she saw him in a moment of vulnerability. Of the two of them, she was always the faster to fall asleep, the last to get out of bed. She took advantage of the rare moment to look at him when he didn't know she was looking.

He hadn't moved since he'd first lain down, the covers still tucked against his chin, the white of her blankets contrasting with the dark stubble on his stubborn jaw.

Josh Tanner really was a beautiful male. The long straight nose, the full lips. Even with the shadows under his eyes, his lashes were straight and full.

She felt like they'd taken some sort of step forward tonight, although she didn't quite know what it meant. Certain as she was now that she loved the damn man, she was glad she hadn't made the declaration. For starters, doing so in a crowded room just moments before midnight on New Year's Eve hadn't been the time.

More than that, though, feminine instinct told her that he wouldn't have said it back, and that would have been crushing.

For the first time in her life she'd fallen in love, and it was with someone who was determined not to love her back, for reasons she still had no clue about.

Heather laid her head on the pillow, her hand searching under the covers until it found his. She twined her fingers with his, smiling when, even in sleep, he easily fit his hand to hers, drawing her hand forward so their linked hands lay across his hard abs.

"You might not love me yet, 4A, but you will," she whispered quietly before sitting up slightly to kiss his too-warm cheek. "You will."

Chapter Twenty-Nine

THE NEXT MORNING, JOSH had gone from feeling slightly under the weather to full-on sick.

His head pounded. His throat was on fire every time he swallowed. He was hot, then cold, then hot again.

His entire body ached, from the tips of his hair all the way down to his toenails.

But he wouldn't admit any of this to Heather.

Hell, he wasn't even letting himself acknowledge it. Not yet.

"Here you go," she said, coming into the bedroom, where he sat miserably slumped against the pillows, trying not to look like death, knowing he was likely failing. "Cinnamon tea."

"I want coffee," he said with no small amount of grump in his voice.

She arched her eyebrows. "Do you really? I know when I'm sick, it's the one time I never want coffee. It just doesn't sound good. But I'm happy to make you some—"

"No, you're right," he said glumly, accepting the mug. "It doesn't sound good. Just sit close to me so I can smell yours while I drink the damn tea."

A moment later, she was curled up beside him, and though he still felt like shit, if he had to be stuck in bed, it was much better to have a beautiful woman by your side, especially one sipping a decadent-smelling Italian roast that she'd stolen from your own stash.

"Did you take the pills?" she asked, studying him as she cupped both hands around her mug and took a sip.

He nodded. "Yes, Mom."

"At least you're not one of those idiot guys who think it's tough and manly to rough it out without medicine."

Josh said nothing as he took a sip of the tea. He hated tea but had to admit it did help the throat. A little.

"I've got nothing against modern medicine," he said quietly.

But while modern medicine had quite literally saved his life, he wasn't holding out hope that the aspirin she'd given him would do much more than maybe take the edge off his headache. *Maybe.*

For one God-awful moment, Josh almost gave in to the fear. He felt a lump in his throat that had nothing to do with his ailment and everything to do with the fact that he was frightened down to his very bones about what this illness could mean. He hadn't had anything like this since . . . before.

He squeezed his eyes shut.

"Hey," she said softly, putting a hand against his stomach. "I'm here."

It's exactly what he didn't want. To need someone else. To take someone else down with him.

But for a moment, he let himself need her. Let himself take her hand in his and squeeze.

It's just a cold, man. Get ahold of yourself.

But now he couldn't stop his mind from going into overdrive, even as his body lay dormant. Potentially ignored warning signs flashed through his mind—had he not been more tired than usual over the past couple weeks? Going to bed earlier, sleeping in later, even taking the occasional nap after a lamer-than-usual session at the gym?

Fuck.

Josh pushed himself up into more of a seated position, desperate to think and talk about anything other than the fact that his body seemed to be turning on him.

"Hey, I wanted to talk to you about something," he said, watching as Heather pulled her newly straightened hair into a sleek ponytail. He loved her curls, but this was nice, too. Hell, she could shave her head, and she'd still be stunning.

"What's up?" she asked as she reached once more for her coffee on the nightstand, sitting cross-legged and shifting to face him.

"I spoke with Logan last night."

"Okay?"

Josh held her gaze. "Why didn't you tell me about the job offer?"

He kept his tone gentle—he didn't want to start a fight.

But Heather didn't even flinch as she met his gaze. "You haven't exactly responded well anytime I've shown interest in your life beyond what the two of us have going on in the here and now."

"What do you mean?" he asked slowly, even though he had a pretty good idea what she was talking about.

"I mean that I'm allowed to talk about a song you're currently playing, but I'm not allowed to talk about what you want to do with that music, if anything. I'm allowed to talk about yesterday, but not two years ago. I'm allowed to talk about your history with Danica, but not your history with your past job. We can talk about tomorrow, but not next month."

Josh opened his mouth to defend himself, but he realized he had nothing to say. Heather was dead-on. It was never fun having a mirror held up, but he couldn't deny that she was right about him avoiding tough topics.

But while his choice not to talk about his past was a conscious one, it was unnerving to realize just how resistant he'd been to discussing his future, and not just with Heather.

He'd clammed up around Trevor. His mom. Jamie.

The pounding in his head increased, and he had a painful, gut-wrenching acknowledgment of why he avoided talking about his future.

He wasn't at all sure that he was going to have one.

A wave of self-loathing rushed over him. He'd been telling himself for the past couple of years that he was living life to the fullest by not going back to work. By not sweating the small stuff, and not letting his weeks pass by in a mind-numbing nine-to-five grind.

But what if he'd been doing the very *opposite* of living life to the fullest? There was living in the moment, but there was also living *only* in the moment, and that was no good. He'd put himself in a goddamn bubble that didn't go beyond yesterday and tomorrow, and he effectively shut down anyone who tried to pop the bubble.

He was living, yes, but he'd gotten so obsessed with survival, so paranoid that each day could be his last, that he hadn't bothered to figure out what he was living for.

Or who he was living for.

"Are you mad?" she asked, biting her lip.

He forced a smile. "No. You were right in thinking I probably would have bit your head off if you'd mentioned it."

Kindly, she didn't rub it in his face.

"How'd Logan take the rejection?" she asked, taking a sip of coffee.

"I didn't turn him down, actually. I told him I was interested."

She froze, bringing her coffee mug back to her lap as she stared at him openmouthed. "Really?"

He shrugged. "I don't know what it is yet, obviously, but I like Logan. More important, I respect him. And if I'm being totally honest, I miss . . ."

"Work?" she supplied when he trailed off.

"Not exactly, although yeah, I suppose I miss the challenge of being busy, of having a set schedule every day. But really, I miss numbers," he said, hearing the sheepishness in his own voice.

Heather grinned. "Do you have any idea how nerdy and sexy that is?"

Josh grunted, feeling anything but sexy at the moment.

"I'm sorry I didn't mention the offer," she said quietly, her smile fading as she met his eyes. "It should have been your choice to say yes or no. And believe it or not, I think I'm getting pretty good at withstanding your man-tantrums."

"I don't blame you," he said. "Really."

"I like you when you're sick," she said, leaning forward and flicking his biceps. "You're all docile and sweet."

"You're going to pay for that when I'm better," he growled softly.

And he would feel better. He would.

It was a cold. Just a cold.

There was a chirp from the kitchen: Heather's text message notification. One of many in the past several minutes, he realized.

"Someone's popular this morning," he said, jerking his chin in the direction of the other room.

"I know, don't these people know they're supposed to be hungover and in bed right now?"

"You want to check on it?"

"Nah, it's probably just the girls reliving the excitement of Brooke getting engaged. I'll join in on the squeeing in a bit. I need to at least finish my first cup of coffee first."

But before she could take another sip, her phone sounded again, this time with the chime of an incoming call.

"Okay, okay, fine," she muttered, kicking her legs around to the side of the bed. Josh wasn't so sick that he couldn't admire the fine curve of her heart-shaped ass beneath those tiny shorts as she headed into the kitchen.

"Alexis, hey" he heard her say in a slightly puzzled tone. Somehow he didn't think an early-morning call on a holiday was typical, even for someone as career-focused as Alexis Morgan.

Josh took advantage of the privacy to rub his head. Whatever brief reprieve the pills had offered hadn't lasted long. His headache seemed to be getting worse.

"Wait, what?" Heather asked in a low, startled voice. *"Seriously?"*

There was a long pause as she listened to whatever Alexis said, and when she spoke next, her voice was small. Tired. "Okay. Thanks for telling me. I'll probably head into the office in a little bit. Some of my files are there, and, well . . . I've got my work cut out for me, don't I?"

Josh went on high alert, trying to block out his pain receptors so he could deduce what was bothering his girl without actually having to move his lethargic body.

Heather said her good-byes, and he waited

impatiently for her to come back into the bedroom. When she didn't, he called out, "Everything okay?"

She appeared in the doorway, her expression barren. Wordlessly she padded over to the bed and handed him her cell phone.

He frowned in confusion, glancing down at what appeared to be a celebrity gossip site.

"Just read it," she said quietly. "The headline says it all."

He glanced back down, and immediately he understood.

"Danica Robinson calls off wedding to Hollywood legend," he read. "Well. Fuck."

Heather said nothing.

"It could be a rumor," he said. "Isn't eighty percent of this stuff BS?"

"This apparently falls in the twenty percent that's not," she said. "Danica's rep has already made a statement."

"What the hell happened, some big New Year's Eve scandal?"

"Not even." Heather snatched the phone out of his hand as he saw the first hints of temper brewing. "Listen to this." She scrolled through the article until she found the spot she wanted and began to read out loud. "'An inside source claims that there's no surprise in the split. In fact, sources close to the Robinson empire claim that the wedding was a hoax from the beginning. A fake engagement agreed to by both sides to aid Mr. Stokes's fading star, as well as the bad press Ms. Robinson had been getting about her serial dating ways.'"

Heather dropped the phone to the bed as though it had burned her. "That bitch used me. No wonder she didn't want to be bothered with the wedding details. She didn't want to waste her time on something that she knew would never happen."

Much as Josh wanted to reassure Heather that there was likely some misunderstanding, he didn't really think there was. He knew Danica all too well, and this was exactly the type of bullshit she would think was within her rights to pull.

"The article also says that the news broke prematurely," Heather said. "Can you believe that? One week before the wedding is premature, apparently. *Way* too much notice. The original plan was probably to end the engagement the day of to really get tongues wagging. Front-page news right there."

"Jesus," he muttered. "What happened to speed it up?"

Heather picked up her phone again, scrolling through once more before handing it to him.

"Ah," Josh said, as he glanced at a picture of Danica kissing a man that was most definitely not her pseudo-fiancé. The champagne and New Year's hats indicated that the make-out session had happened last night.

"So she's on damage control," he said.

"She's going to be seriously damaged when I get my hands on her," Heather ground out, starting to pace the length of the bedroom back and forth.

Josh nearly smiled. He hated that this was happening to her, but feisty Heather was quite the sight to behold.

"I've got to go into the office," she said finally, coming to a stop in front of the bed. "I need to start figuring out my game plan."

"You mean on the cancellation."

She nodded. "It's easy enough on paper, but the trick is figuring out how to do it without burning bridges. I'm not even sure that's possible. We rushed everything. The designer dress is custom. The wine is hand-selected from the top wineries, who all carefully selected their best bottles and already shipped them over. Then there's the handmade centerpieces, the champagne from France, even the freaking ribbon is coming from Italy." She shook her head. "This is a nightmare."

"How can I help?"

She blew out a breath and looked up, a determined gleam in her eyes. "Sleep. Get better. If this doesn't destroy my career—and I won't let it—you can take me out to dinner. We'll have too much to drink and curse Danica Robinson's name. Petty, but it'll make me feel better."

"Sounds like a plan. Maybe we can throw banana bread into the mix?"

She chucked her phone at him before heading into the bathroom, and he laughed, only to stop abruptly at the slight discomfort on his left side.

Josh's smile slowly dropped as icy dread ripped through him. Another symptom that he was all too familiar with. A harmless twinge that he knew from experience could mean something very harmful indeed.

Josh didn't move.

Not as he listened to Heather mutter obscenities in the shower. Not as he listened to her—rightfully so—rage at Danica Robinson as she threw on jeans and a sweater and boots.

Only when she approached the side of the bed, leaning down to kiss his cheek, did he manage to move, his need for Heather stronger than the weakness in his limbs.

He wrapped an arm around her, pulling her awkwardly to his chest. Needing to hold her. Needing to be held, just for a second.

She didn't protest. She wrapped her arms around his neck and buried her face in his hot skin. "You're burning up," she said, sounding worried. "I should stay."

"Nah, just get me a couple pills to combat the fever. I'm just going to sleep," he said, still not releasing her.

"I don't want to leave you," she whispered.

His eyes shut as he stroked her hair, but he didn't say anything.

Finally he let his arm fall away, and she gave him a concerned look as she went into the bathroom and came back with two more pills. "This should help with the fever and the headache, but you need to make sure you're getting enough fluids."

Fluids wouldn't help with what was ailing him, but he played along, rolling his eyes at her bossiness even as he agreed to follow her directions.

She went into the kitchen, and he watched in amusement as she put three water bottles on his nightstand. "I want those all to be gone by the time I get back," she ordered.

"Can we put some whisky in them?" he asked hopefully.

She ignored him, leaning down and kissing his forehead. "I'll be back soon. I hope."

Josh said her name as she was about to leave the bedroom, and she glanced back expectantly, one hand on the doorjamb.

"Yeah?" she said.

Josh swallowed and it hurt. He wanted to tell her how he felt.

"I'm sorry about the Danica thing," he said instead. Lame.

"Eh." She lifted her shoulders. "It stings, but it'll pass. Not life or death, you know?"

Oh, he knew. He definitely knew.

Josh waited until he heard her close the front door, waited until he heard the click of the lock before he forced himself to do what needed to be done.

Slowly, he lifted his hand to his throat, his fingers knowing exactly what to look for.

And he found it.

His hand fell back to the bed as he stared straight ahead, terror mingling with resignation. The sore throat, he could explain away. The headache, a relatively common ailment. Even the body aches and the fever—they happened, right? Grown men got that shit all the time.

But all that plus the fatigue of the past few weeks and the swollen lymph nodes in his neck?

Shit, hell, and *fuck*.

Josh threw the covers back, forcing his stiff limbs over the side of the bed as he walked toward the closet door where Heather had hung his suit the night before.

He found his cell phone in the breast pocket of his suit jacket and scrolled through his contacts until he found the one number he'd hoped he'd never have to call again.

Chapter Thirty

❦

"HOW MUCH PETTY CASH do the Belles keep on hand?" Heather said as she gratefully accepted the large mug of coffee Alexis handed her.

Her boss merely tilted her head in question.

"Bail money," Heather said. "I'm thinking we may need it if and when I ever run into Danica Robinson on the street."

"I'd sell the whole building if I had to," Alexis said grimly. "This woman is dead to me."

"Somehow it's so much scarier when you say that than hearing it from anyone else," Heather said, taking a gulp of the coffee. She'd been at the office for two hours now, and the caffeine from her first cup of coffee back at the apartment was starting to fade.

"I mean it," Alexis said, crossing her arms. "We've had our fair share of called-off weddings, but never anything like this. Never anything so malicious and callous."

"Yeah, well, lifestyles of the rich and famous and all that."

"How are the vendors taking it?" Alexis asked, leaning against the door. She was wearing a pale lavender knit dress, her makeup impeccable as always, belying the fact that Heather knew full well she hadn't gone to bed until the early hours of the morning, and had been awake by six given the time stamp on the texts she'd sent to Heather to break the news.

Heather waved her hand over the iPad and file folders on her desk. "Hardly anyone's picking up. Damn holiday."

"Well, the only good news about this happening with such a famous client is that they'll probably have figured it out by the time they all get back to work tomorrow."

"So they'll be pissed, but not surprised."

"Yes, but not pissed at you," Alexis said.

"I don't know about that. I just keep thinking that a good wedding planner would have figured this out. That *you* would have figured this out."

"Don't be ridiculous. Nobody goes into a wedding-planning endeavor suspecting that it's all a publicity stunt."

"You know what pisses me off the most," Heather said. "That I knew something was up early on, but that I let her play me. I totally bought all that bollocks about her promising her fiancé to be low-key."

"'Bollocks'?" Alexis smirked. "Someone's been spending too much time with Logan."

Heather spun around in her chair, happy to have a change of topic, however brief. "Speaking of Logan, any idea who the boob-tastic broad all over him last night was?"

Alexis lifted her shoulders. "Nope. And I don't care. I *don't*," she insisted when Heather gave her a skeptical look. "He's allowed to date."

"Sure," Heather said. "But he came with *you*."

"Our cabs arrived at the same time and we walked in together," Alexis said in amusement. "What is it with you and Brooke trying to turn us into some grand love story?"

Heather sighed. "I can't help it. I love love."

"Speaking of . . ." Alexis sat down opposite Heather's desk and grinned. "You and Josh seemed mighty cozy at midnight."

Heather looked down at her mug. "I was having . . . an epiphany."

"That you love him," Alexis said in a matter-of-fact tone.

"That obvious?"

"Yes. But it was lovely to see. Did he, ah . . . have a similar epiphany?"

"I thought so? Maybe?" Heather shook her head. "I have no idea. He wanted to say something, and I know that he cares about me. I know it. But he's still holding back. I thought it was just classic bachelor-itis, but I think it's more than that."

"You didn't talk about it after the fact? Or this morning?"

"Nah, he's sick with some nasty cold," Heather said. "I left him in bed with medicine and fluids. One more reason to hate Danica Robinson. It killed me to leave him looking so miserable, which tells you how far gone I am over the guy. I wanted to take care of him and tuck blankets around him and make him homemade soup."

"Why don't you let me take care of all of this," Alexis said, gesturing at Heather's office.

"No way. She was my client. I'm the one that failed to see the signs. The least I can do is take point on my own cleanup duty."

"What do you mean the least you can do?"

Heather bit her lip. "This is bad for the Belles, isn't it?"

"What?"

"We scored the most famous wedding of the year, and then the wedding didn't happen. That can't be good for business."

"Don't take this the wrong way," Alexis said slowly, coming into Heather's office and leaning against her desk, "but it's possible you're taking on a bit too much responsibility here. This reflects badly on two people, and two people only: Danica and Troy. And maybe her team of people who knew about the charade. But it doesn't reflect poorly on you. And certainly not on the company."

"Thousands of dollars," Heather said glumly. "Like thousands and thousands, all for nothing."

"Yes, but we're not taking the hit. That's what Danica's deposit was for, and if the deposit doesn't cover it, you can rest assured she'll be getting an invoice for any spillover, especially for your time."

"It's not the money." Heather fiddled with a paper clip. "This was a test. And I failed."

Alexis frowned. "What do you mean, a test?"

Heather met her boss's eyes. "This was my chance to show you I could make it as a full-blown wedding planner. And I blew it."

"You most definitely did not," Alexis said indignantly. "You honestly think I'd ignore all the hard work you did simply because you got stuck with a bum client? Heck, if anything, the way this turned out and the way you're handling it just proves even more how ready you are for that promotion."

Heather's spine straightened. "Seriously?"

Alexis smiled. "Congratulations. Wedding planner."

Holy crap.

Just like that, she had The Dream. It's what she wanted forever, and she was happy, she really was, it was just . . .

"There's something else," Alexis said quietly.

"I'm thrilled," Heather rushed to say. "Seriously. But there's this weird sadness that this wedding isn't happening. Like I'm taking it personally."

"I can understand that," Alexis said slowly. "This was a unique situation in which you were asked to plan a wedding your way rather than the client's way. You can't keep from putting a bit of yourself into it."

Heather gave an embarrassed nod. "I think somewhere along the line, I planned *my* dream wedding. I mean, not entirely. The dress she picked was way too fussy. I'd have gone with a simple white sheath, cap sleeves, clean lines . . . Pippa Middleton style."

"To show off your great butt," Alexis said with a smile.

Heather snorted. "Well, I don't know about *great*, but it's about the only feature I have to work with. Anyway, the dress wasn't me. And I've always envisioned that my bridal party would just be my mom, not something like Danica's party of twelve. I'd want to honor her, you know? But everything else . . . yeah, pretty much my dream wedding. I figured I might as well do it here, given the unlimited budget."

"Which makes it extra painful to undo," Alexis concluded.

Heather shrugged. "I keep telling myself that this was just the trial run. A chance to work through it all so that when it comes time for me to walk down the aisle, I'll have everything figured out. But the truth is, I'm secretly glad nobody's picking up the phone today. It lets me live in the illusion just a little bit longer that my vision will come to light next week."

"Heather. Let me take care of it, please," Alexis said. "Not as a boss taking over for an employee, but as a friend."

Heather looked up in surprise. She considered Alexis a friend, definitely, but if she was totally honest, she'd never been completely sure that Alexis considered her the same. Alexis was hardly the demonstrative type.

And she was tempted. Tempted to lean on her, to admit that the dissolving of the Robinson wedding felt like a punch to her professional pride *and* her heart.

"You know, there's another way of thinking about it. Relief that your dream wedding won't be wasted on someone who doesn't believe it."

Admittedly, the thought *did* perk Heather up a bit. Come to think of it, it would have been positively wretched to watch someone else go through with her wedding, even if that person wasn't a manipulative socialite.

"Seriously, Heather, let Brooke and me take care of this. Jessie can help, too. Put this behind you and focus on the Sheldon wedding. You're excited about that one, right?"

Heather nodded. Amelia Sheldon was her latest customer and, in addition to being a complete doll, wanted to do a Texas-themed wedding in the middle of the city to honor her and her fiancé's Texas roots. It was a huge challenge and a welcome break from the usual city-esque themes most NYC brides preferred.

As much as Heather chafed at the thought of being a quitter, Alexis's offer was tempting. What would be the harm, really, of leaning on her colleagues to make a few phone calls and unravel the Robinson wedding? It would be a minimal time investment, and unlike her, their hearts weren't all tangled up in the business.

"Let me think about it," Heather said. "At the very least I'll finish putting together the list of everyone who needs to be contacted so starting tomorrow one of us can start making the calls."

"Sure," Alexis said, standing. "Just so you know that when tomorrow comes, it's going to be me making the calls."

Heather was about to protest one last time when her phone rang. She grinned when she saw Josh's name come up on the caller ID and, prompted by Alexis's nod, swiped the green arrow.

"Hey there, sicky, how are you feeling? Which water bottle are you on?"

But it wasn't Josh on the other line.

Heather sat numbly listening to the panicked voice on the other end of the phone for several minutes before she hung up, her hand falling limply to her lap.

"Heather? What's wrong?" Alexis's voice was sharp as she came to Heather's side, kneeling beside her chair. "Talk to me."

Heather turned and looked at her friend. "That was Josh's mom." Her voice cracked as she abruptly stood up from her chair and started gathering papers, stuffing everything into her purse. "He's in the hospital."

Chapter Thirty-One

I CAN'T BELIEVE YOU didn't tell me," Sue Tanner said for the hundredth time, her eyes watering as she reached for his hand. Also for the hundredth time.

"I did tell you, Mom. The second after I hung up the phone with Dr. Rios."

His mom shook her head. "That's not what I meant," she whispered.

Josh squeezed her fingers. Hard. "I know."

Knew that his mom wasn't talking about the most recent sickness—knew that she was referring to the not-so-unlikely possibility that the leukemia could come back. Sue bowed her head, and Josh's father put a hand on his wife's shaking shoulder as she cried, as he met his son's eyes. His dad's brown eyes were shiny with unshed tears, and Josh had to look away as his heart twisted. It was like he was in a time machine. A shitty one.

Four years ago he'd been in this exact position. Lying in a hospital bed while his parents tried desperately not to cry in front of him, succeeding only about half the time.

Just like he tried not to cry in front of them. He'd succeeded 100 percent of the time, although he suspected it might be harder this go-around.

This was everything he hadn't wanted. Everything he'd hoped to avoid.

And yet, he couldn't not tell them. Not when his doctor had suggested he come in right away. There were some secrets one could keep to protect his family and others that would destroy them.

Josh was pretty sure that not telling your parents that you were in the hospital waiting for results on a bone marrow biopsy and blood workup fell into the latter category.

"How much longer?" his mom asked, taking the tissue her husband handed her and dabbing angrily at her eyes.

"Doc said they'd rush it," Josh said. "Given my history."

"And you knew," Sue said accusingly. "You knew that there was a strong likelihood that your particular leukemia was at risk for a relapse."

"Remission is never a sure bet, Ma. For anyone."

"You let us think it was," Sue said, her voice cracking once more. "You let us think you were healed."

"Because I *was* healed. What good would it have done to have you two in a constant state of worrying?"

"We do that anyway," Rob Tanner said wearily. "But . . . I get why you did what you did, son." He put his hand briefly on Josh's shin beneath the thin, ugly blue blanket, and Josh nodded once in gratitude.

His mother glared up accusingly at his father.

"You can't seriously think he was right to keep it from us."

"You meddle enough as it is, Sue. Given what he's been through, can you blame him for wanting a bit of peace and quiet? To be someone other than the sick kid?"

His mother's head dropped slightly, defeated. "No." She turned to Josh and offered him a weak, watery half smile. "I suppose I can't begrudge you that, sweetie."

"There's always the chance that it's nothing," Josh said. "Dr. Rios said it could just be a virus."

His mom forced a smile. His dad looked away.

Josh couldn't blame them. None of them believed it was just a virus.

"Can we get you anything?" his dad asked. "Book? Magazine? Food?"

Josh shook his head. He couldn't eat. And though the medicine they'd given him had taken the edge off the pain, he didn't want to read, either. Unhealthy as he knew it was, he just wanted to sit and try not to think about the news that awaited him.

Try not to think about Heather and what she would think when she got back to her apartment and he wasn't there. She'd knock on his apartment door, and he wouldn't be there, either. She'd call, but . . .

"Hey, have you seen my phone?" he asked.

"With your stuff," his mom said, gesturing to the corner of the room. "You want?"

"Nah."

He didn't want the outside world right now. Couldn't handle it.

"Your sister's on her way," his dad said, glancing at his own phone.

Josh stifled a groan. "Seriously? I told her not to come. The baby shouldn't be in the hospital."

"Josie next door is watching Marian," Sue said, patting his arm. "She has five grandkids of her own; she's perfectly competent with infants." His sister and Kevin had flown up with the baby for Christmas, and Jamie had opted to stay through the New Year so that his parents could help with childcare and get their grandbaby fix.

"She's still flying out tomorrow, right?" Josh asked.

His parents exchanged a glance, and he read their silent communication perfectly. It depended on the test results.

"No, I don't want—" *Fuck*. Josh put both hands over his face. "I can't do this again. I can't put you all through this again."

"Don't be selfish," his father said, in a tone Josh hadn't heard since he got caught with a six-pack of Buds when he was eighteen. Josh dropped his hands and found his dad giving him a stern look. "You think this is about you, and it is, but it's also about the people who care about you. The people who want—need—to be here for you. Because we love you."

Father and son held gazes for several moments, but Josh was the first to look away. His dad was right, of course. If situations were reversed, and any of them were in a hospital bed, there'd be no dragging him out of the building. He'd hop on a plane, train, or unicorn to make it to any one of them, Kevin included, if they were sick.

"You're going to be fine," Sue said as Josh stared blindly at the ceiling and tried to ignore the burn in his throat, the lethargy in his body.

"Can I have a few minutes?" he said, looking back at them. "I'm not asking you to leave, I just . . . I need a moment."

"Of course," Rob said, even as his mother started to protest. "We'll be in the waiting room if you need us. And if the doctor comes back with test results—"

"I'll make sure he finds you," Josh said.

His parents shuffled to the door, looking older than they had when he'd seen them at Christmas just a week earlier. His mom turned back. "Josh, honey, there's something I should probably—"

His mom never finished her sentence, because there was a blur of dark blond hair and blue sweater dashing by the window of his room before coming to stand in the doorway.

Heather.

Out of breath, beautifully disheveled, and *here*.

His heart leapt in joy even as his brain registered outrage. He glared at his parents, and his mom gave a sheepish smile as she crept around Heather, patting the younger woman on the shoulder.

"That's what I was trying to tell you," Sue mock-whispered. "I called her while you were getting the tests."

His mom disappeared before Josh could get good

and properly angry at her, and then he found he wasn't angry at all because Heather was at his side, her face buried in his neck.

A neck that was . . . damp.

Heather was crying.

Motherfucker. Heather was crying. For him.

"Don't," he pleaded. "Please don't."

"You asshole," she muttered against his neck, sniffling, and Josh couldn't help but laugh. She was his same old Heather.

She pulled away and punched him lightly in the shoulder. "Don't laugh at me. How could you not tell me this?" Her eyes flashed even as she swiped at her running nose. "All this time I never knew. Cancer. You had *cancer*?" Her tears seemed to dry and she looked good and pissed. "You don't *keep* something like that from someone that—"

"Someone that what?"

"Cares about you," she said through gritted teeth.

She wanted to say something else, he could sense it. Even more alarming . . . he wanted to hear it.

Wanted to know if she loved him, even though he didn't deserve it.

"Past tense, 4C," he said, reaching out and pushing back a strand of hair that had stuck to her wet face. "I *had* cancer."

"But it might . . . it's back? That's why you're here?"

"They just want to check," he said. "The symptoms I'm having . . . they're similar to what I had before we found out. They're just playing it safe."

She nodded. "Okay. Fair enough. But you don't have cancer."

He smiled grimly. "Heather—"

"You don't," she said emphatically. "And if you do, then we'll—"

And there it was.

He'd known it was coming eventually, but he'd been putting it off. Living on borrowed time.

But it couldn't go on.

It was time.

"There is no we," he said, making his voice go sharp. Firm.

Her lips parted. "What do you mean? I—"

He reached for her hand. He wasn't sure if it was possible to couch rejection in kindness, but he had to try. He cared about her too much not to.

"You get it now, don't you, 4C? Why I didn't want a girlfriend?"

"Actually, no. Not at all," she said.

"Because of this." He gestured down at this hospital-blanket-covered legs. "Because of this." He gestured at the machines around him. "This is my reality, Heather, but it doesn't have to be yours. I won't let it be yours."

She squeezed his hand. "Josh, this could be nothing. It could be the flu—"

"Whether it's cancer this time or later, it'll always be there. The possibility, just looming over us, over any future we might have together. My particular kind of leukemia has a high chance of recurrence."

She swallowed. "Okay. Okay. Wow. So it's a shitty

lot in life, but that doesn't mean you have to get *rid* of me."

"I'm doing it for you, 4C. You're one of the most amazing people I've ever met. And you want to get married and have lots of babies. Don't deny it."

"Of course I won't deny it," she said with a sad smile. "I do want that." She took an audible gulp of air and looked him straight in the eyes. "But I want that with you, Josh."

She might as well have reached over and stabbed him right in the heart, maybe added in a sucker punch to the throat, because Josh suddenly felt faint. "Don't. Heather, please, don't."

"Don't what? Don't love you? Too late, neighbor. It's been too late for that for a long time now."

"We said we wouldn't—"

"Fall in love. I know. But I broke the rules, and now you have to decide what you're going to do about it."

He saw from the familiar cocky smile beginning to shine through her clouded face that she thought she knew what he was going to do with that information.

Heather Fowler loved him.

He lied. He didn't want to hear it.

It nearly broke him.

She was here, holding his hand, even though she knew that their time together might be ripped away by fucking cancer, one of the cruelest of destiny's hands.

"You love me, too," she pressed on. "Or at least you're close. And I have every intention of sealing the deal, so—"

"Heather. Stop."

She broke off, pain flickering across her face before she tried to resume her former smile.

He couldn't do this. He wouldn't do this. Not to her.

Josh shook his head slowly. "This thing we've had . . . it's been fun, and it's like I said, you're one of the best girls I've ever known, but—"

"No," she said quickly. "No buts."

This time it was he who squeezed her hand, wondering how to push her away and not break her heart. But as he looked at her face, a face he knew nearly as well as his own, he knew that she meant what she said. She loved him. There was no way to do this kindly, so he just had to *do* it.

"I can't take care of you and take care of me," he said.

"I'm not asking you to take care of me, Josh," she said, sounding hurt.

Josh winced at her change in tone, but it was too late to go back. "You know what I mean. I've got a rough road ahead, and it'll take all my physical strength just to make it. All my emotional strength is going to go toward helping my family get through it. Helping myself get through this. I won't have anything left to give."

I won't have anything left to give you.

He left it unsaid, but he saw from the widening of her eyes and the fresh onslaught of tears forming in her green irises that she heard it anyway.

"Can you at least wait until you get the test results?" she asked, her voice so quiet and pleading it nearly broke him right then and there. "You may not even need to do this whole weird noble thing."

"Even if the tests come back fine"—*and they won't*—"I'll always be sleeping with one eye open. My life is a solo journey, 4C. I need it to be. For me."

"But why?"

Because when I die, that sure as hell is going to be a solo journey, too.

"Please understand, Heather."

For long minutes they said nothing, and his heart twisted because he knew she was waiting. Giving him a chance to come to his senses and change his mind. To ask her to stay.

He didn't.

He saw the moment she realized it. Her eyes shut down first, turning from vibrant green to shadowy moss. Then her lips, pressing together in the age-old tell of someone trying not to cry.

And then finally, lastly, her hand slipped away. Her fingers releasing his one by one, her palm sliding away from him until her hand was limply at her side. They were no longer touching.

Heather picked up her purse, sliding it onto her shoulder as she stared at him.

For one terrible minute, he was afraid that this was how it ended. With her hating him. And if she did, maybe that was okay. Maybe it was better.

But then she stepped forward, bending at the waist until her lips were near his ear. "I love you. I'll always love you."

She stepped back, holding his gaze for a heartbeat

before she turned and walked out of the hospital room, out of his life.

He waited until he could no longer see her. Until he no longer heard the click of her boots on the squeaky clean hospital hallway.

Only then did he close his eyes and do what he hadn't done once, not a single time since he'd first gotten his diagnosis all those years ago.

Josh Tanner cried.

Chapter Thirty-Two

"Hey, twinny, how goes the kissing disease?" Jamie asked, entering the hospital room just as Josh was buttoning up his shirt.

"Shut up," he muttered.

"Strange," she said, coming all the way into the room without knocking and plopping on the bed, just like she had countless times when they were kids. "I don't recall Dr. Rios listing *asshole* as a symptom of mono . . ."

Mono.

He had fucking mononucleosis. As in the "kissing disease" that went around high schools and colleges like wildfire. Not his high school, apparently. Or if it had, he'd somehow escaped exposure and never developed an immunity.

"I'm glad though," Jamie said quietly, her voice turning serious. "I'm so, so, so, so glad."

Josh felt a tickle in his throat that he knew had nothing to do with the mono. Jesus, was he going to cry at everything now? He reached over and chucked his twin sister gently under the chin. "You and me both, kid."

She held up a finger. "We've talked about this. Me being all of seven minutes younger doesn't warrant the kid moniker."

"I'm taking a free pass today."

"Yeah, it's been a rough one, huh?"

"I feel like a fool," he said, dropping his hands to his sides after he finished with the last button.

"Because you let Heather walk away. No, I'm sorry . . . because you *shoved* Heather away."

Pain tore through him at the reminder of what had transpired hours before. Hours? It felt like fucking days.

"Not about that," he said gruffly. "I did what I had to do."

"Hate to tell you, but I think she's already been exposed to your kissing disease," Jamie said, deliberately misunderstanding him.

Still, she had a point. The doctor had said that mono, benign as it generally was, was wildly contagious. Spread through saliva, hence its nickname.

Josh didn't know where he'd gotten it from. Apparently it stuck around for weeks before showing symptoms, which meant Heather had most definitely been exposed. Chances were she'd be fine. The doctor had said most people were exposed to the virus as children, never exhibiting symptoms beyond the common cold. Most everyone else was exposed in high school or college.

Josh, apparently, was the rare exception.

Still, on the off-chance Heather was also an exception, he'd have to tell her.

Tomorrow. He'd tell her tomorrow.

Right now he wanted a shower, and to be out of the fucking hospital. Maybe a big-boy dose of Ny-Quil and a good night's sleep.

"Heather's not the reason I feel like an idiot," he said, locking hands around the back of his head and looking up at the ugly ceiling of his hospital room. "I dragged you guys down here for nothing. Put you through hell—again—for nothing. For mono."

"Stop," she said quietly. "Don't forget that I was there when the doctor explained how closely mono can resemble the symptoms of something much more serious. You were right to worry. The doctor was right to insist you come here today for tests. And you were right to tell us. You were."

Jamie was at least partially right: The symptoms of mono were easily similar to his early leukemia symptoms, the very ones he had originally dismissed as just a persistent cold. The sore throat, the fever, the persistent, weeks-long fatigue. Even more wily were the swollen lymph nodes and the tender left side courtesy of a swollen spleen. Symptoms of both leukemia and, apparently, fucking *mono*.

But while Jamie had a point about his worries being well-founded, calling his family had been premature. Calling them before he'd had the test results had been downright selfish, and his mom calling Heather on top of that had been downright disastrous.

Still, maybe it was for the best. He and Heather were going to end sometime, might as well be now. Granted, the ripping off of this particular Band-Aid had been horribly painful.

But it was off now, and he could go back to being . . .

What, exactly?

Alone.

"Okay, don't bite my head off for saying this, but you look—"

"Like hell, I know, okay? Give me a break. I've got a fever, my head feels like there's a hammer rattling around inside, and it hurts to talk."

"Not what I was going to say. I mean, yes, you look like you're ready to keel over, but I was going to say that you look lost."

Lost.

Heather had told him the same thing once, and he'd written her off. Correction, he'd bitten her head off.

But here was another woman he cared about saying the same thing, using the exact same word to describe him.

Josh sat down hard on the stiff hospital bed. "How so?" he asked gingerly.

Jamie sighed and stood up, shoving her hands into the back pockets of her black pants before looking at him. "I know you've got the whole 'live like you're dying' thing down pat. I wouldn't be surprised if you told me you'd literally walked on coals and skydived and sang karaoke naked. But Josh . . . you're also *living like you're dying*. You get the distinction, right? The same phrase can have wildly different meanings, and you're heading toward the depressing one."

Every single one of her words struck a painful chord, but he still resisted. "Didn't we just have this talk?"

"Yes!" she said, half shouting. "And you were in *love* when I last saw you, and you're in love now, but you let her walk away. No, you pushed her. All because . . . why?"

"Because I might be dying, Jamie! You got that memo, right? The cancer could come back at any time. I'm not going to leave Heather a"—he struggled to get the word out—"a widow."

"We're all dying, moron. I could get cancer tomorrow. Or Heather could. Or Dr. Rios. Are you a little more likely to get it? Sure. Just like Kevin's more likely to have heart disease because it runs in his family, and just like Dad's more likely than Mom to get hit by a golf ball because he actually golfs. We're all dying of something, but only the cowards among us base their *lives* around that."

Josh reached for his jacket and shrugged it on without responding.

"You can ignore me," she said quietly, "but it won't go away. You are lost. You won't let yourself care about anything, and it's getting tiring. You're boring."

After her whole speech—and it was a good one— for some reason it was that last line that gave him the most pause. "Boring," he repeated slowly.

She nodded emphatically. "Yup. You're a cancer

survivor, but you're not being one of the cool ones who keeps on trucking, waving your 'I beat it' flag and taking on the world. You're one of the scared ones who's letting it beat you. Not physically, but mentally and emotionally, the leukemia is *whipping* your ass."

He let out a surprised laugh. "I swear to God, having a twin is the worst."

But even as he said it, a strange sense of calm was settling over him. He wished that the self-realization would have come from within. That he could have figured shit out for himself. But having it come from the sibling he'd shared a womb with was probably the next best thing.

And Jamie was absolutely right. Josh had been patting himself on the back for being a survivor for years, but he'd only physically bested the cancer.

He'd let it mess with his mind. And definitely his heart.

A heart that absolutely knew what it wanted. And what it wanted was a certain curly-haired wedding planner with green eyes and a heart of gold.

But he didn't deserve Heather as he was now.

Heather was a go-getter. A firecracker. She deserved a man who knew he had his shit together. A man who did something more than amble through his day from breakfast to dinner with zero purpose beyond doing it all again tomorrow.

He rose from the bed and stomped toward his sister, wrapping both arms around her. He intended to lift her off her feet, but he settled for a bear hug instead. "Thank you," he whispered.

She swatted the back of his head, then hugged him back. Hard. "You're welcome."

He released her and stepped back before heading toward the door.

"You going after Heather?" she asked.

"Of course," he replied. "But there's something I have to do first."

"Wait, you're not *leaving*," she said. "I know you sweet-talked the doctor into discharging you as long as you monitored the fever, but mom's already been talking about how she's going to make your favorite chicken parmesan tonight. Let them take you home with them. Take care of you."

Josh paused and sucked in his cheeks as he thought. It wasn't right to drag his family all the way out to Manhattan and then bail. Not to mention, it would serve his rapidly forming plan well if he avoided his own apartment for a few days.

"I'd love to," he said, meaning it. "But I need to make one phone call first."

Seven minutes later, Josh had made his phone call.

He also had received and accepted a job offer from Logan Harris.

His body would do what it wanted. He was dealing with that.

His brain though, he could do better by. With one phone call, he'd just taken the first step.

Now for the last, and most important.

It was time to do right by his heart.

"Actually, guys, is it cool if I make one more phone call?" Josh asked as he left the hospital with his family and headed toward the train station.

"Honey, you can make as many phone calls as you want," his mother gushed.

Jamie rolled her eyes.

Josh pulled out his phone and made the call.

By the time he hung up, he was grinning. The girl in 4C didn't stand a chance.

Chapter Thirty-Three

HEATHER FLIPPED YET ANOTHER gossip magazine closed with a frustrated huff, tossing it on the countertop next to her drink with more force than was probably necessary.

She'd gotten to JFK a full hour before the customary two-hour window recommended by the airlines. It wasn't her usual MO. She was more of a run-up-right-before-last-call kind of girl. But when you were on a temporary hiatus from work, getting ready to board a plane to hide out in Nowhere, Michigan, while you licked the wounds of a broken heart, why not get to the airport earlier, grab a drink, and read guilty-pleasure magazines?

She'd been half-successful. The pear martini was a hit, the magazines were a bust. Every single one headlined the Danica Robinson wedding that hadn't happened.

Pass.

On the heels of Josh's earth-shattering rejection, Heather had wanted to lose herself in work, but

Alexis had refused, insisting that Heather take some time off.

It was an order.

And one Heather hadn't wanted all that much to push back against. She'd always thought that when she finally got that promotion, everything would change. That life would be better.

And though she was still ecstatic that the professional dream she'd been chasing for years was finally becoming a reality, it wasn't the game changer she'd thought it would be. The earth hadn't shaken. The heavens hadn't parted.

At the end of the day, it was just a job. A job she loved, but still . . . a job.

Her mom had been so devastatingly right. It wasn't the wedding-planner role Heather had wanted so much as the wedding.

The wedding with the right guy, and the right guy didn't want her.

She'd heard from Josh only once since he'd dumped her a week earlier. Could you be dumped by someone who had never really been your boyfriend to begin with? Whatever, it didn't matter. She'd been dumped by Josh and had heard from him only once via text.

A concise message that had informed her that his symptoms had been the result of mono rather than a cancer recurrence.

Her heart had soared. Really, it had. Josh wasn't dying. He was okay. He was alive.

But the text had hardly contained a mea culpa.

In fact, she was pretty damn sure that if mono

(really?) hadn't been a contagious virus, he wouldn't have contacted her at all.

Lucky for both of them, Heather had already had mono her sophomore year of high school, courtesy of a badly made decision involving several wine coolers she'd bummed off her unsuspecting mother and a willing accomplice by the name of Dylan Haven.

She texted him back that she was fine, and he hadn't written back.

Heart. Meet Break.

The airport intercom rambled something, and Heather leaned back slightly on her barstool to peek at her gate across the way. Her flight was starting to board.

Since Heather was reasonably sure that she could maneuver the shattered pieces of her heart into her seat at 24E without assistance, she was in no rush. But just to be safe, she signaled for her check as she drained the last sip of her rather delicious pear martini.

Heather paid her bill and gathered her bags as she made her way to the gate to wait for her section to be called. Normally going back to Michigan came with a little surge of bittersweet reluctance to leave New York, which she loved so dearly, combined with excitement to see her mother. Tonight though, she could have been flying anywhere. She just needed to get away. Needed a break from the hurt of the past week.

She'd told him she loved him.

So, that was big. And a surprise. She hadn't even realized it until the words were out there, but the second they'd left her lips, she'd known the truth in them.

It was the first time she'd said the words to anyone aside from her mother, and he'd all but shooed her away, out of his hospital room, when she'd thought he'd had cancer.

No *wonder* people were hesitant about falling in love. Here she'd been all whiny about never experiencing it, when really, she should have been grateful.

It sucked. Big-time.

Heather opted to hover around the outskirts of the loading area rather than rush to get in line. She was in a middle seat, so there was exactly zero point of getting on the plane earlier than she had to.

Eventually, however, the line whittled down, the crowd shrunk, and it was last call.

Heather reached for the handle of her carry-on, preparing to wheel it forward, when a large male figure stepped in front of her.

"Excuse me," Heather murmured by default even as the New Yorker in her bristled at the disturbance. Still, airports were crowded, people got oblivious.

She stepped to the side, and the man stepped with her.

Okay. Now she was annoyed.

She lifted her eyes, prepared to communicate her irritation with a proper glare.

Instead she froze.

"Josh?" Her voice wobbled. The man she loved—the man who'd rejected her—was standing in front of her in a New York City airport, wearing a tux of all things.

"Hey, 4C." His voice was low, easy and casual, as though this wasn't the most absurd thing to ever happen to either of them.

"What are you doing here?" she hissed.

"Wanted to know if you were okay."

"You mean did I catch your mono? No, I told you I'm fine," she said, more than a little confused and pissed off at his sudden appearance.

"But how are you fine? Did you catch the kissing disease from someone else?"

"Yes," she snapped. "A JV basketball center with braces who played the clarinet in our high school band during the off season." She tried to push past him. "Now that we've got that all cleared up, if you'll excuse me, I have a flight to catch."

But Josh blocked her path with one strong, muscled arm. "Names, 4C. I'm going to need a name, and address if you have it, so I can beat this motherfucker down."

Heather gave him a quick once-over, wanting—needing—to make sure that he was okay.

He looked . . . great. A little tired, maybe, but mostly he was the pinnacle of health.

"I still have to take an afternoon nap," he said, reading her thoughts. "And I wouldn't say no to a sponge bath. But I'm fine. Fever gone, yada yada."

"I'm glad."

She meant the statement to come out snippy and sharp, but instead it was softly uttered, like a wish.

Because she did mean it. This man had hurt her badly, but she still loved him. She was relieved that the only thing currently ailing him was a brush with an adolescent virus.

She glanced back up at him, noticing for the first time the bouquet he held in his hands. "What's with the peonies?"

He glanced down, seeming to realize for the first time that he was carrying pink flowers, and shoving them against her chest. "For you."

She barely caught them with one arm, since her other was still on her luggage. "Um, thank you?"

Wary as she was, she couldn't resist admiring them. She did love her some pink peonies.

"4C, there's something I need to say to you."

Heather's gaze snapped back from the flowers to Josh's face, but all she saw in front of her was empty space.

Because Josh Tanner was on one knee.

In front of her. In an airport. In a tux.

And there was a ring.

Oh, the ring.

She stared down at him, and he smiled half-nervously, half-cockily.

"I love you," he said. "I had this whole speech planned out, and Alexis and Brooke and my sister proofread it with a red pen and everything, but as I'm kneeling here awkwardly, I realize it's all unnecessary. I love you. I love you more than is sane for any man to love any woman. All the way, to the ends of the earth. Damn, is that cheesy?" He shook his head slightly. "Maybe I should have brought the speech after all."

"Josh." She knelt down slightly, trying to tug him upward. "What are you doing? Get up."

"Not until I get an answer."

"I don't even know what you're asking!" But of course, she did. It was written all over his posture.

And his face.

Oh, and the ring.

"Marry me," he commanded.

Heather's heart lifted and then fell and then did some sort of somersault.

"Josh—"

"I know it's soon. I'm probably rushing it. But if battling that damn leukemia taught me anything, it's that life is fucking short. And if recovering from cancer taught me anything, it's that a life spent thinking just about tomorrow, even if tomorrow's all there is, is a half life. I need you, Heather. I need you, I want you, I love you for always. For all the todays and all the tomorrows."

She blinked. "You didn't really forget that speech your sister wrote for you, did you? There was a little bit of it in there just then."

He grinned. "I have an excellent memory. And a pretty decent-sized package. Honestly, woman, you have to marry me."

The moment was insanity. He was insanity. Proposing in an airport, dressed in a—

"Wait, why are you wearing that?" she asked.

"Oh my God, she still hasn't said yes," someone whispered. Heather glanced up from Josh's gaze to see a rapt semicircle of airport dwellers gathered nearby, gaping. A few women were looking at her accusingly, and Heather had to stifle a laugh. If they'd had to put up with Josh's shtick like she had, they, too, might be given some pause.

Josh, however, seemed unfazed as the pull of his hand tugged her attention back down. Minus the increasingly panicked look in his eye, and the way his fingers were slick with sweat beneath hers.

"Let's just say I meant that whole bit about life being short," he said earnestly. "If you say yes—and by God, woman, you'd better—we're getting married immediately. Today."

Her mouth dropped open. "I am not getting married today. You're proposing to a wedding planner. Have you forgotten that I live to build the perfect wedding?"

"And you have, haven't you?" He lifted an eyebrow.

"What are you—"

Everything clicked into place.

Heather breathed outward. "Oh, my God. The Robinson wedding."

Her wedding. The wedding she'd planned. It was supposed to have been today.

"I talked to Alexis. Not a single thing has changed except for, like, four details. Maybe six, if you count the bride and groom."

Heather's breath was shallow. Her wedding. Her dream wedding was a forty-minute drive away.

But that wasn't what was important.

The man in front of her was important.

And the man was *here*. And she loved him. Always.

For better or worse.

Very slowly, Heather lowered to her knees in front of him, ignoring someone's reference to Chandler and Monica from behind her.

"Yes," she said softly, lifting her free hand to touch his face. "I'll marry you. I'll marry you yesterday, I'll marry you tomorrow, or five years from now, or in a barn or in this airport."

Josh's mouth closed on hers, and the people who'd crowded around them finally got what they wanted. A chorus of clapping sounded as he slid the ring onto her finger without ever breaking contact with her mouth.

When they pulled apart, the crowd was still cheering, and the airline employee looked torn between being charmed and being frustrated that they were holding up her boarding process.

"Ma'am, are you Fowler, Heather? Are you boarding or not?"

"Oh gosh," Heather said, the attendant's question jarring her back to reality. "I can't get married today. I'm all for a small wedding, but my mom—"

"Is already in New York," he said, kissing her softly as he helped her to her feet. "Brooke and Jessie have her at the salon right now while Alexis gets everything else get coordinated."

Her heart melted. She was marrying a man who'd proposed in an airport and had flown her mom into town.

And that meant her mom was in New York. Finally. All of her dreams were coming true, except . . .

Heather frowned. "You can't get through security

without a ticket, which means you had to buy one. And you bought my mom a ticket. And Danica's wedding—"

"Our wedding," he corrected.

"—was crazy expensive."

"Well then, good thing I'm loaded."

Her eyes narrowed.

"Seriously, 4C, don't be weird. Don't overthink this." He picked up her left hand. "Look, big diamond. Swoon."

She laughed. "Trust me, I will, and I am, I just—"

"I'm about to be more loaded," he interrupted. "I signed on with Logan. I called him from the hospital and let him know I'd like to join him. We're probably going to take over the world, no big deal. But I'll tell you about it later."

He offered her arm. "How about it, 4C. Marry me?"

"Absolutely, 4A." She grinned, taking his arm.

"Oh, that reminds me." He began leading her through the airport as the crowd parted for them, fairy-tale style. "We'll need to pick one or the other."

"Pick one or the other what?"

"4A or 4C."

"Why's that?"

"Contractors are at our place now, figuring out which wall to tear down to join our two units."

"Wait, what?" She held up a hand. "Can you do that? The landlord's going to be pissed."

"The landlord just manages the place. It's the owner who will care."

"Well, whatever. Point is, we're going to get in trouble."

He smiled. "Yeah, I don't think so."

Heather's eyes narrowed. "Why do I get the feeling I'm missing something?"

He reached for her left hand, lifted it to his lips as his thumb played with the ring on her finger. "One thing I may have forgotten to mention. I sort of own the building."

She stared at him. "What?"

Josh shrugged. "Why do you think I had no qualms about playing my music so loud?"

"Because you're an ass?"

"At first, maybe," he said, wrapping both arms around her and pulling her close. "After that, it was all about getting the girl in 4C to notice me."

"Did she?" Heather asked innocently.

His mouth lowered to hers. "Oh yeah."

Epilogue

THE WEDDING WAS PERFECT.

But then again, Heather knew it would be—after all, she'd planned it.

From the flowers to the music, all the way down to her mother's pale pink maid of honor dress that Alexis had somehow managed to secure same day, the wedding was everything she'd dreamed of. Everything she'd wanted.

Good old Alexis had surprised exactly nobody by making a couple of crucial modifications. For one, there was no sign of Danica Robinson's gaudy, over-priced dress. Instead Heather walked down the aisle to the man of her dreams wearing her perfect satin white sheath, her butt looking every bit as amazing as she'd envisioned.

Or so Josh told her.

And the wedding was small. Tiny, even: just a handful of close friends, the Belles, Heather's mom, and of course Josh's family.

His band was there too. Ex-band.

Trevor had winked at her as her mom had walked her down the aisle, and she'd winked back. Which had made Josh's eyes narrow, and that was just down-right sexy.

But as Heather stood at the altar, listening to the pastor talk about love and forever, she realized that none of this mattered. Not really. Not the dress or the flowers, or even the color of her mom's gorgeous dress.

What mattered was Josh. And her.

And the fact that her heart had never felt so full, and the moment had never felt so right. He was hers, and she was his, and they had the rest of their lives to make each other laugh, and she had no doubt they'd rise to the occasion, no matter what fate threw at them.

But it wasn't until the end of the evening when they were cutting the cake that Heather realized that Alexis wasn't the only one who'd made some tweaks to Heather's dream wedding.

Josh had made some changes of his own. Most of them for her sake, but as she opened her mouth to receive the proverbial first bite of cake that he shoved in her mouth, she realized that one of the changes had been just for him.

"Josh! What is that?" she said, barely managing to choke it down.

Her husband—*husband!*—merely grinned as she forced herself to swallow the god-awful piece of wedding cake.

Josh Tanner had finally gotten his banana bread.

Acknowledgments

THANK YOU TO THE amazing team at Pocket Books who helped turn my scrappy story idea into the gorgeous book you're holding:

Especially Elana Cohen, for always knowing exactly what the story and characters need.

For the production team, who never judge me for an overreliance on elipses.

The cover designer, for creating one of the most gorgeous covers I've ever seen.

The sales and marketing gurus who work endless magic to make sure you know about this book.

And all the other behind-the-scenes folks whose names I might never know, but whose commitment to quality gives us book addicts the best of the best.

Next up, a shout-out to my friends and family, especially my husband, who not only tolerates me wallowing for hours in the writing cave, but actually moves mountains so that I can do so.

For my agent, Nicole Resciniti, who said, "Let's

do it," when I told her I *had* to write a series about wedding planners.

And lastly, for Kristi Yanta, for believing in my writing since the very beginning and helping it be the best that it can be.

Keep reading for an exclusive sneak peek of
Book Three in the Wedding Belles series,

TO LOVE AND
TO CHERISH

Available Fall 2016 from
Pocket Books!

Eight Years Earlier

WHAT CAN I GET you, miss?"

Alexis settled at the barstool, unwinding the scarf from around her neck and placing it on top of her warm puffy coat before smiling at the bartender. "Pinot grigio?"

"You got it. Which one? We've got two by the glass."

"Um . . ." She glanced down at the menu, scanning for the wine list. "I had one the other day . . . I think it was four dollars?"

"Ah, yup. That's our happy-hour white. I can still give it to you, but it'll be eight fifty now as it's past seven."

"Oh," Alexis said, trying to hide the stab of dismay. "That's fine."

She'd just have to drink it slow, make it last.

"Food menu?"

"Yes, please," she said. "You mind if I work on my laptop here at the bar?"

The bartender shrugged, her blue eyes completely disinterested. "Fine by me. Tuesdays in January are slow. You could pretty much sleep here, and nobody would notice or care."

A few days ago, the offer might have been somewhat tempting, but as of yesterday morning, Alexis was officially a New York resident.

Well, sort of. Did subletting count? She'd signed a three-month sublease on a two-bedroom place in Harlem with a sweet, if slightly ditzy, roommate named Mary.

It wasn't quite where she wanted to be, but it beat the cheap hotels she'd been staying at before now, at least budget-wise. Enough so that she was fully intending to eat something with protein in it tonight.

She flipped open the menu and winced as she saw the price of a cheeseburger. *Or not.*

Even hole-in-the-wall pubs were pricey in Manhattan. Alexis thought she'd been prepared, but she was running through her allotted spending money a hell of a lot faster than she'd expected. Especially considering she hadn't made any traction on a potential investor in her business idea: an elite, full-service wedding-planning agency.

Alexis glanced at the bartender, hoping she wasn't too late to cancel her wine order, but the bored-looking redhead had already poured her wine and was heading her way.

At least the glass was filled to the brim. Alexis must have looked like she'd needed it. Still, she'd have to offset the wine price with the cheapest food item. *Again.* Just a few months ago, she wouldn't have thought it possible to be sick of French fries, but she'd passed that point about a week ago.

"You know what you want to eat, or need a few?" the bartender asked.

"Still deciding."

"No prob." Her attention was on her phone. "Just holler when you're ready."

The bartender wandered away, still typing on her phone, and Alexis opened up her laptop and pulled out the ever-present file folder where she kept a printed copy of the most recent proposal.

Generally speaking, the electronic version of her business plan was more practical, but you never knew when someone who mattered was going to ask you for more information, and she wanted to be ready.

Alexis was *always* ready.

Her stomach rumbled in hunger, and hard as she tried to ignore it, it wasn't the first time a tiny part of her wished that she'd taken her father up on his offer of a loan. Then her company would be a reality instead of a dream, and maybe she'd be able to eat something other than cereal and ramen.

But though she had a reasonably good relationship with her sometimes-cold father, his stipulations had just been too much.

For starters, the loan came with a location requirement. *Stay in Boston.*

That wasn't the dream. New York was the dream.

The other stipulation had been even harder to swallow. *You could hire your sister, you know . . .*

Yeah, no.

She didn't want to hire her sister. She loved Roxanne, but her sister wasn't the type of person she was looking to bring on to help get this business off the ground. Alexis needed someone with drive and business acumen. Roxie, while smart and savvy, was easily bored when it came to her career choices. Alexis needed someone who'd be in it for the long haul.

Plus, there was the bigger elephant in the room—it was just too damn hard to be around her sister right now.

The wound would heal, eventually. Alexis knew that. It was just a little too fresh, and Boston was just a little too painful.

She took a sip of wine as she opened her spreadsheet. The potential investor she'd spoken with today had been polite and shown token interest but was concerned with her growth model, specifically with the size of her team.

It was a valid point—a tiny number of employees would mean they could only support so much business. Still, Alexis was hesitant to change it. What the company would lack in scalability, it would make up for with consistency. Perfection every time, even if there were *fewer* times.

She left the column as is. Alexis knew it was unrealistic to think she wouldn't have to make some compromises, but she kept holding out hope that someone would *get* it. That someone would hear her, see what she was trying to do, and understand.

"Hello."

The sexy British accented startled Alexis out of her thoughts, and she glanced up, both alarmed and intrigued to find that the face that awaited her was every bit as appealing as the voice.

The man was about her age—early, maybe midtwenties—and ridiculously cute. His hair was dark and maybe just a touch too long, as though he intended to get a haircut but kept forgetting. The eyes were brown and friendly, accented by trendy black-framed glasses.

The chunky cable-knit sweater with elbow patches—*for real*—bordered on dorky, but then, Alexis had always had a soft spot for dorky. He had a bit of the Clark Kent thing going on, which had always been far more her type than the overrated Superman.

"Hi," she replied quickly, realizing that she'd been staring.

His smile grew wider as he extended a hand. "Logan Harris."

Darn. Even the name was good.

"Alexis," she said.

"Does that come with a last name?" he teased, lowering himself to the vacant barstool beside her.

"Not to strange men," she retorted.

"I could buy you a drink. Get rid of the 'strange' part."

Alexis's smile slipped as she remembered that romance, even flirting, wasn't part of her plan. She'd learned the hard way that she could have one or the other—her own business or a boyfriend—not both. *And even if she wanted the latter, the latter didn't want her back.*

"No thanks; I'm fine," she said, letting the slightest amount of chill enter her voice. The ice-princess treatment, Roxanne called it.

Logan shrugged, undeterred. "All right then. May I borrow your menu?"

She nodded, and he picked it up, perusing it for several moments and paying her no attention.

It was both a relief and also a bit of an insult, if she was being entirely honest, to be given up on so easily.

Alexis tried to turn her attention back to her laptop but watched out of the corner of her eye as he finally shut the menu and waited patiently to catch the bartender's eye.

"Hi there," he said, when the bartender ambled back over. "I'd like a Stella, and maybe a bite to eat?"

Alexis didn't miss the once-over that the bartender gave Logan before the curvy redhead leaned over the bar, displaying perky boobs as she clicked her pen and pulled a notepad out of her back pocket.

"Shoot," the bartender said flirtatiously, looking a good deal friendlier than she had when she'd spoken to Alexis.

Not that Alexis blamed her. A cute Brit could do that to a girl.

"All right then," Logan said. "I'd like the burger, medium, with Swiss. Fish and chips, extra tartar, and . . . how's your chicken club?"

The bartender blinked. "It's good. But you want all that?"

"I do. Thank you."

"Suit yourself," she said, scribbling Logan's order on the pad.

"Hungry?" Alexis couldn't resist asking after the bartender moved away.

Logan gave a sheepish smile. "I'm a recovering student. I sometimes get so wrapped up in my day that I forget to eat."

"A *recovering* student. What does that mean?"

He turned slightly toward her. "Someone's showing plenty of interest in a *strange* man."

She bit her lip. "I'm sorry if I was rude before. I'm just not really in the market for . . . you know."

He gave her an easy smile. "Everyone's in the market for a friend, Alexis."

She opened her mouth and then shut it as she realized he was right. She *could* use a friend. She'd spent her entire life in Boston and knew almost nobody in New York. This guy seemed nice and nonthreatening enough—what would be the harm in a little conversation over dinner? It had been too long since she'd had somebody to share a meal with.

Logan seemed to know the moment she capitulated, because he turned more fully toward her. "A recovering student, Alexis, is a recent graduate. One who hasn't quite absorbed that there will be no more finals, no more requisite all-nighters, and no more dorm sex."

Alexis laughed. "Undergrad, then?"

He gave her a wry look. "How young do I look, darling? MBA from Columbia. Just finished up end of last year."

She felt a little stab of relief that he wasn't twenty-two.

He leaned toward her slightly. "Twenty-five next month, just in case you were wondering. *As a friend.*"

She tried to hide her smile and failed. "Columbia, huh? You're a long way from home."

"Noticed that, did ya?" He winked. "I came out here for undergrad, also Columbia. Always figured I'd go back to London and maybe someday I will, but . . ." He shrugged. "Seems I have stuff to do here first."

"Such as?" She took a sip of her wine, dismayed to see that it was half-empty.

"Well, this will probably shock you, given my vast amount of brawn, but I'm an accountant. Or at least I will be, once I get my business up and running."

Alexis was impressed. "Your own business?"

Most twentysomethings, even those with an entrepreneurial bent, opted to get a few years of work for someone else under their belts before branching out on their own.

He nodded. "I'm working out of my flat for now, but I'm hoping to lease some office space soon, get some legitimacy. If nothing else to get my father off my back."

"He's not a fan of your plan?" Alexis asked.

Logan's shoulder lifted, and for the first time he seemed a little sad. "Both parents have had it in their head that I'd come home. Run the family business in London."

"Which is . . . ?"

He spun his beer glass idly. "Financial consulting firm. My father's the CEO, Mum's the COO."

"Wow, that's . . ."

"Scary?" Logan supplied.

"I was going to say impressive. That they work together—without killing each other, I mean."

"They're in love. It's atrocious," he said with a wink. "What about your folks?"

Alexis laughed. "*Not* in love. They divorced when I was in high school. Dad's remarried and happy now, I think. Mom not so much."

"And you?" he said. "Are you happy, Alexis?"

She pursed her lips, surprised and yet not entirely unsettled by the personal question. "It's been a while since anyone asked me that. Since I even thought about it, really."

"Think it out. I'll wait," he said with a wink.

She didn't have to think that long. "I'm *almost* happy."

"You sound quite confident on that."

She shrugged. "Let's just say that I need a few things to fall into place in my professional life, but once that happens . . . yeah, I'll be happy."

She'd make sure of it.

"You're starting your own business."

Her head whipped around. "How'd you know that?"

Logan reached over and tapped her laptop. "I can spot an Excel spreadsheet from a mile away."

"Is that why you came over here?"

"No, darling. That would be your smile."

"I don't remember smiling."

He burst out laughing. "You're unusual. I like that. And you *did* smile. At the bartender, when you ordered your wine."

"You were watching me," Alexis said, eyebrows lifting. "Rather creepy for a *friend*."

Instead of acknowledging her comment, he nodded his chin at her laptop. "What are you working on, if you don't mind my asking? Dare I hold out hope you're also an accountant and we can have darling, glasses-wearing babies together?"

"My eyesight is twenty-twenty," she retorted.

"So that's a maybe, then?"

Alexis couldn't help the laugh, a *full* laugh, the first in a long time, and his eyes crinkled a little at the corners as he watched her. "Tell me about you, Alexis, my new best friend."

Damn, he was charming.

"Well," she said slowly. "I'm not an accountant—sorry to break your number-crunching heart. But I, too, am a 're-covering student.' "

"Do tell."

"I finished up my master's program at Boston College end of last year. Marketing and business administration."

"Boston," he said, the word sounding ridiculously appealing in his clipped accent. "And what brings you to New York?"

Alexis waved a hand over her laptop and the folder holding her business proposal. "This."

"And *this* would be . . . ?"

She shoved the folder his way and took another sip of her wine—a big one.

He pulled it toward him, opened it, and began to read.

Having the entire thing memorized, Alexis couldn't help but "read" along with him inside her own head.

The Wedding Belles is a boutique wedding-planning company committed to providing carefully curated weddings for the discerning bride . . . The Wedding Belles ensures the perfect combination of classic elegance and innovative modernity, promising a wedding that's both timeless and contemporary . . .

Logan turned the page, and Alexis expected him to lose interest once he was past the marketing fluff, but to her surprise, he read every last page, analyzed every last chart she'd painstakingly created.

His food arrived and Logan gestured with one finger for another round of drinks, before absently pulling a fry off one of the plates and shoving the plate in her direction.

She bit her lip. She couldn't. She *shouldn't*.

But the smell of the chicken club, with melted cheese and ripe avocado between buttery, toasty bread, was too much to resist. She picked up a knife and cut off a quarter of the sandwich.

"Oh my God," she whispered around the first heavenly bite.

Out of the corner of her eye she thought she saw him smile, but he never looked up from her proposal, careful to wipe his fingers between fries and turning her pages.

Finally, he'd read the entire thing, and Alexis was mortified to realize she'd eaten half his chicken sandwich, a quarter of the burger, a good two-thirds of the fish, and more than a few fries.

Logan didn't seem to mind as he picked up the remaining half of his chicken sandwich and took a thoughtful bite.

He chewed slowly, methodically. Took a sip of beer. Then turned toward her once more. "Where are you with this?"

"How do you mean?"

"You need funding, yes?"

She nodded, reaching for the second glass of wine the

bartender had brought along with Logan's beer. She couldn't afford it, but . . . what the hell?

"Yes. I'm envisioning a three-story, multiuse brownstone that could serve as both office space for the team, reception, as well as my living quarters. It'll be more money up front, but I've done the math, and it makes more financial sense in the long run when you factor in the cost of moving, inflation, lease renewal."

"You want to start it off right," he said. "From the very beginning."

She nodded, grateful that someone finally understood. "I know conventional wisdom suggests that I should start it out of my home and sort of build up, but the entire brand of the Belles is elite. The clients I want aren't the ones who will meet in the living room of my Harlem apartment."

"Any nibbles?"

She lifted a shoulder and pulled another fry off the plate, long past the point of playing coy about being desperately hungry. "I've had a few meetings. Nobody's laughed me out of the conference room yet—just a lot of noncommittal 'We'll be in touch.'"

He nodded. "You have a location in mind."

She smiled, loving that it wasn't a question so much as a statement. As though he knew the way her mind worked, putting the cart before the horse and touring Manhattan real estate when she couldn't even afford a second glass of eight-dollar wine.

"Aha," he said, with an answering smile.

"Okay, fine," she said. "It's on Seventy-Third between Broadway and West End, and it's just . . . perfect."

"Upper West Side," he said in surprise.

"Yes. It feels right for the Belles. Classic but up-and-coming, upscale but not stuffy, expensive but not too expensive . . ."

"You really have thought it all out." Logan was studying her.

"Since I was, like, twelve," she admitted.

"Never wavered?"

Alexis shook her head. "Nope. The vision became more precise over time, not less."

He turned away, watching his beer glass as he spun it idly on the bar top. "I had a great aunt. Margaret. Great old lady, great sense of humor. She passed away a few months back."

"Oh," Alexis said, a little confused by the change of subject but sympathetic all the same. She touched his arm consolingly. "I'm sorry."

"Thank you," he said. "Although she was ninety-two and passed in her sleep. Definitely the way to go, don't you think?"

"Can't say I've put too much thought into dying. Quite the opposite, actually."

"Yes, I can see that about you, Alexis," he said thoughtfully.

She liked the way he said her name, embracing all the syllables. *Uh-lex-iss.*

"Aunt Margaret left me some money. Quite a lot of it, actually," Logan said, still not looking at her.

"Um, congratulations?"

Logan's shoulders didn't move, but he turned his head, resting his chin on his shoulder as he pinned her with an intense gaze. "I'd like to make you an offer, Alexis Morgan."

She stilled. "What kind of offer?"

He used his elbow to indicate her proposal. "I'd like to fund the Wedding Belles."

Her breath caught in her throat. "Why would you do that?"

Instead of answering, he turned to face her more fully, and all traces of the casual postgrad vanished, and she realized she was seeing the accountant version of Logan Harris—the shrewd businessman.

"There's a catch."

She tried not to let her deflation become visible. Of course there was a catch. There always was.

"I don't want to just offer you a loan. I want to be part owner. Fifty percent."

She was already shaking her head. "That's not in the plan. It's *my* business."

He smiled. "That won't change. I won't tell you how to run it. You'll do things your way. But this business plan is legit, and I want to be a part of it."

"I'd pay you back every penny with interest," she said. "I expect I can be profitable in two years, I already have a handful of socialite connections, all engaged or *almost* engaged, and—"

"No deal," he said. "I own fifty percent or I'm not involved at all."

Fifty percent.

This complete stranger wanted to own fifty percent of her business. Fifty percent of her *dream*.

She shook her head. "I can't. Thank you, but no."

His gaze shuttered just for a moment before his smile returned, just slightly more restrained than before. "Fair enough."

Logan shifted his weight, and she felt a little bite of disappointment when he pulled his wallet out of his back pocket. He was leaving.

The urge to tell him to stay was strong, and for the life of her, she couldn't figure out if it was for personal or professional reasons. She didn't know what she wanted from Logan Harris, but she wanted *something*.

The thought scared her, and was exactly what had her biting her tongue.

She watched as he put several bills on the counter, saw immediately that it was more than enough to cover all of the food, plus her drinks and a hefty tip.

"No, Logan, please." She reached forward to pick up some of the bills and return them to him, but he caught her hand.

Alexis gasped at the contact. His thumb found the center of her palm, his long, strong fingers closing around the back of her hand.

"Let me, Alexis." It was a command.

Her first instinct was to scratch back at his high-handedness, but she couldn't seem to think when he was touching her, didn't want to do anything other than what he wanted her to do.

Not like her at all.

No doubt about it, this was a man she needed to guard herself against.

She slowly nodded. "Okay. Thank you."

"There," he said softly. "That wasn't so hard, now, was it?"

"Actually, it nearly killed me," she grumbled.

His smile was slow and intimate. "I know."

Logan's gaze dropped to their joined hands, and his thumb brushed against her palm, lingering as though reluctant to release her, before he finally let go.

He pulled something else out of his wallet, set it purposely in front of her. A business card. *His* business card.

"You'll call me if you change your mind." Again, it was a command. She was starting to gather that beneath the quiet smile and charming accent was a man accustomed to exercising control in all things. *Much like her.*

Alexis picked up the card. It was heavy white card stock with nothing but his name, phone number, and email. The card suited him. Simple and to the point, but the midnight-blue font rather than the expected black belied just a hint of unconventional that appealed to her far too much.

"I can't," she whispered again, eyes locked on his card.

She felt his gaze on her profile but didn't meet his eyes, and he finally gave up, pulling on his heavy wool coat.

"It was lovely meeting you, Alexis."

She finally looked up, met his piercing gaze. "You, too."

He opened his mouth as though to say something but then shook his head and slowly started to walk away. Alexis felt something twist inside her at the thought of him leaving, and she gave in to the urge.

"Logan."

He turned around, hands shoved into his pockets, eyes unreadable.

"Why?" she asked, lifting his business card slightly. "Why would you offer this?"

He jerked his head in the direction of her folder. "It's a good plan. Worth the risk."

She shook her head slowly, searching his face. "No, it's something more than that. Another reason. I'd like to know what."

The outer corners of his eyes crinkled a bit, and he gave a fleeting smile before walking back to her, crowding her against the bar.

For a moment she feared—hoped?—that he would kiss her, and from the way his mouth dropped to just inches from hers, she thought maybe he wanted to.

Then his face turned, his lips brushing against her cheek instead. "Say yes to my proposal, Alexis. Say yes, and maybe someday I'll tell you the other reason."

Logan pulled away, held her gaze for a heartbeat.

Then he stepped back, gave her a sly wink, and walked away without a backward glance.

Alexis sat there for a long time after, his card in her fingers, her heart in her throat, and her life in the hands of a stranger who somehow didn't feel like a stranger at all.